WHAT TO DO WITH LOBSTERS IN A PLACE LIKE KLIPPIESFONTEIN

COLETTE VICTOR

What To Do With Lobsters In A Place Like Klippiesfontein
Colette Victor
First Published by Cargo Publishing in 2015
SC376700
© Colette Victor 2015

ISBN 978-1-908885-70-8

Printed & Bound in Scotland by Bell & Bain Ltd
Cover design by Kaajal Modi
Illustration by Ottavia Pasta
www.cargopublishing.com

Also available as:
Kindle Ebook
EPUB Ebook

Dedicated to the memory of Lucky Tsomo
12/05/1994 – 03/01/2015
Loved by all

Chapter One

No one in town had ever seen anything like it. Well, except for that advert on TV about the bottled water. Of course, Fanus' aquarium with the exotic fish that everyone ogled over was sort of down the same line. But a lobster tank with a bright blue background and brown lobsters, their claws taped up with yellow sticky tape... Not in a million years would anyone have guessed that something like that would end up in Klippiesfontein.

At first, the supply van pulling up outside Oom Marius' General Store evoked the same kind of mild interest it did every week. Familiar stragglers hanging out on the street ambled over lazily to see what this week's load had brought. That's when it appeared. The delivery guy took his cart to the back of the lorry, hitched the forked teeth under the tank, and lowered it to street level. Interest was piqued. An excited murmur passed through the small crowd.

"Oom Marius," Lenny called, trusting the stagnant air to carry his voice all the way inside the shop, "what's this tank thingy you've got here?"

"Oh that," Oom Marius called back. "It's a lobster tank."

His voice was calculatedly casual. It was at that point that everyone knew something big was at hand. Fake-casual was simply not Oom Marius' way of doing things. Clearly, they concluded, this had something to do with Patty.

Five or six men followed the delivery guy into the dark shop smelling of washing powder and paraffin. They watched intently as Oom Marius plugged the thing into a socket and filled it with water.

"What you mean, Oom Marius?" Frikkie asked. "You going to throw lobsters in there? Aren't they going to start stinking the place out after two days?"

"Don't you know anything?" Oom Marius snapped. "You don't throw dead lobsters in there."

"You mean they're..."

Just then the delivery guy returned with another load. In his arms he held a white polystyrene box which he placed carefully at Oom Marius' feet. He handed him a clipboard and waited for the cheque.

After he'd left, Oom Marius nodded at Petrus, his faithful assistant, to start unpacking the boxes.

"This one you leave for me, you hear?" Oom Marius called, gesturing to the white box.

The mute Petrus nodded.

Oom Marius spent the whole afternoon fussing with his lobster tank. Reading the instructions, shoving a thermometer in and out of the water every so many minutes, acting as if this was what he did all day, every day. The crowd both inside the shop and outside on the blistering veranda, grew. At twenty to two school was let out and the throng filled out even more with barefoot boys in grey shorts and shirts and girls in red pinafores. They carried the smell of dust inside with them.

"*Oom, wat het Oom daar binne in die boks?*" a little one ventured.

"Come then, let me show you what I have in the box, child," he relented. Like the Pied Piper, the giggling kids followed him from counter to lobster tank where the mysterious box still stood untouched.

Taking his penknife from his belt, Oom Marius deftly slit open the tape holding the lid down. With the flair of a circus ringleader, he yanked off the lid and held it above his head. The smell of sea trapped too long inside plastic overwhelmed the children standing in front. As everyone caught a glimpse of the inside of the white box, a chorus of *aaahs* went up from youngsters and adults alike.

With the sudden exposure to light, the four lobsters started wriggling and moving about and the *aaahs* turned to excited yelps. Gingerly (though by watching him no one would've guessed he'd never touched a lobster before in his life), Oom Marius stuck his hand into the box, took hold of one of the creatures' shiny backs and picked it up. He swung it close to his audience. The thing squirmed in his hands. Everyone stepped back. Holding it above the tank, he dropped the animal into the water. With the same showmanship, Oom Marius proceeded to plunge the other three in as well.

"You going to sell these things here in the shop?" Frikkie asked.

"Of course. Modern supermarkets all over the world sell lobsters like these. Why should Klippiesfontein be any different?" he proclaimed proudly.

"Who's going to buy them, Oom?" young Daan's blue eyes stared trustingly at the proprietor.

"What are you supposed to *do* with them? Are they like puppies?"

"They're to eat, child. To eat."

Spontaneously the group broke out laughing. The tension that had been hanging in the shop all day was broken. Oom Marius had finally provided proof that he was *mal*. Crazy. The band of kids broke loose and rushed outside to find something better to do than stare at giant water cockroaches that somebody was supposed to eat. The adults drifted away too. Only Frikkie and Lenny hung around on the veranda, smoking cigarettes and calling greetings to passersby.

It was dark and cool inside the late afternoon shop. This was the time of day Oom Marius loved best. A temporary lull in business, the only sound was Petrus' rhythmic swishing of the broom for the tenth time that day. You could call that Petrus many things, but the one thing you couldn't say about him was that he was lazy.

As far as anyone in town knew, Petrus had never spoken a word in his life. Of course, no one had bothered asking Petrus' mother because, at the time he came to work for Oom Marius twenty-two years ago, white people didn't bother asking black people much. Barking commands was more the order of the day.

It had been at the time Oom Marius was looking for someone to clean his shop, help unpack the shelves, and do his bidding and calling. He'd taken pity on a scraggly black woman who spent her days struggling around town asking people for spare change so she could feed herself and her idiot boy. One look at the wretched woman and Oom Marius knew he couldn't have her standing in the shop. She'd chase away the customers with that malnourished look of hers.

He walked up to her, "Hey you, what's the child's name?"

"This is Petrus, Baas," she answered.

"How old is he?"

"He's eight, Baas."

"Is he strong?"

"He's strong, Baas."

"Have him here at seven tomorrow morning so he can start work. And make sure you bath him tonight. I don't want him smelling of wood fire."

"Thank you, Baas. Thank you, Baas," she tried to grab Oom Marius' hand.

"Go home now. And here, take this," he grunted, shoving a plastic bag with a loaf of bread, a block of bright orange cheddar cheese and a litre of milk into her hands. "Now don't tell anyone where you got this from, you hear me?" he barked. "Or else I'll have every bastard from the township on my front step tomorrow morning."

"Thank you, Baas. No, Baas, I won't say anything."

As the afternoon wore on and the hour hand ticked closer to five, Oom Marius became more agitated like he did every afternoon round the same time. Petrus noticed that the glances at the wall clock and quick spurts from behind the wooden counter at the back of the store out to the veranda to peer down Main Street were more frequent today, more frenzied.

It had to have something to do with Missies Patty, Petrus concluded. At five o'clock the school bus would pull in from Springbok where she worked as a secretary for the high school. The students would spill out onto the pavement in front of Baas Botha's Butchery in their green and white uniforms. Then Missies

Patty would step off the bus in that deft way of hers and cross the road to the General Store for her and her husband's cigarettes. This, as everyone in town knew, was Oom Marius' favourite part of the day.

No one could remember when it became public knowledge – the way Oom Marius felt about Missies Patty. It seemed it had always just been that way. Of course, Oom Marius didn't tell Missies Patty how he felt and she pretended she didn't know. In fact, the pretending in this town was so good that even Missies Patty's husband, Shawn, and Oom Marius' wife, Tannie Hettie, pretended they didn't know. It was a good town for pretenders, this Klippiesfontein.

Even though no one could remember *when* he started feeling this way, everyone knew *why* he did. It was because Missies Patty had lived in the big city for many years and knew big city things that no one in Klippiesfontein knew. It was because Oom Marius had always dreamed of living in the big city himself and learning big city ways. It was like it always is in life. One person has something that another one wants. And normally they'll go far to get it. At least, that's the way Petrus saw it. Missies Patty had big city ways. Oom Marius longed for big city ways. And now there was a lobster tank inside the shop.

At five to five Oom Marius barked at Petrus, "Go sweep the veranda and tell me when you see her coming."

With patience born from years of servitude, Petrus nodded, collected his broom and ambled slowly out onto the shaded veranda.

Swish, swish, swish went the rhythm of the broom. From force of habit, Petrus took in the details of the slow happenings of the crossroads. On the veranda of the Royal Hotel, white men, usually the same white men, sat drinking their cold beers. And they said that black men were lazy, Petrus scoffed. On the opposite side of the street, a farmer was parked at the petrol pump with his *bakkie,* filling jerry cans with red diesel for his tractor. And at Henk Coetzee's Hunting and Fishing Store, he could see the owner staring out the window, probably thinking about some or other animal he'd shot over the weekend. *Swish, swish* went the broom.

"Petrus," came Oom Marius' slightly frenzied voice from inside. "Where's that yellow *lappie*? There are kids' fingerprints all over this bloody tank."

Leaning his broom against the wall, Petrus ambled inside and went into the small storeroom at the back of the store. He emerged with a bottle of Windowleen and the yellow duster which he proffered silently to Oom Marius.

"Who's keeping an eye on the bloody bus if you're in here?" snapped Oom Marius.

Dragging his feet, Petrus went back outside, picked up his broom and continued his sweeping. He heard the *spssht, spssht* inside as Oom Marius sprayed Windowleen on his precious tank. Then he heard the heavy gears of the bus moaning their way up the road. Leaning on his broomstick, he watched the usual faces disembarking, holding up hands in casual salutations, shouting goodbyes and crossing the street without looking for cars. Klippiesfontein wasn't the kind of town where you had to pay too much attention to cars. At last he saw Missies Patty coming down the bus steps. She rubbed her palms over her thighs to get the creases out of her pencil skirt, tossed her blond hair over her shoulder, and headed for the General Store.

Broom up against the wall again, Petrus walked back inside. He crossed the floor until he was standing right behind Oom Marius who was still polishing the tank. He touched his shoulder.

Oom Marius spun round, "Is she there? Is she coming?"

Petrus nodded.

"Come. Get out. Take out the rubbish or something. Come on. Get a move on, you lazy bastard."

Petrus heard this line spoken to him every afternoon when Missies Patty was crossing the road on her way to the General Store. Other men, they might have been angry to hear words like this spoken to them but Petrus... he didn't get angry. Petrus understood Oom Marius' excitement at seeing Missies Patty. Petrus felt the same way when he saw Precious. Maybe he'd also swear at anyone hanging around if she ever walked up to him.

Petrus carried the rubbish out to the dark, narrow alley between the General Store and the video shop next door.

He heard the bell above the door ring as Missies Patty walked into the store.

"Afternoon, Oom Marius," she called with her voice full of music.

Oom Marius laughed his pretend-shy laugh. "How many times must I tell you Patty, just call me Marius."

"OK," she answered. Friendly, like Missies Patty always was. "Can I have a pack of Bennies and Hennies and some Camel Filters for Shawn, Marius?"

Petrus heard a rustle from behind the counter as cigarettes and money were exchanged.

"Is Tannie Hettie feeling better today?" Missies Patty asked.

Petrus knew what was coming now. The only thing Oom Marius couldn't stand of Missies Patty was when she mentioned his wife. And Oom Marius wasn't much good at hiding things he couldn't stand.

"Better? What's she got to feel better about?" he snapped.

"I saw her coming out of Doctor Brown's office yesterday afternoon," Missies Patty explained.

"*Ag*, it was just her routine check-up, Patty. It was nothing. You know Hettie, she likes to be on time with these things. But tell me, why were *you* at the doctor's off..."

"No, Oom. She was crying when she came out. There was definitely something wrong."

"Hettie? Crying?"

"Yes, Oom. She was crying."

Oom Marius stood quietly for a few seconds. Petrus knew he was thinking about Missies Patty's words. He spoke again. "It's probably just some of this depression thing going around. You know, women and doctors are very fond of it. I'm sure if Hettie was sick she'd tell me."

"If you say so, Oom. Look, thanks for the ciggies," she called. Her departing heels sounded on the wooden floor.

"You see what I got today?" Oom Marius called rather desperately after her.

"What have you got?" Petrus could hear a smile in her voice.

"Look there, in the corner," he replied proudly.

"Oh my God, Marius," Petrus heard her squeal in obvious distress. "That's just awful. Where did you get that from?"

"From the sea, Patty. They've got divers and metal cages and they go down really deep to catch them. You used to live by the sea. Why do you say it's awful?"

"Marius, it's terribly cruel. They throw them live into pots of boiling water and you hear them scream as they boil to death. Oh I can't stand it, Marius. Promise me you'll get rid of them?"

"Of course, Patty. Of course. I didn't know. I genuinely didn't know."

Petrus heard the tapping of Missies Patty's high heels grow fainter as she headed for the door.

"I'll see you tomorrow, Oom Marius," she called.

"How many times must I tell you, just call me..."

But he never finished his sentence.

Petrus waited for the sound of his name.

"Petrus," came Oom Marius' gruff voice, "get inside here and pack out those bloody pilchards. That box has been standing here since this morning."

Petrus let the lid of the rubbish bin clang shut. Shrugging his shoulders, he headed back inside.

Chapter Two

"Jissus God, wat gaan ek nou met die blerrie goed doen?" Oom Marius called after the delivery guy.

Jesus, God, what am I going to do with these bloody things now?

Oom Marius watched him cross the dusty veranda, take the three steps down to road level and head for his supply van parked out front under the Acacia for the bit of shade it so sadly offered.

Acacias, or thorn trees, as they were generally known, were just about the only things that grew here in Klippiesfontein. And grass. Of course, there were vast plains of arid, yellow grass interspersed with outcroppings of haphazard rock piles and lonely steel windmills trying to suck what little moisture there was out of the red earth. Space – that's how most people would describe the area. There wasn't much more that could be said about it other than that it had a lot of space. Oom Marius hoped the delivery guy would have an especially hot and long journey back to the closest town, Springbok, one hundred and sixty-seven kilometres to the east.

Damn him, thought Oom Marius. Now he was stuck with it. With them. The four leather-coloured creatures staring out of their prison at him all day long. What was he going to say to Patty? What about the rest of the townsfolk? Oom Marius was no longer a respected businessman of Klippiesfontein. No. Now he was its laughing stock. Lobster babysitter. That's what his rash decision had reduced him to. He didn't even know what the damned things ate, but one thing was sure, if he let them starve to death, Patty would stop talking to him.

Oom Marius heard the door between the shop and his home creak open. He should tell Petrus to put some oil on the hinges, he reminded himself. He turned round to see Hettie, his wife, shuffling into the shop. He raised his eyebrows. Hettie never came into the shop. If she wanted anything she invariably sent Anna, her domestic, to ask for it.

"*Dag vrou*," he said.

Good day, wife.

Hettie had never been much of a looker. Even when he married her thirty-nine years ago. Yes, she'd been young and soft and round. She'd had that shy giggle about her that some girls had that made things move down there for a man. But most importantly, she'd been approved of by his father, his mother, and the dominie. And in those days, that was the best reason to get married.

Now his parents were long gone. And so were Hettie's. Also her shy giggle and any hint of prettiness had left their marriage many years ago. She was a stout, strong Afrikaans woman. She'd borne him three robust sons and had the hips to show for it. Once a week she went to the hairdresser who set her hair in a halo of earthquake-proof curls. She wore wrinkles under her eyes, a faint moustache on her upper lip, and green eyes that still twinkled youthfully, making up for the rest of her features. Hettie was his wife and a wife was there until death did you part. That's what it said in the Bible.

Tannie Hettie had been born sixty-three years ago to a karakul sheep farmer and his wife. She was their fourth child and a girl at that. Marrying an upstanding young Afrikaans man from the district was her inescapable fate and that's exactly what her mother prepared her for. From the age of four, Tannie Hettie was trained in the vital skills of cooking, baking, needlework and bossing around black servants.

The young girl did well at school, achieving marks at the top end of her class, but her parents took little notice of such an irrelevant detail. As long as she could read the *Huisgenoot*, a national magazine which provided as good as compulsory reading matter to any self-respecting Afrikaans housewife, and balance the household budget, she had no further need of an education. Although, as a girl, Tannie Hettie had harboured dreams of becoming a teacher or a nurse, she'd never voiced these out loud. A young woman going away to study was hardly an acceptable convention in small-town Klippiesfontein, unless, of course, it was as a ploy to catch a husband with respectable prospects. But Tannie Hettie wasn't in the business of catching respectable prospects. She believed, naively enough, in ideas like love and romance, so she stayed put on her father's karakul sheep farm and waited for the right boy to come along.

Marius was two years older than Hettie. He was both blond and strong and it could be said that the old saying, the one about necessity being the mother of invention, was particularly relevant when it came to him. His entrepreneurship did not stem from an inborn sense of business like many people thought, but rather from the very practical issue of being the third son. His eldest brother would inherit their father's small *rooibos* tea farm, while his second brother had taken over their paternal grandfather's sisal processing plant close to De Aar. There was nothing left for the young Marius to do besides become inventive. Inheritance had been ruled out. There was no talk of further studies after Marius' less-than-shining high school career. Finding a cushy office job in some government agency, as was the practise in those days for many white South African men, was just about as attractive to him as taking a swim in the Limpopo River with all its crocodiles. No, being resourceful was the only way Marius was going to earn a living.

Townsfolk and local farmers had been used to, up to that point, buying the goods which their land couldn't provide like coffee, sugar and Marie Biscuits from the delivery truck that pulled into the centre of town every week. Marius had been given the chore to drive his mother to Klippiesfontein so she could collect her weekly supplies. Soon after he'd helped her load the groceries onto the back of the bakkie, they watched the truck set off back to Springbok. On their way home to the farm, Marius' mother remembered that she'd forgotten to buy soap powder. She sat next to her son, practically in tears because she'd be unable to wash her family's clothes in time for church on Sunday. That's when the idea had first taken hold in his head. The idea of supplies being available all day long, every day, except of course, on Sundays.

"Imagine if you could buy a box of washing powder whenever you ran out," Marius had suggested to the young Hettie that Sunday after church. "A man could make some real money doing something like that."

Hettie had nodded fiercely, terribly impressed with this strapping man's business visions.

So he'd gone ahead, fuelled by the enthusiasm of the karakul sheep farmer's daughter. He took out a small loan from the bank in Springbok and opened up the General Store. A year later, when it appeared as if his venture would provide a decent income, he proposed to her and, another year after that, they were married in the Dutch Reformed Church of Klippiesfontein.

Tannie Hettie's arms, thick and freckled, were wringing a dishtowel she'd brought with her from the kitchen. "Marius, I need to talk to you about something."

"Have you spoken to Andre today?" he interrupted, a fresh idea having taken hold in his head.

"No, I'll phone him tonight. I wanted to speak to you first."

"Hettie, go back inside and phone him. You need to ask him something for me."

"He's at work now, Marius. I don't like to disturb him there."

"You're his mother, for God's sake. You can disturb him any time of day or night and he should be grateful for it."

Tannie Hettie smiled. She loved it when Marius exaggerated the boys' duty to her like that. "Alright, I'll phone him. What do you want me to ask?"

"Ask him what lobsters eat," he said.

"I thought you were going to send those things back with the supply truck?"

"They don't want them back." Oom Marius looked down at the floor.

"And now what?" she demanded.

"And now you're going to ask Andre to look up on the internet what I'm supposed to feed these things. Charlie tells me there's nothing you can't learn from it. It's like the library of the world..."

"I'll ask him Marius, but I just want you to understand one thing here today: I don't want those creatures anywhere near my house. Do you hear me?"

Oom Marius nodded. It was true that a man should make the decisions in the household. But then it was also true that there were times when a man had to listen to his wife. And one of those times was when he bought a tank with four lobsters in a town where people thought fish fingers were exotic.

Tannie Hettie shuffled back through the door. "When I come back we need to talk, Marius," she called over her shoulder.

Oom Marius didn't hear her. He was on the look-out for something to release his frustration on. The pots and pans in the kitchenware aisle had been polished. The shards from the broken plate swept up. On the opposite shelf he saw the mops and brooms standing proudly in a row, the dusters and dishtowels stacked neatly, one on top of the other.

"Petrus," he yelled.

Petrus came into the shop.

"How many times have I told you to oil the hinge on that door?" he shouted, gesturing to the squeaky culprit.

Never, thought Petrus. But he shrugged and started moving towards the storeroom to fetch the small oil can.

"And while you're in there, bring out that cardboard advertisement for washing powder that we used last year. I want you to put it there in the corner. And move that bloody tank behind it! Do you hear?"

Oom Marius saw the back of Petrus' head nodding.

Taking the calculator and the heavy black ledger out from under the counter, Oom Marius busied himself with the VAT returns for the month. He heard Petrus moving around the shop. First he worked on the squeaking door. Then he moved to the darkest corner, between the counter and the storeroom, and positioned the large cardboard cut-out in front of the lobster tank.

Oom Marius caught sight of himself in the mirror behind

the counter. Just like they'd done with Hettie, the years had taken their toll on him too. Gone was the tall, muscular, blond man he'd once been; the one staring back at him, although still tall, sported a serious *boepens,* potbelly, that strained at the buttons of his checked shirt tucked into a leather belt. His arms, though they could still lift a small sheep, looked flabby and depleted, just like the jowls of his leather-brown face. Though thankfully he didn't have a receding hairline like his late father had had, his temples were grey and his blond mane was substantially thinner. When he'd been younger, depending on the angle and the observer, it had been possible to describe him as handsome but the word hardly applied to him anymore. Perhaps it was nothing more than sheer vanity to expect to be handsome at sixty-five. Just like a woman, he thought. He shook his head, irritated at his momentary lapse of self-inspection, and returned his attention to the books.

Two customers came in during the next twenty minutes. One was Lenny. At first he dawdled in the toiletries aisle, touching the bottles of deodorant without much interest, before he came up to the counter to fetch the dirty magazine he ordered from the city each week. He'd obviously been keeping an eye out to see when the supply van drove past his house, on its way out of Klippiesfontein. The other was Agnes, Sarie's domestic, sent to buy five kilos of self-raising flour. Sarie was Hettie's oldest friend.

There'd been a time, back in the day, when Oom Marius had thought about marrying Sarie. She'd been a lot prettier than Hettie. But then the dominie pointed out that Sarie had a cousin who had fallen pregnant out of wedlock. She'd been shipped off to live with a spinster aunt to avoid the *skande.* The shame. It was hardly Sarie's fault, Oom Marius had thought at the time, but he'd known better than to voice his opinion out loud. It was a dangerous thing to have the dominie's anger directed at you.

So he'd settled for Hettie instead. Thirty-nine years married, until death did them part and all that stuff. She didn't deserve a husband reminiscing about her best friend's good looks forty years previously, Oom Marius reprimanded himself. He felt himself blush – just like a bloody teenager, he thought.

He heard the door between the shop and his home open, this time with significantly less creaking, and turned to face his wife. Luckily for him, Oom Marius' skin was so brown and leathery from the remorseless sun that Tannie Hettie didn't pick up on his blush. It would surely have raised a question from her.

"What did he say?" Oom Marius demanded.

Tannie Hettie crossed her arms and stared at her husband, "Don't you want to know how Andre is? And Suzan and the little ones?"

"*Lieve God* Hettie, these bloody creatures are starving and you want to talk to me about the children? Do you know how it's going to stink in here if they start dying?"

"It's already smelling, Marius," she answered.

"Just tell me woman, what do lobsters eat?"

"Crabs, sea stars, sea urchins, plankton, and small fish. They can turn into cannibals when they're kept in crowded conditions, Andre says. Sometimes you even find partially eaten animals in the live-tank. Do you have any idea what you've started here, Marius?"

Oom Marius ignored his wife, "*Jissus*, where am I going to get those things from?"

Then he had another idea. "Petrus," he barked.

The black man, still busy with the tank in the corner, looked up.

"Petrus, your people eat lobsters?" Oom Marius barked angrily because, of course, he already knew the answer.

Petrus shook his head.

"*You* want to eat the lobsters?" he continued. "Fancy people in the city, they pay hundreds of rands to eat these things."

Again Petrus shook his head.

"Uneducated fool," Oom Marius muttered.

He looked back at his wife.

She continued, "They'll eat any type of saltwater seafood, Andre said. They especially like chunks of fresh fish and squids."

"*Jissus* Hettie, the way you talk it sounds like I can just walk over to the fridge and take out a couple of squids. How am I supposed to feed these things?"

Tannie Hettie was smiling. "Andre couldn't stop laughing when I told him. I had to hold the phone away from my ear for a whole minute. He says to say thank you. He hasn't laughed that much in years. He also said you should tell Petrus to dig a hole out back and throw them in there."

"I'm not going to bury them alive, Hettie. They never asked me to bring them here."

"I think Andre is right," Tannie Hettie pushed on.

"Who asked you to think, woman?" Oom Marius snapped. "Now, how am I supposed to feed these things?"

"Are you asking me to think again now Marius?"

"*Ag*, you're right Hettie. You know I didn't mean it. You got any ideas?"

"I've got some I&J hake portions in the deepfreeze. I could defrost them in the microwave for you. Then you just make sure you tell the delivery guy to bring you some fresh seafood next week. Are you going to keep their claws taped up like that?"

"You heard what Andre said. They start eating each other up when they're kept in confined spaces. So, no, I'm not going to let them tear chunks out of one another."

Tannie Hettie nodded, her expression turning serious again, "Do you have time to talk now?"

"What's with you today, woman? All you want to do is talk? Can't we talk tonight in front of the TV?"

"No Marius, we can't."

He nodded.

"Go outside and sweep the stoep, Petrus."

Both watched as Petrus disappeared out the front door. They waited until they heard the familiar *swish-swishing* of the broom.

"I went to the doctor two weeks ago for a check-up. He took some blood. Then he phoned me and said I needed to come in for more tests. I went back yesterday for the results, Marius. I have the cancer. I have to go to a hospital in Cape Town for treatment."

Oom Marius looked earnestly at his wife. He saw the mother of his three sons staring up at him with her twinkling green eyes. He saw a woman for whom, through no fault of her own, practically all feelings of attraction had been eroded by almost four decades of marriage. He saw the karakul sheep farmer's daughter who had chosen to love a third son with no inheritance. His Adam's apple moved up and down. He swallowed a little pool of saliva that had formed beneath his tongue.

"I'll find someone to look after the shop for me while we're gone," he said.

Tannie Hettie nodded.

Oom Marius nodded.

Until death did them part. Like it said in the Bible. And that was just the way it was. After thirty-nine years there was nothing more to say.

"You think you can put that fish in the microwave for me now, Hettie? I'm going mad thinking about these lobsters."

Tannie Hettie turned round and went back inside their home.

Chapter Three

"Thanks Willem. No, no. Of course I understand. I appreciate that you tried," Oom Marius spoke, over-emphasising his consonants in a way typical of Afrikaans speakers. He rubbed heavily over his furrowed brow with thumb and forefinger, "Say hello to your Elaine from Hettie and me."

Oom Marius slammed down the telephone, causing Petrus to look up from the shelf where he was packing out a box of creamed sweetcorn. The glass bottles on the counter, filled with sweets, shuddered from the ferocity of Oom Marius' actions.

"*Wat kyk jy so?*" Oom Marius snapped.

What are you looking at?

Petrus was used to being the butt of Oom Marius' irritation. There was no one else around most of the time. And, of course, Petrus knew it would be bad for business if his baas started shouting at customers instead of at him. He shrugged and continued his unpacking.

The weekly delivery had arrived that morning and Petrus had many boxes to unpack before he went home to the township, Rifilwe, at the end of the day. Plus, Oom Marius had asked him to chop up the squid the delivery guy had brought and feed it to the lobsters.

Petrus had been working for Oom Marius now for twenty-two years. He'd started there as a petrified eight-year-old, confused as to why his mother had thrust him into the care of the big, blond white man. He'd spent the whole of his first day trembling, peering out the window to spot his mother's scraggly figure coming back up the road to take him home. Baas Marius asked him to unpack some boxes onto shelves already straining with produce. The boy had never seen so much food in his life. He didn't even know what half of it was. At lunchtime he was given a plate of soft white bread spread with peanut butter by a white woman who appeared through the door. It was the most delicious thing he'd ever tasted. That night, after the longest day of his life, his mother arrived, at last, to fetch him. The boy was so relieved he started crying. In his hand he clutched a plastic bag full of food his new baas had given him to take home. His mother was almost just as glad about the contents of that bag as she was about getting her boy back. When he learnt he was to go back again the next day, when he thought about the white bread sandwiches and the food he could take home to his mother, he didn't think it was too bad.

Over the next few weeks, Petrus learnt that Baas Marius was a kinder man than his loud and impatient voice would make you believe. He learnt that the white woman who appeared through the door every now and then was, in fact, the baas' wife and that she didn't bother to hide her kindness like Baas Marius tried to do. She even took a new writing book and pencil from one of the shelves and gave them to Petrus. Each afternoon, when the shop was quiet, she'd call the child into her kitchen where she taught him to read words, to write those words, and to do sums. Baas Marius, he would get impatient sometimes that it was taking too long and he needed Petrus in the shop, but Missies Hettie wouldn't take any notice of him. Whenever Baas Marius looked through the door between the shop and the kitchen, she would shake her head sternly and the baas would disappear again. This school in Missies Hettie's kitchen went on for eight years. When he was sixteen, she decided he knew enough words and numbers and capital cities and the lessons stopped, but by then Petrus was every bit as educated as his peers in Rifilwe. Plus he earned a salary every month which no other black child could claim. He had stopped feeling less than the township children and it was all because of Baas Marius and Missies Hettie. Petrus had learned to be grateful from a young age.

So long had he known Baas Marius and he'd never done something so stupid before as buying that lobster tank. At first Petrus thought it was just another strange habit of the white people, because he trusted Oom Marius and believed he knew what he was doing. But even the white people didn't want to eat those lobsters, and who could blame them? Petrus wouldn't put something that ugly into his mouth even if someone offered him a thousand rand. For the first time he found himself wondering about Oom Marius.

His baas had been on the telephone all morning. Repeating his request to at least six different people. This last one had been Willem, Oom Marius' brother-in-law who lived two hundred kilometres away. It was the same request he'd been putting to all the clever people in Klippiesfontein.

Yesterday morning Oom Marius had spoken to Mister Scott, the retired English teacher. He'd turned Oom Marius down but his baas wasn't one to give up easily. He'd spoken to Mrs Joubert, the widow, about his request, but he must have known she'd say no from the beginning because even Petrus had known that.

That afternoon he'd approached Charlie. Charlie who'd been accepted to the University of Cape Town last year where he'd studied for seven whole months before coming back to Klippiesfontein. Now he worked for Telcom and fixed people's computers so they'd get that internet thing everyone seemed to want. They'd given him a car that said Telcom on the side so he could drive to nearby towns to help the people there with their computers. Petrus had heard Charlie say they even paid for his petrol. Yes, that Charlie was a bright one, Petrus nodded to himself. But he hadn't wanted to do it either.

Petrus heard a pair of shoes scuffling up the three wooden steps that lead from the street level to the veranda, stamping hard to rid themselves of the ever-present red dust before entering the shop.

Habitually, Petrus and Oom Marius turned their heads in the direction of the door to see who was about to enter.

Shawn walked into the shop. Missies Patty's husband. He was a short, stocky man, with thick arms and spiky blond hair. He'd probably run out of cigarettes. Shawn stayed home during the day, taking the odd job here and there, helping out when one of the farmers put up a new shed or when the time for sowing or harvesting came. He wasn't too fond of working, that one. That's why Missies Patty had to go on the bus every day to Springbok to work as a secretary.

Oom Marius' face took on a determined look and Petrus realised just how desperate his baas really was. He was actually going to put his request across to Shawn.

"A lazy white man is worse than a lazy black," Oom Marius would always mutter when Shawn walked out of the shop and no one but Petrus was in earshot.

Shawn ambled over to the counter.

"*Môre*, Oom Marius," he spoke just as slowly as he did everything else.

"*Môre*, Shawn."

Good morning, Shawn.

"A pack of Camel Filters please, Oom?"

Oom Marius had the cigarettes ready and slid them across the counter. Shawn tried to hand over his money but Oom Marius pulled back his hand.

"What's wrong?" Shawn asked.

"Nothing. Nothing's wrong, my boy. But I want to talk to you about something. Come, let's go stand outside on the stoep and you can smoke your cigarette."

Oom Marius came out from behind the counter and put his arm across Shawn's surprised shoulders, steering him gently down the wide aisle to the doorway. Petrus stared after them. The younger man's eyebrows were pulled up almost into his hairline. Hurriedly abandoning his position, Petrus moved to the front of the shop where a box of cornflakes was waiting for him on the floor. He held the pricing gun in his hand just in case Oom Marius came back. Petrus positioned himself at just the right angle to keep the two men in view, straining to hear what they were saying. Oom Marius and Shawn were leaning up against the wooden railing, their backs to the street.

"You've been looking for work for a long time now Shawn, haven't you?"

"I was just over at Oom Hans' farm last week helping him with the lambing," Shawn explained nervously.

"*Ag*, no man," Oom Marius snapped edgily.

Petrus saw the look on his baas' face as he tried to compose himself and shrug off his usual impatience. It was a look Petrus knew well. It was a look Oom Marius never bothered to use on Petrus.

"You know what I mean. Steady work. Every day. Not piece jobs like you've been doing. Not like the blacks from the township. I'm talking about a regular-hour job where you can take care of that pretty wife of yours. Or buy the parts for your motorbike you're always scrounging around for."

"Ja, Oom, that would be nice but you know there's no steady work up here in Klippiesfontein. I've been looking for years and you see where it's gotten me."

"And what if I offered you a job? A steady, well-paid job? What would you say?"

"Are you going to fire Petrus, Oom Marius?" Shawn asked puzzled, "Because I don't want to do a black man's job. I haven't fallen that low yet."

"*Nou my God.* Why would I want to fire Petrus? He knows almost as much about running this shop as I do. I'm talking about taking over my place. For a few weeks. Maximum a few months. I'll pay you well. I need someone I can trust."

"Where are you going then, Oom?"

"Tannie Hettie is sick, Shawn. She has the cancer. I have to go with her to the city to their big fancy hospital."

"Is Tannie Hettie going to die, Oom?"

"*Jissus Shawn, nou nou klap ek vir jou hier dat jy vlieg, hoor jy my.*"

Jesus Shawn, just now I'm going to slap you and send you flying, do you hear me?

"Of course she's not going to die and I don't want to hear you speaking like that again. Is that clear?"

"Sorry, Oom Marius. That was a stupid thing to say," he mumbled sheepishly.

This wasn't going very well, Petrus thought.

"Why must she go to the hospital for so long, Oom?"

"It's called the treatment. It's like a kind of poison they put into Tannie Hettie's body that isn't strong enough to kill her but it's strong enough to kill the cancer. Sometimes..." Oom Marius looked down at the floor.

Poison, thought Petrus. That couldn't be good. Poison was never good. But you never knew with the white man's medicine.

"Poison?" asked Shawn. "Is that a good idea, Oom Marius?"

"How the bloody hell should I know? Do I look like a doctor to you? But if that's what they say Hettie needs then that's what we're going to do. Now do you want the job or not?"

Shawn shifted his weight from one foot to the next, "What time must I start?"

"I open up at six."

"That's what I thought, Oom. Six o'clock is very early. And what time do you close?"

"You know what time I close, Shawn. Stop shooting crap with me. Seven o' clock on weekdays and eight on Fridays and Saturdays."

"That's a very long time, Oom Marius. Can't you ask Petrus to open up in the mornings and then I come in later? And maybe he can cover for me for a few hours at lunchtime too? Wouldn't that be possible?"

"If Petrus has to do all the work, why do I have to bother paying you? You know what Shawn, forget it. It was a dumb idea."

Just as Oom Marius spoke, Petrus had an idea of his own. It was also a dumb idea so he shook his head to get rid of it.

"I think you're right, Oom. I'm not really cut out to be a businessman."

"Good. Good. As long as we both agree," Oom Marius' arm was back over Shawn's shoulder in a fatherly-like way. "Is there anyone else in this town you can think of who could run the shop for a few weeks? Maximum a few months? I'll pay well."

"I'll think about it and get back to you."

"You do that Shawn, but don't take too long. Tannie Hettie needs to start this treatment as soon as possible."

Shawn nodded knowingly and wriggled out from beneath

Oom Marius' arm. He made his way to the wooden steps leading down to the street. On the bottom one he paused and looked back at the older man, "You won't tell Patty about this, will you, Oom?"

Oom Marius shook his head distractedly.

Petrus could tell he'd already forgotten about Shawn and was thinking about who he'd approach next. He turned to come back inside and Petrus quickly grabbed a box of cereal.

Oom Marius stamped in and cast an impatient glance at Petrus. He clenched his jaw as he turned to his assistant.

"Have you fed the bloody lobsters yet?" he snapped.

Petrus shook his head. This was a bad time not to have done what Oom Marius had asked.

"*Jissus, vandag is die dag wat ek jou klap,*" he started.

Jesus, today's the day I slap you.

Quickly, the shop assistant abandoned his unpacking and made his way to the dark corner at the back of the shop where the squid things were defrosting. The smell reminded him of that time he'd forgotten his plate of tinned pilchards in tomato sauce out in the sun. He picked up the first icy, slimy creature and threw it down on the wooden chopping board. Just as ugly as the stupid lobsters, thought Petrus. He brought down the silver blade and started slicing.

Petrus was a thin man. He was always going to be a thin man. The chance of being overfed or having too little physical activity to burn off his food didn't exist in his world. His tight black curls were cropped close to his skull, his eyes shone big and white from his dark black face, made shiny with a daily layer of Vaseline. He had a large, flat nose, and big sticking-out ears. Petrus was not a good looking man. He'd often stared at the only photograph he had of his father, a strapping, handsome black man, and wondered why he hadn't inherited any of his fine features. But Petrus wouldn't allow this wondering to stay in his head too long. He tried not to think too much about sad stuff. He had a job, he had a house, and he was able to look after his mother. What more could a thirty-year-old man ask for?

While he was cutting the squid, Petrus' dumb idea came back.

He shook his head to get it out of there. It was a bad idea. A very bad idea. But it was stuck now like the red dust that stuck to his shoes. It got into everything and could never be gotten rid of, no matter how often he dusted or washed. Petrus shook his head again and again but it only seemed to make the idea grow stronger.

"What are you doing, standing there shaking like a bloody thorn tree in a storm?" Oom Marius called out from behind the counter.

Petrus forced his head to stay still but inside the idea was taking over everything. He went back to the boxes on the floor and packed out the remaining tins. He flattened the cardboard box and took it into the alley where they stored old paper. Still the idea was there. Petrus finished unpacking the corn flakes and then moved on to the maize meal. But the idea came with him. He worked faster, packing out all the boxes in record time, but it didn't help to leave the idea behind. He tried thinking about Precious but today it seemed impossible to conjure up the image of her jaunty walk and pretty, smiling face.

So, he decided, if even Precious couldn't chase away this idea in his head, then the only way to get rid of it was to go to Oom Marius.

The shop was quiet again. The usual rush when the primary school was let out had subsided. All the little kids who'd gotten money from their mothers for chores or good behaviour had spent it on sweets. Others had been sent to buy bread for sandwiches. Now they were all at home munching away on their purchases. The only sound was the rhythmic swishing of the ceiling fan.

Shuffling nervously, Petrus moved closer to the counter where Oom Marius was bent over one of his ledgers.

"Baas?" Petrus tried out his voice timidly.

It had obviously been too soft. Oom Marius didn't look up.

"Baas?" Petrus tried again, this time louder.

Oom Marius looked up and stared him straight in the face.

"Did you just call me, Petrus?" he asked slowly.

Petrus nodded.

"*My lieve God!*" Oom Marius said, unhurried. "Did you just speak?" His mouth hung slightly open and his eyebrows knitted together to become one.

"Yes, Baas," Petrus repeated.

"When did you learn to talk?"

"I've always been able to talk, Baas," Petrus replied.

"What? You mean you could talk when you were eight years old and you first came to work for me?"

"Yes, Baas."

"For twenty-two years you've been able to speak and you haven't said a word? Not a single word?" Oom Marius' voice was sounding more like a woman's each time he asked a question.

Petrus was angry with the idea for having taken hold in his head. Today was the day he was finally going to get the beating he'd been promised so often. Of that he was sure. And it was all the idea's fault.

"Why haven't you said anything until now?" his voice was just a touch lower. Was he starting to calm down, Petrus wondered.

"You never asked me anything, Baas."

"And today I asked you something?"

The pitch was going up again.

"I was thinking about something. Something that would help you. Something…"

Petrus stopped. He could see on Oom Marius' face that he wasn't hearing a word he was saying. He could see him thinking back to all those times when it might have been easier if Petrus had just answered him. Petrus could see by his face that there had been many, many times. And he could see that Oom Marius was very, very, angry.

"All these years you've been lying to me?"

"No Baas, I haven't been lying," Petrus shook his head profusely.

Oom Marius' face was, by this time, almost as red as the uniforms the little girls wore to school. Petrus had never seen this particular shade of red on his baas' face before and he was very familiar with all of his shades. Oom Marius was making his way out from behind the counter. Warily, Petrus started walking backwards, past the sieves, the chopping boards, the bright plastic salad bowls, trying to put some space between himself and his baas.

Petrus needed to say something quickly before Oom Marius reached him. He'd seen with his own eyes how hard he could hit. Last year Oom Marius had caught old Abel from the township stealing beer. He'd dragged him out back and given him a hiding. Petrus had heard later that the doctor had had to stitch him up in several places or his insides would have fallen out. Petrus didn't want his insides falling out today.

Petrus kept walking backwards and Oom Marius kept coming forward. He saw his baas clench both his fists. Oom Marius was getting closer.

Petrus felt his foot catch on something behind him. He stumbled backwards and just managed to keep his balance. It was the pricing gun. When he looked up again, Oom Marius was right in front of him. He smelt peanut butter on Oom Marius' breath. Saw drops of sweat in the furrows of his brow. His hand stretched out towards Petrus and grabbed hold of his shirt collar. The skin on Petrus' chest burned as Oom Marius twisted the fabric into a tight ball. He raised his other hand in a fist above his shoulder.

The idea was back in Petrus' head.

"Baas, I can look after the shop when you take Missies Hettie to the hospital," he spoke faster than he ever had in his life.

"What?"

Oom Marius' raised hand dropped slightly. His grip on Petrus' shirt relaxed.

Petrus breathed shallowly. His heels could touch the ground again.

"I know how you do everything in the shop. I can't do all the numbers you write in that book but I can count and I can give change and I can check the delivery man has brought everything that stands on the paper and I can help the customers and I don't steal Baas, you know I don't steal."

The look on Oom Marius' face told Petrus his baas was thinking about his words. The angry look hid away for a few seconds. It was making a place for new thoughts that were in Oom Marius' head.

His baas spoke again, very slowly. Petrus made sure the look on his own face told Oom Marius he was paying very close attention.

"You know I should give you a bloody good *paksla*?"

"Yes, Baas."

Without warning, Oom Marius released his hold on Petrus' collar. Petrus stumbled over the pricing gun again and this time he landed on the floor, his arms behind him for support, his legs stretched out in front. Still he stared up at Oom Marius' face. This wouldn't be the right time to give the impression that he didn't respect him.

"Get up off the floor and go home before I change my mind."

"Yes, Baas."

Petrus scrambled upright and allowed his feet to carry him backwards again. Towards the door. He wasn't going to be stupid and fetch his things from the storeroom. His sandwiches and his wallet and his bottle of water. He would just walk back to Rifilwe, he decided. There'd be no mini-bus taxi today.

Petrus reached the open doorway. Again he tripped and stumbled out onto the veranda. He was about to turn round when Oom Marius' voice called out from inside, "*Jou bliksem!*"

You scoundrel!

"Yes, Baas," Petrus called out. He turned round and hurried down the steps.

"Twenty-two years!"

"Yes, Baas."

"Not one word!"

"Sorry Baas."

On his way home, his shoes covered with the red dust of the dirt road that lead to the township, tired black faces staring out of the taxis speeding past him, Petrus decided that maybe the idea hadn't been such a bad one after all.

Chapter Four

Tannie Hettie laid down the last fork next to the flower-bedecked dinner plate. Taking a step back, she admired her handiwork. The back door was open to let in a bit of a breeze but she wasn't sure whether, at this time of the day, it was more heat than breeze pouring into the kitchen. She smoothed down the corner of the white tablecloth, thin with age, which she'd embroidered with daisies round the edges all those years ago when she and Marius were just married.

At the start of their life together, she'd spent a lot of time trying to impress her new husband with her housekeeping skills: she embroidered pillow cases and table cloths, knitted Marius a jersey for the winter time, bought scatter cushions the same colour as the curtains, she even tried making the boys matching shirts for Sunday school, though this venture couldn't be said to have been a wild success. Oom Marius had never, not once, during those early years, praised her for any of her feminine talents. The only thing he voiced any kind of appreciation for was her cooking skills. And he was right, even if she had to admit it herself; she was a good cook. Embroidery, knitting, interior decorating and needlework had slowly drifted out of their home.

It was just as well, actually. Tannie Hettie had never been too fond of these pastimes. But despite having no particular affinity with the handiworks, she would often imagine herself sitting side by side with the daughter she'd never had, each with a needle in their hand, cross-stitching flowers onto their handkerchiefs while they sipped tea and dunked home-made rusks. Female company, that's probably what she missed most in her home. Whenever these wistful thoughts overcame her, she'd shake her head sternly and tell herself it was time to get over to Sarie's place for a visit. There was always some good, solid female company to be had over there. Why, she'd just been to see her best friend yesterday and felt so much better for it.

Her three boys were coming home today. Oom Marius had

phoned them during the week, told them to cancel their plans and get over to Klippiesfontein for Sunday lunch. Good boys they were, the way they still listened to their father despite being grown men. Tannie Hettie looked down at the pretty fabric of her dress, little blue forget-me-nots against a yellow background, and wondered if anyone would notice she'd bought it new, specially for today. One thing was certain; Marius wouldn't. The small efforts she made to keep herself attractive – trips to Alan's Hair Salon, forcing herself into passion-killer underwear to hide those extra kilos, tweaking the pesky hairs from her upper lip with her tweezers – they were all lost on him.

These were the days Tannie Hettie liked best of all. They didn't come round often, mind you. Only three or four times a year but, as everyone knew, the most worthwhile things in life were scarce. Only today… well, even the prospect of seeing her sons couldn't lift the weight hanging over her. The weight of the announcement she and Marius would have to make. She'd be grateful when this day was over and they'd all gone home.

How could she even think that! She shook her head to get rid of the thought. The smell of meat simmering in thick gravy drifted into her nostrils and reminded her to check on her pies.

They were browning nicely, she nodded, even if she said so herself. The one, a succulent lamb pie made from one of Hans' day-old lambs, the other, a guinea fowl and chicken pie. Henk Coetzee had gone hunting last week and he'd given her a few of the wild birds. Satisfied, she straightened up and let her hands rest briefly on each of the dishes on top of the green enamel stove, just to assure herself everything was ready; the stewed sweet potatoes, the yellow rice with raisins, the glazed beetroot salad…

A part of her couldn't wait to hear the first car drive up, but then another part was grateful as long as she heard nothing. Who would arrive first? Probably Johan with his wife, Karien, and little Johan. They had the furthest drive so they'd possibly left home nice and early. Tannie Hettie couldn't wait to take baby Johan in her arms and smother the little guy with kisses. She didn't see him as often as she did her other grandchildren because of the distance. Those fat little cheeks of his, she laughed softly to herself, weren't they just made to bite in?

A car pulled up in the driveway behind the shop. Tannie Hettie's heart lurched into her throat. They were here. The time had come. There was no going back. Four doors slammed in quick succession and a clatter of voices drifted in through the open door. Wiping her hands on her apron, she undid the bow at the back and hung it up on the hook behind the door. Looking down at the angry, cracked skin on her fleshy fingers, she wondered if there was enough time to put on some Ingram's Camphor Cream.

She heard Oom Marius outside greeting their youngest son Stefaan and his family, and she knew she should go out there too, but somehow she couldn't convince her feet to move. She felt cold beads of sweat on her upper lip and in her eyebrows. Why couldn't it leave her alone? Just for a few hours? Just long enough to enjoy her sons' company for a while? Wiping her brow, she realised it was probably the only thing they'd talk about for the rest of the day. The cancer. Tannie Hettie stretched out her hand and took hold of the back of the kitchen chair to steady herself.

"*Waar is Ma?*" she could hear Stafaan's voice.

"In the kitchen, getting lunch ready," Oom Marius answered.

She could hear the voices coming closer to the open door.

"Pull yourself together, Hettie," she reprimanded herself. Tugging one last time at the folds in her dress to hide her fat rolls, she forced her lips into a smile and waited for her son to appear in the doorway.

An hour later, Tannie Hettie's entire family was seated at the two tables, the little ones in the kitchen, except for baby Johan who was in his high chair with the adults in the dining room. She could still remember when the boys were young and the five of them would eat in the kitchen every evening. When they would look up at her like she was the only woman in the world. Had Marius ever thought about her in that way? What had happened to those days? Where had they gone?

Her daughters-in-law dished up for the children and took their seats next to their husbands. Tannie Hettie sat at the end of the table, across from Oom Marius, and watched her family as they passed dishes to and fro between one another. She was quiet. There was no way she could take part in the banter around the table today. Oom Marius' eyes met hers and he gave her a curt nod of encouragement. Despite the wear of years of living on each other's lips, he still managed, occasionally, to know just what she was feeling. She smiled wanly in return.

"Pass me the sweet potatoes?"

"Could you give me the rice?"

"What about this drought we're having?"

"Ma, what's wrong? You're so quite today."

"It's nothing," she said, shaking her head in abject denial. "Just the heat that's getting to me."

Her sons nodded, only half convinced, and turned their attention back to one another.

"Remember that time…" Andre had started with the boys' favourite pastime as soon as they set foot in their childhood home – reminiscing with his brothers about their younger years. She watched him laughing out loud as the recollections flooded back. "Remember when Blackie Swart was after Lynette? He couldn't give a damn that she was my girl."

Tannie Hettie closed her eyes. She had no appetite. Not for the food, not for the conversation around the table. If it wasn't for the fact she'd draw unwelcome attention to herself, she'd have pushed her plate away. Shaking her head to compose herself, she opened her eyes again.

"Ja," Johan joined in, "he even bought her chocolates from Pa's shop. Can you believe his nerve?"

"Isn't he the one who made that tape for her with a whole bunch of love songs on? And then… and then you found it instead of Lynette?" Stefaan was laughing.

"We really let him have it, didn't we?" Andre said. "Knocked his front teeth right out of his mouth. Do you still remember how he lay there, blood pouring down his chin, shocked that we jumped him like that?"

"As if we were going to let him get away with going after one of our girls."

Tannie Hettie looked across the table at Anne-Marie. She suspected her daughter-in-law wouldn't be too impressed with all this violent talk from her husband and his brothers. Tannie Hettie was right. The younger woman was rolling her eyes.

"Ja man," Stefaan carried on obliviously, "what about that year you blokes got into a fight with the guys from Prieska High? What was that about again?"

Tannie Hettie heard herself being summoned gingerly from the kitchen doorway by her granddaughter, "*Ouma,* may we be excused? Can we go to the shop?" She was grateful for the distraction.

"Have you finished all your food, sweetheart?"

"I have, but Gerrie and Kobus didn't eat their beans. They said it was gross."

Tannie Hettie knew she had to react quickly before the children's parents sent them back to the table and made them sit there until their plates were empty. It was her house and she didn't want any unpleasantness this afternoon. "Yes, you can go. The green beans probably were a bit too peppery."

"And don't eat up all my sweets," Oom Marius piped up from the other end of the table with a wink.

The little girl nodded solemnly.

The children didn't need a second invitation. Jumping up from their chairs, they rushed to the door separating the kitchen from the shop and stormed through it. For the first time, Tannie Hettie managed a smile.

"Close the door," the youngest one squealed, "so they can't see."

"We really gave them a *paksla* that night, didn't we?" Johan picked up the conversation again. "How many of them were there? Eight? Ten? They didn't know what hit them."

Anne-Marie laid her knife and fork pronouncedly down on her plate. She was glaring at her husband but he didn't notice. He raised his fork with a steaming bite of pie, the crust golden and crispy, to his mouth. "Ma, this guinea fowl's excellent," he said.

Anne-Marie was looking straight at Stefaan. Impatience and fury dripped from the young woman's eyes. Not this too, thought Tannie Hettie. She didn't have the strength for one of their family squabbles today. She wished she was sitting closer to her youngest son so she could nudge him in the ribs to let him know it was enough. Her two other daughters-in-law, Suzan and Karien, exchanged meaningful glances with each other.

"Teach them to mess with the Klippiesfontein blokes, hey," Stefaan snorted. "Didn't one of them end up going to hospital?"

The laughter that erupted from the three men at the table was cut short by the sound of a chair scraping loudly on the floor. A squeak of panic escaped Karien's lips. Anne-Marie had pushed her plate away and was standing upright, her white knuckles clutching the edge of the table. "Can't the three of you find something else to do for once?" she pronounced every word slowly and with emphasis. "I'm sick of listening to the same stories over and over again. Didn't you do anything except fight when you were boys?"

Everyone was quiet. The food steamed undisturbed from the eight plates around the table. Eyes glanced nervously back and forth at one another to determine alliance or discord. The only audible sound was the laughter of the children drifting in from the shop.

Andre put down his knife and fork and looked up at his sister-in-law's angry, red face. "That's what we do, Anne-Marie, we fight. It's what we've been doing since we arrived on this continent over four hundred years ago. We fight. Because if we didn't fight we would've been wiped out centuries ago. We are Afrikaners. It's in our blood."

If she'd had the strength, Tannie Hettie would've said something in Anne-Marie's defence. She had also had her fill of young men with more testosterone than sense. On the other hand, what Andre said was true as well. If it wasn't for the Afrikaners' fighting spirit, they would've been annihilated by the

British or the native tribes many years ago. She remained frozen in the discomfort of the moment.

Tannie Hettie looked across to the opposite end of the table. Oom Marius was looking straight back at her and she knew he could read the look in her eyes, "Help!"

But before he could say anything, a high-pitched scream erupted from somewhere on the other side of the wall, from inside the shop. There it was again. The scream. Over and over it sounded. A hysterical little girl.

Her sons and their wives shot simultaneously out of their seats, chairs clattering on the floor behind them, and rushed into the kitchen. Tannie Hettie heard the dividing door between the shop being ripped open and the clatter of six adult pairs of feet as they followed their children into the screaming depths of the Sunday afternoon store. A muffle of voices as adults urgently questioned children.

Tannie Hettie and Oom Marius stayed calmly seated at the two ends of the table. They even had the faint beginnings of smiles on their faces. Oom Marius looked at his wife and nodded his head knowingly, "They've found the lobster tank."

"Right on time," answered his wife.

Now, Tannie Hettie was renowned for being a good cook. Her daughters-in-law were always asking for her family recipes so they could prepare her famous dishes for their husbands. But the one area where her cooking skills, any self-respecting Afrikaans woman's badge of pride, surpassed all others was her preparations of sweet, sticky South African puddings. It was the highlight of all family gatherings. She'd make one big one for the family and three smaller puddings for her sons to take home with them. At the next gathering, her empty dishes would be dutifully returned because they knew, at the end of the day, they'd be presented with another of her mouth-watering creations.

But Tannie Hettie was going to have to disappoint them today. Yes, she'd spent the afternoon before baking a traditional Cape brandy pudding. She'd left it to rest and grow rich with flavour overnight but she hadn't baked three smaller ones. Even though she'd fully intended to, when it actually came to breaking the extra eggs, measuring out the flour, melting the farm butter... well, she simply hadn't been able to summon up the energy. The pills Doctor Brown had given her seemed to do that to her. Standing in the kitchen, pouring the hot custard into the jug, she didn't know how she was going to tell them.

"*Ouma,* what pudding did you make today?"

"A Cape brandy pudding, my love," Tannie Hettie explained to her little grandson standing next to her at the stove.

"Did you make a lot?"

"I made enough."

"Enough to have seconds?" he wanted to know.

"Enough to have seconds," she confirmed with a smile. "Now go inside and wait with your mother. This is hot."

The pudding bowls were arranged on the dining room table. Children gathered round their parents, waiting for their grandmother to make her customary entrance, carrying a huge wooden tray with the dish of pudding and a steaming jug of custard.

Tannie Hettie started her slow walk towards the dining room, anticipating the little faces that would stare at her in awe and wonder that she could create something so scrumptious. She smiled to herself. Six grandchildren in total.

Getting closer to the doorway, a new thought took hold in her brain. Would there be any more grandchildren, she wondered. Would she get to see them? What on earth was Marius going to do without her?

Tannie Hettie's usually strong arms and hands were shaking. The earthenware dish and porcelain jug rattled against each other. Her steps hesitant. The time was getting closer to tell them. Everyone knew they'd been summoned to Klippiesfontein for a reason. It was no one's birthday. It wasn't Christmas or Easter. So why were they here? Conversation had faded to a trickle as everyone waited for the announcement.

Suddenly, for no explicable reason, Tannie Hettie's hands

seemed to turn to pudding themselves and she let go of the tray. The dish and the jug clattered onto the floor, breaking into hundreds of shards. Loud, it's so loud, she thought. Tannie Hettie looked down at her chubby feet bulging out of their neatly cased white low-heeled shoes, her camel-coloured stockings, and saw steaming hot custard all over them. She realised she was in pain but wasn't sure how to react. A chunk of pudding lay limply on the toe of one shoe. Should she shout? Should she sit down? Her children were jumping up from the table, coming towards her in slow motion. Expressions of concern. Tannie Hettie just stood there.

Twenty minutes later she was sitting on a chair. Her nylon stockings had been removed by one of her daughters-in-law. Her burns had been smeared with butter. She was wearing slippers. At the dining room table! Tannie Hettie was embarrassed. They'd never seen her like this before. The women had finally stopped fussing and were all three looking directly ahead of them, clutching their children on their laps. Andre, Johan and Stefaan however, were not so discreet. They stared straight at their mother. Questions on their lips they didn't dare ask.

Oom Marius pushed his chair a little way back and wiped his mouth on his embroidered serviette. Clearing his throat, he took hold of the edge of the table with both hands and raised his eyes to look at his family. Tannie Hettie noticed the left corner of his lower lip quivering. It only did that when he was upset. Her heart went out to him. She knew how much he despised any show of emotion in front of his sons, how he was dreading the next few minutes. She imagined she could even hear his heart beating at her end of the table.

"It's alright, Marius," she spoke in a quiet but certain voice, "I'll tell them the news."

Chapter Five

"*Kom vrou, ons gaan laat wees,*" Tannie Hettie heard Oom Marius calling through the door separating the shop and their home.

Come wife, we're going to be late.

Was it time already? She'd got out of bed half an hour earlier that morning to make sure she had enough time. Dusting her cheeks with a last sprinkling of beige powder, she dropped the brush on her dressing table, cast one last look at her apricot-coloured bed-spread to assure herself she'd made the bed, and rushed through to the kitchen.

Tannie Hettie had stopped noticing the way Marius spoke to her. He didn't mean it, she knew that, and that was enough for her. If almost forty years of marriage had taught her one thing it was that she couldn't change him. She'd stopped nitpicking over little details like expecting attention from him or being spoken to decently a long time ago. All the same, she sighed.

"I'm coming," she called, lifting the cake off the plate and lowering it into the cake tin.

Doubt skirted across her brain – was she dressed appropriately? She was wearing the dress she'd worn to Stefaan's wedding. Had it been six years ago already? She could hardly believe it. Time seemed to go so much faster when one got older. She looked down at her bosoms, saw them straining against the white buttons down the front. A little neck scarf would hide that, she decided. She'd even put on the pearl earrings Marius had bought her on their honeymoon in Cape Town all those years ago, though she doubted if he'd notice. With a final straightening of her shoulders and jutting out of chin, she picked up the cake tin.

Pushing the door open, she walked into the shop.

Oom Marius was examining his face in a small hand mirror encased in shiny red plastic – the one Petrus kept in the back with his belongings now he was paying more attention to his appearance. He straightened his tie and slicked down his blonde fringe with a lick of spit to his finger.

He looked up at her.

"Pineapple upside down tart," she smiled nervously in answer to the question she thought she read on his face. "Last year at the church fête, Dalene said it was the best she'd ever eaten. I added some coconut this time."

"We're going to be late," he grunted.

"I'm ready," she said. Then, turning her attention to her husband's assistant, "Good morning, Petrus."

"Good morning, Missies."

Petrus was wearing a pair of beige trousers and a white shirt he'd bought from Oom Marius on tick three days previously. The red dust had been washed from his face and he'd smeared it with a fresh layer of Vaseline. She was glad to see he was making an effort. What with the news they were bringing to the townsfolk, it was important he looked presentable.

"Come, let's go. We don't want to keep him waiting," Oom Marius said.

Tannie Hettie scuttled over to him and hooked her free arm through his. They set off towards the door.

"You watch the shop now, Petrus," Oom Marius called over his shoulder.

His assistant, who'd been checking out his reflection in the glass of the lobster tank, nodded fiercely and hurried behind the counter to take up Oom Marius' place.

"I don't want to hear any nonsense when I get back. You hear me?"

"Yes, Baas."

As they left the shop, Petrus stood stiffly behind the counter, staring straight ahead of him.

Arm in arm, Oom Marius and Tannie Hettie went down the steps and out onto Church Street. Nodding at the regulars nursing their brandies and coke on the veranda of the Royal Hotel, past Boutique Nadine claiming to sell *suitable formal and everyday wear for today's woman*, past Alan's Hair Salon, on their way to the yellow brick house that stood next to the church.

Now Dominie Andries was not an easy man to approach, even with the simplest of requests, and this one was as far from simple as the Kalahari Dessert was from the tropical shores of Natal. In fact, Tannie Hettie thought it might just turn out to be the most controversial request anyone had ever made in Klippiesfontein. It was even worse than the time when the preacher from the ZCC Church asked the Dutch Reformed congregation to pray for the mysterious deaths in the township, believing prayers in vast numbers would summons the Lord's mercy.

In the first place, Tannie Hettie had known, just like the other members of the Dutch Reformed Church, that theirs was the chosen church of the Lord and therefore no one really approved of fraternising with other faiths. But then again, she had to concede that belonging to the ZCC Church was better than belonging to no church at all. And here the congregation agreed with her one and all.

In the second place, no one was foolish enough to believe that the deaths were in any way mysterious. Not even Tannie Hettie, and she knew she could be gullible at times. It was AIDS killing off the blacks like that but they were simply too superstitious to call the disease by its name. And surely AIDS was God's scourge on people of low morals? Or wasn't it?

But then again, as Mrs Joubert, the widow, had pointed out during the weekly prayer group, God wouldn't mind if they prayed for the innocent children and pregnant mothers who were suffering from the disease. So, after three weeks of heated debate around Klippiesfontein, Dominie Andries finally relented and called on his flock to take up the women and children suffering from the disease in their daily prayers. Tannie Hettie had felt better when they came to that conclusion.

But today there would be no Mrs Joubert with her sensible way of seeing things in the dominie's living room. Today it would just be Oom Marius and Tannie Hettie sipping their tea and nibbling their cake. Today it would be only their two feeble voices putting across this outrageous request, facing the dominie's Christian decency and his unpredictable wrath. Tannie Hettie thrust her shoulders back and her chin forward as she tried to put on a brave face she wasn't really feeling. She scurried along on her husband's arm, having to take almost two steps for each of his.

Ten minutes later, perched nervously on the edge of the floral sofa in the living room, Tannie Hettie watched as Dalene, the dominie's wife, poured four cups of *rooibos* tea into her tea set. It was a very pretty tea set, sighed Tannie Hettie. Her grandmother had had one almost like it but it hadn't been passed down to Hettie. It had gone to her brother's wife instead.

"Now tell me, Brother Marius," Dominie Andries started slowly. His voice, used to projecting from the pulpit, boomed in this small space, "What is it you have come to my home about today? I hope it is good news you bring."

Tannie Hettie reached over, grabbed hold of her husband's clammy hand lying in his lap and gave it a little squeeze.

The next morning, Oom Marius and Tannie Hettie sat bolt upright in their usual pew, four rows from the front. The lines of the church were stark, the walls white, the decoration minimal, keeping to the Calvinistic teachings of the church. Even though she realised she was being irrational, Tannie Hettie imagined the whispers they were hearing from the expectant worshippers were directed at them. That their secret was out before the dominie had even said a word.

A chorus of *sshh's* arose from the congregation as Dominie Andries made his way into the church from a side door. It was followed by a rustle of Sunday's best as everyone rose to their feet. Tannie Hettie straightened her skirt and stood up.

"*Goeie môre kinders van die Here,*" the dominie greeted his congregation.

Good morning, children of the Lord.

"*Goeie môre* Dominie," they replied in unison.

"Come, let us start this morning's service with a prayer."

There was another rustle as people took their seats and bowed their heads.

"We join in prayer to celebrate our coming together this morning and surrender our destiny to you, oh Lord. We give thanks in our hearts for the founding of this vibrant nation of diverse peoples."

A few coughs interrupted the prayer.

Dominie Andries raised his voice and continued, "We give thanks for and bless the souls of those who came before us and prepared this nation, to nurture and to save it; because so many gave their lives for it, some selflessly and many needlessly. We ask that God's Holy Spirit now fill the hearts of all of Klippiesfontein's citizens with thoughts of goodwill, acceptance and respect for others. In this may we be cleansed of all destructive thoughts. May judgement of others, bigotry, racism and intolerance be washed clean from our hearts, like the blood of our forefathers. May our children be blessed. May we be renewed. May each one of us be filled with the spirit of the Almighty, the Divine. We thank you Lord, for hearing our prayer this day. Amen."

"Amen," chorused the congregation before all heads jerked up in question to face the dominie.

What on earth was this new message he was preaching?

It felt to Tannie Hettie as if a hundred pairs of eyes were boring into her and her husband's backs. Of course, the congregation could have no idea what was to unfold but still, she couldn't shake the feeling. She scratched around in her handbag, took out a tissue, and dabbed at the beads of sweat on her upper lip. She saw Oom Marius push his finger in beneath his collar and tug at it.

Dominie Andries' sermon went on and on in the same vein, preaching a brand of tolerance not often heard inside their Dutch Reformed Church. Having the dominie behind them was the best weapon they could have in this town, but still, Tannie Hettie doubted whether it was likely to have much effect in the face of Klippiesfontein's small town ways.

She thought back to the meeting in the dominie's living room the day before. She was grateful to him for eventually seeing Oom Marius' side of the matter. Even if it had taken two and half hours, four cups of tea, a shot of *brandewyn*, burning wine, for the men and, as a last resort, Tannie Hettie's breaking down in uncontrollable tears to convince him that they had no other choice. Petrus was going to run the General Store. There was no way around it. Tannie Hettie had the cancer and they had to go to Cape Town for treatment.

"Until death do us part like it stands in the Bible, Dominie," Oom Marius had told him.

And that had been the bit that finally drew the dominie over onto their side.

Now Tannie Hettie knew the dominie's blessing of a black man running a white man's shop would go a long way in convincing the more charitable folk of Klippiesfontein. But it wasn't the charitable folk she feared. It was the likes of Oom Hans and Herman and Karel, the local leader of the AWB, the Afrikaans Resistance Movement. It was the Frikkies and Shawns of this town who were always looking for a leader no matter who that leader turned out to be.

She'd spotted them, one by one, sitting amongst the worshippers that morning and she knew there'd be a confrontation. *They* knew there'd be a confrontation even if they didn't yet know with whom. They listened seethingly to the dominie carrying on about that most hated of virtues: tolerance. They didn't know the details yet but they knew they were going to fight it. Patience was a feature the Afrikaners were renowned for and they exercised it in an exemplary fashion that morning. The fine points, everyone knew, would be in the part of the sermon where the dominie called for various church members to be taken up in the prayers of the flock.

Tannie Hettie sat anxiously through the Bible reading. She knew she had large wet patches showing under her armpits and there was nothing she could do about it. The dominie proceeded to interpret the reading to a moral lesson especially cut out for the residents of Klippiesfontein. He asked them to stand and join him in song.

"Now thank we all our God. With hearts and hands and

voices..."

Tannie Hettie belted out the words rigorously. Of course, today wasn't the day to be showing off her singing prowess, but the song was helping her release some of the tension she was feeling.

"Who wondrous things hath done, In whom his world rejoices..."

She felt a sudden easing of pressure at her bosoms. She looked down and saw two buttons had popped open. Raising the hymnbook in front of her chest, she quickly redid the buttons and continued to sing, a little less enthusiastically.

"Who from our mothers' arms, Hath blessed us on our way..."

She glanced over at Oom Marius, saw he wasn't singing and discreetly elbowed him in the ribs. He glared at her. She looked up at the dominie to see if he'd noticed. Oom Marius opened his mouth and started miming the words.

"With countless gifts of love..."

Staring down at the hymnbook, she saw a drop of perspiration fall onto the page.

"And still is ours today."

"Thank you. You can take your seats," the dominie said.

It was time, Tannie Hettie realised, for the dominie to make his announcements.

"Shall we take a moment now, children of the Lord, to think about the people in our congregation who are less fortunate than ourselves? I urge you all to carry these people with you in your hearts and prayers this week."

A faint murmur rose from the crowd.

"I ask you, members of the congregation, to think about Sister Babs and her family at this time of suffering. Her sister-in-law is in hospital in Prieska where she is undergoing a hip replacement. Then there is young Dawid and Hester. As you all know, there was a fire in their barn last week and they lost most of the farming equipment. We pray for them and we ask the Lord to let the insurance people make the right decision. I would also like to ask you to carry Brother Marius and Sister Hettie to the Lord in our prayers..."

A faint gasp from several matrons – a new fact was about to be revealed that had somehow escaped their notice.

"Hettie is suffering from the cancer and must go to Cape Town where she can get specialist treatment. Brother Marius will be leaving us for a short while to be with his wife at this difficult time. I ask you to pray for them and for their sons, Andre, Johan, and Stefaan. And because the people of Klippiesfontein must eat, even at a time like this, Marius has decided to leave the store in the capable hands of Petrus, whom you all know."

For a few seconds there wasn't a sound to be heard inside the church. Then the rustling started as people turned their heads to check one another's reactions.

A voice rang out, "*Wat sê jy daar Dominie?*"

What did you just say?

It was Oom Hans. Prominent sheep farmer and regular donor to the church.

Oom Marius and Tannie Hettie twisted round to see the speaker. They saw the short, stocky man who, without trying to, conjured up the word bulldog in everyone who looked at him. Blond hair, freckled arms and a skin with the look and consistency of leather. He was standing upright.

"I am asking the good people of Klippiesfontein to lend their support to Brother Marius at this difficult time," answered the dominie.

Tannie Hettie looked back. She could see beads of sweat running down the dominie's greying temples.

"Yes, that's what I thought you said. You're asking us to support a kaffir running our local shop?"

Tannie Hettie looked down at her white high-heeled shoes and noticed with distaste that they were covered in red dust. Oom Marius was squirming next to her.

"Petrus is a God-fearing man, Brother Hans, and I would ask you not to refer to him with that word. You know it is no longer tolerated in this country of ours."

"I don't give a damn what is tolerated by this new banana republic. A kaffir is a kaffir and will always be a kaffir. You know that as well as I do, Dominie, and yet you stand here in front of us, in the house of the Lord, asking us to send our wives and children to buy our daily bread from him?"

Here and there indignant men rose to their feet in support of Oom Hans.

"In all honesty, Brother Hans, your wives and children have been buying more than just bread from him for many years now."

"No!" sounded a new voice. It was Karel. He was upright too. All necks jerked round simultaneously to get a full view of him. "We have been buying our groceries from Marius. A white man. A brother. Petrus is a cleaner and that's the way it should be. He's always known his place and we've accepted him. But when people start getting airs and graces, that's where our acceptance stops. Next week you'll be telling us that some *moent* from the township is going to run our children's school. This might be the way they do things in the city, Dominie, but it's not the way we do things here."

Oom Marius cleared his throat and stood up. Tannie Hettie noticed his hands shaking. "In all honesty Karel, this is a very difficult time for us. Hettie and I need your support. We cannot afford to close the shop and there is no one else who wants to take over. Ask Charlie. Ask Mister Scott. Ask Mrs Joubert. I spoke to all of them and asked them to run the shop but they couldn't do it. I even asked Shawn, for God's sake. I have no other choice."

Tannie Hettie noticed Shawn three pews back, sitting next to Patty. His wife gave him an enquiring look and he smiled apologetically.

"What about one of those employment agencies? Can't you phone one of them and ask them to send you a suitable person?"

"That will cost me a small fortune. And they employ people on the basis of affirmative action too, you know. There's no guarantee they will send me a white person. Anyway, no one knows the shop like Petrus. And it will take at least a couple of weeks before they find someone. Hettie needs to get to the hospital right away."

Tannie Hettie sniffed quietly into her lace-trimmed handkerchief. She felt so proud of her husband but she knew now wasn't the time to show it. Others might see it as gloating. She felt Marius' hand rest lightly on her shoulder.

"Then I have no choice either, Marius. I will drive my wife to Springbok once a week and we will do our groceries there," said Karel.

"And so will I," echoed Oom Hans.

A chorus of *me too's* echoed from the other men standing. Several women's voices joined in.

"You may be a prominent man in Klippiesfontein, Oom Marius," Bertie was talking now, standing next to his father, Oom Hans, "but that doesn't mean you can just stroll in here and start changing the way we've been doing things for generations."

Tears stung Tannie Hettie's eyes but she'd be damned if she let them pour out here. Her husband's voice had a hint of pleading to it, "Our medical aid won't cover all the costs for the treatment. I'm going to have to use our savings. Where will we be if the shop closes, Bertie?"

"It is our Christian duty to support our brothers of the church in times of need," the dominie tried again.

"I am sorry for your troubles, Marius," Oom Hans interrupted, "but you have no right to ask us to sell out our principles because your wife got sick."

"Since when is racism a principle?" Oom Marius snapped.

"What one man calls racism another calls self-preservation, and that's what I'm calling it here today. Self-preservation," said Oom Hans.

A chorus of approvals rose up from the congregation.

Suddenly Mrs Joubert stood up. The only woman amongst the standing men.

"You can call it any pretty word you want Hans, but you're a bigot. Marius, I for one, will be in front of your shop tomorrow morning when it opens up to buy my bread from Petrus. And I will do what the dominie asks. I will pray for you and Hettie and the boys every night. I will pray for Petrus too and hope this town finds the sense to support you."

A few voices were raised in appreciation of Mrs Joubert's words, but they were substantially fewer than the supporters of the other side.

"Thank you. Everyone," Oom Marius mumbled, before dropping back into his seat.

Mrs Joubert shuffled past the knees in her pew to get to the aisle. Others were taking her lead, standing up to leave. The discussion waiting outside over tea and slices of home baked cakes promised to be much more interesting than the one inside the church.

"Go in peace, children of the Lord," the dominie called after his disappearing congregation before coming out from behind the pulpit and hurrying outside too.

Only Oom Marius and Tannie Hettie were left inside. She felt his hand close over hers. It was still shaking.

Chapter Six

Petrus was sitting on a plastic crate outside his mother's front door, getting a bit of sunlight because it was good for his bones. He spent far too many hours inside the General Store every day. That's what his mother told him and Petrus always listened to his mother. Even if he was a grown man. He was sipping on a glass of Koolaid she had poured for him. Grape. His favourite.

The sun baked down ruthlessly but Petrus stayed sitting all the same. Sweat poured from his temples and trickled down his back. He stared at the pack of stray dogs running across the potholed street in front of his house. When it rained the whole thing was impassable, a mire of mud, but luckily that didn't happen too often around here. Across the road was a little house, identical to their own except that it had been painted a different colour, and the few sad shrubs sticking out of the rock hard red earth were different to the few sad shrubs in their own rock hard red earth. In fact, all the houses in his street, in half of Rifilwe for that matter, were identical. Built by the government when Mandela came to power, when he promised to take better care of his people, these rows and rows of identical little houses were proof that it had happened, that Mandela had existed and tried to keep his promise to them. It was a good thing to be reminded of this promise. Almost twenty years on, it seemed the politicians had forgotten that their job was taking care of the people.

Petrus started thinking about the important place Baas Marius and Missies Hettie had been to the day before. He knew it was important because Baas Marius had looked in the mirror and Missies Hettie she had baked a cake on a Saturday. And she'd come back without it. What this important thing was, Petrus didn't know. The baas and the missies they didn't tell him important things. But if he had to guess, and Petrus was a good one for guessing, he would've thought it had something to do with Missies Hettie's sickness and Petrus being in charge.

Now this was an important thing, this being in charge. And

not just important for Baas Marius and Missies Hettie and all the white people of Klippiesfontein. No, it was an important thing for Petrus too. It was so important that he'd never even dreamed of it happening to him. It was so important that he needed to tell his mother.

Petrus was nervous about this because he was never sure how she'd react. Her behaviour could be very erratic at times, though Petrus would never dream of holding her accountable for this. He tried to be a good son in this respect. She'd been through a lot, he always reminded himself, so he tried not to have unrealistic expectations.

He understood he wasn't the kind of man other people considered to be worthy of hearing important news. He accepted this. Even his own mother sometimes forgot to tell him important news. Like that time she went to visit her sister, Petrus' aunt, in Bloemfontein for a week, and she forgot to tell him. Or the time she bought a new television with monthly instalments and even though Petrus was the one who had to pay the monthly instalments, she'd still forgotten to tell him. Yes, most people people didn't think it was necessary to tell Petrus important news.

But Petrus wasn't like that. He liked to share his important news with others. Especially with his friend, Jacob, who got kicked in the head by a donkey when he was small and everyone said he was simple, but still he was Petrus' best friend. His only friend. Yes, Petrus would tell Jacob later that afternoon after the church meeting under the big tree in the veldt. But first he was going to be brave and tell his mother.

He stood up from his crate in the sun and went inside the three-roomed brick house he'd bought for her in the early days of the RDP – the *reconstructionanddevelopmentprogram*. It was dark inside the house but it was cool. He could hear the television on in her room so he went in.

"Mma?" Petrus spoke.

His mother was lying on her double bed which took up most of the floor space in the tiny bedroom. There was only enough place for a wire to be strung from one wall to the other on which she hung her clothes and a small crate in the corner that served as a stand for the TV. There was no place for a chair and that was why his mother had to watch her programmes lying down.

"Yes, son? What is it?"

"Mma, I want to tell you about something at my work."

"Sit down and keep quiet until this is finished. Queen is going to find out that Ruby is sleeping with her husband."

Petrus sighed and sat down gingerly on the edge of the bed. He watched the screen without much interest. He didn't understand why people wanted to watch actors doing bad things like sleeping with one another's husbands when you could see all of that stuff happening in real life in Klippiesfontein. At last the credits rolled down the screen and Petrus pulled himself into an upright position. He hoped his mother would not disapprove of his important news.

"Yes son," she turned her attention to him at last. "What is it? Be quick. I must make us lunch."

"Mma, Missies Hettie she is very sick."

"Yes?"

"The baas he must go to the hospital in the city to look after her."

"Get to the point Petrus. I have to get ready for church."

"I will be in charge of the shop while they are gone."

"What? You?" she scoffed. "You don't even speak to them. How can you be in charge?"

"I speak to them, Mma."

"What!"

"I speak to Baas Marius. I will speak to the customers also."

"No. No! I cannot believe what my ears are telling me. You mean to say you have broken your promise to me? Your promise never to speak to a white man?"

"Mma, it was time for me to speak. It was necessary."

That night. It was Petrus' first memory. Sometimes he wasn't sure if he actually remembered the event itself, or if he'd reconstructed it in his mind based on the facts his mother had told him again and again.

He was four years old and had been fast asleep. Something had gone wrong in the hospital after his birth and his mother wasn't able to have more children. That's why Petrus was allowed more than other children who had many brothers and sisters. That's why he was in his parents' bed that night.

He was woken up by a loud bang, probably the sound of the door smashing into the wall as they bombarded into his parents' bedroom. He was briefly blinded by the strong sharp light from one of their torches shining right into his eyes before he felt his body gathered up in his mother's arms and his face pushed between her breasts. He could still remember the sweet, musky smell of wood fire and porridge in her pyjamas. He tried turning his head to look at the men but his father's body was shielding his view.

The next thing Petrus heard was his mother's scream – a sound that seemed to travel right into the very centre of his bones and was still there all these years later. He recalled that scream as clearly as if it was still escaping her throat this minute and the mere memory of it never failed to turn his body cold all over. He saw outstretched blue-uniformed arms tugging at his father's shimmering black ones. His father's body was lifted from the blankets. Petrus saw more blue legs, arms, torsos, a cap, the twinkling of metal as torchlight fell on a badge – everything strangely disconnected. His father was shouting something and then Petrus heard a dull thud and his father's shouting stopped.

"You stay right there and watch the child," one of the men barked at Petrus' mother.

Leaving him frozen in bed, she scurried after them only to be stopped at the door by a white fist in her face and blood pouring from her mouth.

"Now don't make this more difficult than it has to be, woman. Stay here with the child."

His mother crumpled into a heap on the floor and Petrus stared over her bulk into the living room where the men were dragging his father's limp body out the front door.

That was the last time Petrus saw his father.

It was the only memory of him that he had.

Petrus could remember the next day too. The day after his father had disappeared. Carelessly, his mother had thrust him into the care of a neighbour who had seven children and no man, while she set off to Springbok to find out what had happened to her husband. She came back late that night and collected her frightened, hungry boy. She had nothing to tell him.

The next day was the same. And the day after that. And the day after that. Petrus was hungry and dirty and sat in the corner of his neighbour's yard with his eyes fixed on the dusty road that would bring his mother back to him, a little more broken every night. For two years she kept going back to Springbok, using any money she could scrounge for the taxi fare. Petrus learned to be content with table scraps that other mothers passed his way. He heard them, the other mothers, whispering to one another that his father was long dead, that his mother should give it up, accept it, and take care of her boy instead. He watched his former playmates when they came home from trips to Springbok to buy school uniforms so they could start in Class One after the New Year. He didn't bother asking his mother where his school uniform was. He knew there'd be none. Where once she'd been a beautiful woman, she was now a scraggly, dirty wisp, with hollow eyes and an outstretched hand begging for coins for the taxi fare to Springbok.

Then one day she turned to Petrus as if she'd suddenly remembered he was there. She gathered him up in her arms again like she had that night they'd taken his father. "You're growing up, my boy," she said.

Petrus nodded into her bosom which smelt sour and dusty at the same time. He wondered if he would ever smell wood fire and porridge again.

"Will you promise me one thing?" she demanded urgently.

Petrus nodded fiercely into his mother's chest. He would promise her anything in the world, he thought, as long as she held onto him like that.

"Promise me you'll never speak to a white man. Ever."

"Why, Mma? Why must I never speak to a white man?"

"Your father, he was one who couldn't keep his mouth shut. Had to complain about how he was treated at the railroads. Had to talk about standing up to them. The white men. And do you see what happened to him?"

Petrus nodded.

"Promise me," his mother insisted.

"I promise," he mumbled.

"Louder," she ordered.

"I promise I will never speak to a white man, Mma."

"Good, good," she nodded distractedly and let go of Petrus. He looked up at her and saw that distant look start to creep back into her eyes, "because I couldn't bear to lose you like I lost your father."

"I couldn't bear to lose you either," he said.

"I know. I know. Now be a good boy and go search in the veldt for some firewood for tonight's supper. Maybe I can make us some porridge."

His mother clutched her tight black curls. Tears coursed down her cheeks. "Your mother, Petrus. A helpless widow. The woman who has devoted her whole life to taking care of you, never taking a new man into her bed after your father disappeared. Alright, except that one, but it didn't last long, and you sit here on my bed and tell me you couldn't keep one little promise to me? One promise. One promise! Have I ever asked you for more than that?"

Petrus leaned forward and put a trembling hand on his mother's ample thigh. "Mma, I have a life outside the walls of this house. I have a job at the General Store. It is from this money that we eat, that we pay for this house. I had to talk to them, Mma, to help Baas Marius."

"Baas Marius. Missies Hettie. All the money they pay you. Yes, I see that is more important to you than your poor mother who lives every day with a broken heart..."

Every day taking care of her one and only son – Petrus knew what was coming. It was a tirade he heard regularly. A tirade he'd been hearing since he was a little boy. He had no defence against it. No defence against his mother. He was just grateful when he found her waiting at home for him with a warm plate of food every night when he got back from work. He sat quietly and waited until her words and her tears were spent.

When she had nothing more to say, when the accusations dried up, Petrus spoke gently, "It is the right thing to do, Mma. To help Baas Marius after all the many times he has helped us. I must do this."

A fresh wave of tears erupted from his mother. He stood up from the bed and went back outside to sit on his crate in the sun. Maybe he had upset her too much for her to make lunch now. He would buy them some *pap,* a porridge made from maize meal, and chicken from the eating-stand around the corner. After that he would go to church. Then he would speak to Jacob. Maybe he would be pleased to hear Petrus' important news.

Petrus stood under the sprawling wild fig tree dressed in his church uniform of a khaki jacket and trousers. Pinned to his lapel was a small silver star, like a sheriff's badge, etched with the letters Z.C.C. The women at the service wore calf-length straight skirts, daffodil-yellow tunics with rounded collars and neat bottle-green headscarves. The Zionist Christian Church was one of the biggest churches in Africa and Petrus was a proud member of it. Only people who had made the annual million-strong pilgrimage up to Moria over the Easter weekend, had feasted with the church and had been plunged under the waters of the river, were entitled to wear this uniform. Together they sang and danced, prayed, and listened to the minister's teachings.

After the service there was a chance for socialising amongst the members but Petrus and Jacob didn't usually wait around for this part. No, Sunday was Petrus' only day off except for Good Friday, Christmas and New Year, so he didn't have many hours to spend with his friend. Instead they wandered over to the township's soccer field – bare of grass, dry red-baked earth, two shallow hollows in front of the dilapidated goal posts – to watch the Sunday afternoon match.

Petrus would buy him and Jacob each a coke and something good to snack on like mealie cobs baked over the open fire or a bag of Mopani worms. Then the two men would enjoy the match and catch up on the goings-on of the past week. Jacob would tell him about what everyone in the township had been getting up to; who had broken up with whom, who was in love or pregnant, who had died... In turn, Petrus would bring his friend up to date on what Jacob perceived to be the glamorous happenings of the townsfolk – new cars purchased, computers that could do magical things, cellphones that seemed to be cleverer than people. He'd try to bring his friend a gift every week; a chocolate bar, a new pair of shoelaces, a packet of Space Dust that crackled on Jacob's tongue and made him laugh so much he almost wet himself.

Today they were sitting down on the red soil, leaning up against an old car wreck, too far away from the soccer field to follow the action but content just to be in each other's company. They were reaching the end of a big bag of Nik Naks and were licking the orange cheese-flavoured crumbs off their fingers. Always the best bit.

Petrus was telling Jacob his good news when he heard a gaggle of women's voices coming closer. He didn't look up because he was used to women gathering around the soccer field, decked out in their Sunday best, trying to catch the eye of any number of young men about. But never Petrus' eye. Or Jacob's, for that matter. The two of them, it seemed, were invisible to these young women.

But then Petrus heard one particular sound that made his head jerk up. A sound that cut straight through his flesh and made his skin cold. A familiar sound. A beautiful sound. A peal of laughter that had just erupted from Precious' throat.

Petrus stood bolt upright. His hands attacked his trousers,

his bottom, to swat off the layer of red dust that was stuck to him. That's what you got for sitting around on the ground like a pair of good-for-nothings. He stretched his hand out to his friend.

"Get up!"

"What?" Jacob asked.

"Get up," Petrus insisted, the whites of his eyes bulging with urgency in his black face.

"Why?"

They were getting closer. A group of four or five women, hips swaying, earrings jangling, words jabbering. And in their midst was Precious. A vision. Her cheeks shone, her eyelids batted, her teeth flashed momentarily. Her black curls had been straightened and brushed back, shiny with some or other oil that Petrus knew would smell wonderful if he got close enough. She wore a pleated pink skirt that danced when she walked and, even though he only saw her approach, he knew the skirt would dance extra joyfully at the back where it hung over her bum.

"Get up you idiot!" he urged, grabbing hold of Jacob's confused hand and yanking him up. His friend stared at him, injured, but Petrus didn't have patience for that look today.

"Do I look alright?"

Jacob looked him up and down, not sure what he should suddenly be seeing that hadn't been there before. He nodded uncertainly.

There they were. The women had reached them. Looks were exchanged. Polite acknowledging nods. And there she was. In the middle. Her lips broke into a smile.

"Good afternoon, brother," she said.

Petrus could do nothing but nod in return and even that took super-human effort.

Precious had greeted Petrus.

Precious had greeted Petrus!

Chapter Seven

At four o' clock Precious' boss approached her, "Would you mind staying a bit later today? My wife used to help me with the tax returns but now that she's not well, you know…"

Precious acquiesced. Truth be told, what choice did she have? It was because of him that she had her degree in bookkeeping, so staying late at work kind of came with the package. Usually she wouldn't have minded but it had been a long day and she was exhausted. She wouldn't show it, of course.

Done at last, Precious dragged her tired body into the waiting minibus taxi. Taking off her dangly pink earrings, she shoved them into her little white handbag. She loved those earrings but after a day like this they were simply too heavy. That's when she heard her cellphone give its familiar beep to announce she had a new message.

Precious' father had disappeared seven years ago when she was sixteen. Up until then her parents had been a two-income family who worked hard to pay the school fees of the formerly white high school in Springbok for their bright eldest child. But the lure of drink and loose women had proven too hard for her father to resist and he'd taken off, leaving her mother behind with five children and another one on the way.

Precious' mother had been adamant that her daughter finish her schooling at the high school in Springbok. She wouldn't be able to offer the same opportunities to her sons, now that her husband had left, but one way or the other she would see to it that her daughter got a decent matric. She'd started; she was going to finish it, even if she was a girl. She took on extra ironing work and there were days at the end of each month, before pay-day, when they had nothing to eat, but Precious' school fees never went unpaid.

When she was seventeen, Precious started working in white people's homes over weekends and school holidays so she could help her mother out with the cost of her education. She matriculated at eighteen amongst the brightest of her year, and could easily have gone to university if there'd been the money for it. Even if she'd won a bursary, her help was needed at home. So Precious found herself a job as a cashier in the shop at the Shell Service Station out on the highway.

After a year her boss suggested she register at Unisa, a correspondence university, and take a course in bookkeeping. His own wife was ill and she couldn't do the accounting anymore. He would deduct a sum off her salary each month that would go towards the cost of her studies.

Even though the thought of becoming a bookkeeper had never entered Precious' head, she agreed to his suggestion without a moment's hesitation. Passing up the chance to learn would have been ludicrous.

It took Precious four years to complete her diploma. She was invited to the graduation ceremony at the university in Pretoria but there was simply no way they could afford to pinch off that much money from the family budget to pay for the trip. For although Precious' next brother, seventeen-year-old Given, had had to be content with attending high school in the township, Precious and her mother had managed to scrounge enough money together to send her second brother, fourteen-year-old Blessing, to the same high school as Precious had gone to. That was simply the way it was: family members made sacrifices for one another to help them get ahead. In the end it would benefit the entire family.

Precious scooted over to a window in the taxi where she could stare out at the endless sea of grass and think of nothing until she arrived in Rifilwe. She took out her cellphone to read the message from her mother: she had no bread for the boys for school the following day. Could Precious bring some home?

If only she had sent it ten minutes earlier, Precious could have bought a bread at work. Now she'd have to get off the taxi in Klippiesfontein to buy one there and she was already exhausted.

Her feet throbbed in these shoes she'd got from her cousin. They were as good as brand new – her cousin had only worn them once but they'd been too small for her. She, in turn, had got them from the white woman for whom she worked – apparently they weren't quite the right colour to match the woman's outfit. Feeling a headache coming on, Precious could hardly keep her eyes open. She only hoped the shop would still be open when she got there. It was almost eight o'clock.

Climbing out in the centre of town, Precious stared languidly after the taxi as it carried its weary passengers off to their families; to their *pap* and gravy, to an hour in front of the TV watching *Generations,* to their beds… It was going to be late tonight. She only hoped her mother had got home early enough to prepare dinner. Precious was famished and the idea of still having to start supper made her weak with hunger.

"I'll buy two breads," she thought. "That way if Mother hasn't started supper, we can eat bread with jam instead. The boys will like that."

Satisfied with her foresight, she mounted the first of the three wooden steps leading up to the stoep of Klippiesfontein General Store.

Just as she took the last step, Precious heard the turn of a key in a lock. She glanced at her small white wrist watch and, almost simultaneously, at the glass pane of the shop's front door. Petrus' dark face stared at her from the other side.

Now if it hadn't been Petrus' face in the glass pane, if it had been Baas Marius', she would have broken out in a hunger-fuelled panic. The thin coating of sweat covering her body would have gone cold, she'd have turned round, taken the three steps back down to street level and waited for the next taxi, the whole time thinking about her hungry brothers and their empty lunchboxes at school the next day. But it wasn't Baas Marius. It was Petrus, so Precious stayed calm.

Looking up, she batted her eyelashes a few times and flashed him what she knew was a captivating smile. Even though she didn't like depending on it too much, there were times when female wiles were useful, and this was one of them. She had no doubt she'd hear the key turn back in the lock and she was right. Precious knew Petrus from seeing him around the football pitch at weekends. She knew him from the township and also the shop. He was a good, kind man. She'd often heard people speaking about the devotion and patience with which he took care of his sometimes less than sane mother. At twenty-three she also knew enough about men to know the way Petrus smiled at her would make him open up that door.

"You forgot something, sister?" he asked, sticking his head out the door.

"I didn't realise it was so late. I need two loaves of brown bread to take home."

"I will go ask the baas," Petrus' head disappeared back inside the door.

Precious waited. Would that door open up to let her in to quickly grab the two loaves? Would Baas Marius care enough about a simple black girl to switch on his till again? Did Petrus like her enough to insist or would he be too docile? She waited. Why couldn't her mother just have texted ten minutes earlier?

After standing there for what felt like ages, she eventually realised they weren't going to let her in. Petrus was probably too ashamed to face her, to tell her that Baas Marius had said no, so he'd ducked round the back and was already out on the street.

"I hope I get to sit on the same taxi as him," she thought, her footsteps heavy as she descended the stairs, "so I can give him a piece of my mind."

Just then he appeared alongside her. He'd come round the back of the building. In his hands he carried two loaves of bread and on his face, a grin. "Here, sister," he beamed and thrust the bread towards her as if it was his first born son. Gladly she took it from him.

"Thank you. How much do I owe you?"

"Owe *me*? They are not my breads, sister. They belong to Baas Marius."

"Yes, I know that. How much do I owe him?"

"Nothing," he continued beaming.

"Nothing? How can that be?" she frowned.

"When I went inside to ask the baas for two breads, I remembered that you learnt about money and about writing everything down that's got to do with money. Jacob's mother, she told me that. She sometimes works with your mother. She said you sent letters to the university and they sent letters back telling you what to do and this is how you learnt about money."

"That's correct, brother. This is how I learnt. It is called correspondence. But what does this have to do with paying for my bread?"

"I will tell you something that I have not told many people. I have told my mother and I have told Jacob. Do you know Jacob?"

"Your friend? The one who got kicked in the head by a donkey when he was small?"

"Yes, that Jacob."

"What did you tell Jacob that you want to tell me?"

"Baas Marius he is going to Cape Town for some weeks. He is going to leave me in charge of the shop, sister, because no white person wants to do it."

"That's good news. You must be very proud? You've worked for Baas Marius now for a long time."

"Twenty-two years," Petrus said, as if time itself was an achievement.

"But I still don't understand what this has got to do with the bread?"

"Baas Marius he asks me if I know anyone who is smart enough to help me in the shop when he is gone. I say no because when he ask me this, I can't think of anyone smart enough. I think of Jacob. I think of my mother. But they are not smart enough to help me so I say to Baas Marius, no."

"And then?" Precious suppressed the urge to roll her eyes. Why couldn't this man just say what he wanted to say?

"Then I see your face on the stoep and I remember that I do know someone who is smart enough. So I go inside and ask Baas Marius for two loaves of brown bread and I tell him I know a girl from Rifilwe who learnt about money."

"What did he say?" Precious was suddenly enthusiastic, her mind instantly filled with the possibilities a second job could offer. She didn't want to smile – she knew what they said about counting chickens before they hatch – but she smiled all the same.

"He say you don't have to pay for the bread and can you come into the shop tomorrow to talk to him. This is what he says, sister."

"I can do that, brother. I can do that."

Precious linked her arm through Petrus' and marched off to meet the next taxi.

Chapter Eight

It was the big day. The sun wasn't up yet. No thin line of light on the horizon. But then, it was only five in the morning. Oom Marius was swinging the suitcases onto the back of the bakkie, parked in front of shop. It was probably for the best, thought Petrus as he handed up Missies Hettie's beauty case, to get an early start. Less chance of being noticed.

Oom Marius had allowed Petrus to sleep in the storeroom the night before. "You never know what they'll do to you on your way from Rifilwe," he'd offered as explanation.

Well, sleep was a big word on a night like this. Just like him, Petrus didn't think his baas had been able to get a wink of it.

Oom Marius went back inside to have an early breakfast with Missies Hettie. Petrus sat down on the stoep and ate his *pap* with milk and sugar that the missies had made him. It was his favourite time of day this, before the sun managed to get its claws into everything, but on this particular morning there was just too much going on for him to enjoy it. Even his *pap* tasted like nothing, and Petrus loved his *pap*.

That's when he saw them: silhouetted against the dark shops of Klippiesfontein, strolling down the road as if they were going for a Sunday afternoon walk in the veldt. Lit up by the lone street lamp that stood at the intersection of Main and Church Street. All of them next to each other, taking up the entire width of the road. Thirteen, Petrus counted. Carrying two wooden poles with flags attached to the ends. Although they were rolled up, Petrus knew exactly which flags they were. The red one, when it was opened out, would bear the three-pronged black swastika of the AWB. The other one, with the flashes of orange, white and blue, was the old South African flag that some white men loved so much they refused to give it up. These flags, Petrus knew well enough, meant only one thing. Trouble.

He jumped up from the step, upsetting his plate of *pap* and milk, and ran into the shop.

"Baas, Baas!" he shouted.

He heard the scraping of a chair inside the house and the door was flung open, slamming into the shelf and causing the bottles of liquor to tinkle against one another. Oom Marius stared at Petrus. His jaw was clamped down, his eyes wild.

"What is it?"

Petrus jerked his head in the direction of the door. Oom Marius rushed out onto the stoep. He said nothing. From behind the tins of coffee creamer, Petrus watched his baas standing in the open doorway, his feet planted firmly apart and his arms crossed. He could see Oom Marius' eyeballs bulging in his head.

Petrus sucked in his breath as he watched the men walk up the steps without a word. Men whom his baas had known his whole life. They didn't even look at him. Frikkie tried to give Oom Marius a discreet nod when he thought no one was looking but Oom Hans flashed him an angry glance and Frikkie quickly looked down again. Oom Marius stared silently at the traitors who'd taken up his top step.

The men had a roll of red striped cordoning-off tape that Baas Piet had probably gotten from his job at the Roads Department. Calmly, as if Oom Marius wasn't even there, they spun their tape between the two wooden poles on both sides of the steps. Against one pole they leaned the Afrikaner Resistance Movement's flag, on the other, the former colonialist colours. They positioned themselves across the length of the stoep, legs spread, arms folded, and looked out across a just waking Klippiesfontein. It was only then that Karel turned round to face Oom Marius.

"We have closed your shop for business, Marius. For the good of all the people in this town. One day, when this whole business with Hettie and the cancer is behind you, you will see that what we did was for the best. The day will come that you will thank us for this."

"*Julle bliksems*," was all Oom Marius said.

You bastards.

Oom Marius turned round and went back inside. Behind the counter he picked up the receiver and punched in a number.

Petrus listened nervously as his baas told the police what was happening. He wondered whether it was such a good idea to phone them. Everybody knew that the police were *skelms*. But then again, thought Petrus, maybe they were only crooked when black men phoned. Maybe they'd help if they heard a white man's voice.

Oom Marius walked slowly up to where Petrus was cowering behind the shelf, "You're sure that Precious is coming in today?"

Petrus felt himself getting warm at the mere mention of her name. He pushed his finger in under his shirt collar and tugged at it. Soon she'd be here and he would spend all day working by her side. He would only need to glance at her to take in her skin, the colour of an ox after it had rained, or her lovely round bottom and her smell of perfume, like roses. That would make all this trouble worthwhile.

"She can help out for a small time in the mornings before she must go to her other job," he explained again.

"What time will she be here?"

"She said eight o'clock, Baas."

"Good. Good," Oom Marius nodded. "Now listen to me Petrus, this won't last long. They all have farms to look after or jobs to go to. After a week the excitement will die down and everyone will start coming to the shop again. We just need to be patient. Wait it out. No yelling. No fighting. No touching these men because that's when it will get out of hand. And don't speak to them. Do you hear me?"

Petrus nodded urgently.

"Now, back to business. Don't forget to phone the delivery guy. Don't order too many perishables. We won't be selling much this week. If everything goes well at the hospital then I'll try to drive down on Friday night to check on things. We have to go now, Petrus. It's a long drive to Cape Town and I don't want Missies Hettie to be late for her appointment."

"Ja, Baas."

Oom Marius let his eyes travel languidly through his shop, where they rested at last on the silently humming blue tank,

"And look after those bloody lobsters. Jesus, I'm going to eat the damn things myself when this whole business is over."

He walked to the back of the shop and disappeared through the door.

Petrus turned his fevered eye back to the open doorway in front. Fixed on the men. After a few minutes he saw his baas outside in the street. Popping open the bonnet of his bakkie, he checked the oil. He slammed it closed again, took a *lappie* out of his back pocket and wiped the dead insects off the windscreen, not once looking up at the men who'd taken over his top step.

Tannie Hettie had followed her husband round the back onto the street. She stood wide-eyed behind him, clutching her handbag and a Tupperware container with their sandwiches for the road. She dabbed at her eyes with a little lace handkerchief.

Petrus saw Oom Marius turn to his wife and nod, "*Dis tyd om te gaan vrouw.*"

It's time to go, wife.

Oom Marius opened the passenger door for Missies Hettie and helped her in. Walking round to get to his own door, he stopped suddenly and looked at something on the other side of the road. Petrus' heart froze over. He edged gingerly forward so he could make out what the baas was staring at. That's when he saw her: Mrs Joubert. Standing there in the first rays of the sun, her arms crossed, looking silently at Baas Marius. He saw her nod at him and his baas nodded back. What those nods meant, Petrus wasn't exactly sure, but he knew the nods were on their side. Mrs Joubert was probably the smartest woman in all of Klippiesfontein and if she nodded knowingly like that, then things might not be quite as bad as Petrus feared. He nodded too, even though no one could see him.

And just like that it was over. Baas Marius climbed into the bakkie and started the engine. They drove off. Petrus watched the backs of their heads grow smaller. Oom Marius' head stayed up high. He didn't turn to look back.

"Come back soon," he spoke out loud because the silence in the shop was too much to bear.

When Petrus looked across the road again to where Mrs Joubert had been standing, she was gone. He saw her prim figure making its lone way down Main Street towards her house. He hoped she'd be back.

Would Precious come in early, he wondered. It wasn't that he felt scared exactly, but having someone else inside the shop with him would make him feel braver. Braver than he felt now with only those evil lobsters for company. He went to stand behind the counter where his baas usually stood, opened the till and counted the money. The smell of the coins filled his nostrils. At least it was better than the everlasting smell of dust.

Chapter Nine

"How does this bloody thing work?" Oom Marius snapped before tossing the cellphone into his wife's lap. He shoved the gear stick into first, dropped the handbrake and skidded away from the side of the road, leaving a cloud of red dust behind the bakkie.

Tannie Hettie picked up the offending object and examined it carefully. "The protection is on, Marius. So you don't phone someone by accident when you press against it."

"I've never phoned anyone by accident in my life and I'm not going to start now."

"Do you want me to phone him, Marius?"

"*Ag,* I don't know Hettie. We haven't been gone long. The last thing he needs is me on the phone every five minutes like a bloody woman."

"Do you want me to phone him?" she asked more forcefully.

Oom Marius pressed his lips together and nodded.

He watched as Tannie Hettie lightly tapped the buttons. "You make me think of the teenagers who hang out on my stoep in the afternoons, Hettie," he smiled. Sometimes, only very rarely, that old smile that had been there when they first got married would creep back into his face. This was one of those times.

She smiled back.

"It's Missies Hettie here, Petrus. I'm phoning for Baas Marius to hear how it's going."

Her husband was looking at her, thin-lipped with concentration, his forehead wrinkled with a frown.

"Look in front of you, Marius," she scolded, and stretched out her hand to touch his chin and turn it in the direction of the road. She saw his eyes turn back to the shimmering black line stretching to the horizon. A mirage was rising from its surface, blurring a skinny brown cow grazing at the roadside.

"And haven't they arrived yet?" she asked.

She listened to Petrus' reply.

"But we phoned them two-and-a-half hours ago?"

Tannie Hettie jerked her head up in fright as the car veered to the right. Oom Marius had yanked the steering wheel sideways and was skidding to a stop again. He turned off the ignition and held his palm out to his wife. With a sigh she handed him the phone.

"Who's in the shop now, Petrus?" Oom Marius barked.

Tannie Hettie looked at her husband. She saw the sweat in the grey of his temples, the furrows in his forehead. "Turn around and go home, Marius," she sighed.

"Hold on, Petrus." Oom Marius turned to face his wife.

"Go home," she repeated. "I'll phone the doctor and tell him we can't make it today. We'll go when all this trouble has blown over."

"No Hettie, we've postponed this thing for as long as we could. Your appointment is for two o'clock and I'll have you there on time if it's the last thing I do. I don't want to hear anything more about this. Is that clear?"

He didn't wait to see her nod. His attention was back to the phone, concentrating on the details Petrus was relaying. Oom Marius gave a short, bitter laugh, "Only Mrs Joubert has been in. She cut through their tape with her sewing scissors and walked right past them. They didn't dare open their mouths to her."

Tannie Hettie recognised a sparkle of hope in the corner of his eye.

"What about Patty? Did she come for her cigarettes before she got on the bus?" he asked Petrus. Oom Marius nodded as he listened to the answer, his features hard as stone.

"At least tell me they let the kids in to buy their sweets before they went to school?" He shook his head. "OK Petrus, I have to go now. I'll speak to you later."

Tannie Hettie reached down for the Tupperware container at her feet. Clicking the plastic lid open and shut again with her neatly filed fingernails, she released a little waft of sulphurous egg each time. Not used to seeing disillusion on her husband's face, she didn't dare look at him.

Oom Marius sat quietly for a few moments before he reached for the key and started the car again.

Tannie Hettie stared at a cluster of tin shacks as they drove past. She saw a shiny black toddler playing in the dust out front. Finally she pulled the lid off the container and turned to her husband, "Sandwich, Marius? I made chicken mayonnaise."

"Not now, Hettie. I can't eat a thing."

The last sign they passed said there were only twenty-five kilometres left before they got to Cape Town. The vast stretches of farmland were interspersed more frequently with farmhouses, farm stalls and clusters of tin shacks. Tannie Hettie hoped they'd see a roadside shop soon. She'd ask Marius to pull off so they could buy some cold drinks. Maybe some nice ripe peaches. She wasn't quite ready for this trip to reach its end.

The radio was playing a song she usually liked to sing to. But not today. It wasn't a day for singing no matter how hard the radio tried. A shrill squeal escaped the cellphone lying in her lap. Both Oom Marius and Tannie Hettie jumped.

"It's Precious," Tannie Hettie told her husband. "Turn that thing off," she gestured to the radio. He quickly complied.

Tannie Hettie listened carefully while the young woman spoke. She saw her husband's eyes fixed on the road, full of concentration.

"The police have just been, Missies Hettie," Precious started.

There was almost no trace of the thick accent that characterised many blacks' speech, a sign she'd been educated well past primary school level. And not simply a township school either, Tannie Hettie noted, but somewhere further afield where she might even have been taught by white teachers. That wasn't necessarily a bad thing, someone with their wits about them was exactly what everyone needed at a time like this. Petrus was a good man, that much was true, but a bright girl like Precious couldn't be underestimated.

"They treated Petrus like an idiot," Precious continued. "They were shouting at him, laughing at him, poking him in the shoulder until he was so confused he didn't know what to say. I didn't know what to do either Missies, to help him, so I ran out the back and went to Mrs Joubert's house. She followed me back to the shop and spoke to the police. In the beginning they didn't want to listen to her. They said they would only speak to the owner. Then Mrs Joubert she said something about abstention of duty and the police grew nervous because she was using big words from their training manuals. I wanted to laugh when I saw the look on their faces but I didn't think it was a good idea. You know, it's easy for them to find out where I live Missies Hettie, and I don't want to make trouble for my mother.

"But then they went outside. They said to the men that it was private property, that they couldn't stand on Baas Marius' stoep without his permission. So the men they moved their tape and flags down to the ground and they stood there.

"The policemen came back inside and told Mrs Joubert that now they were acting within the law. They got into their van, drove a little way off and parked the car. They're still sitting there. Under that little tree just outside Baas Botha's butchery. They're watching the shop but I don't think they're really interested."

"Just hold on, Precious. Let me tell the baas what you said," Tannie Hettie covered the phone with her palm and relayed what Precious had told her.

Oom Marius muttered an expletive under his breath and hit the steering wheel with his fist, "I should have known they'd never go up against Hans. The police captain in Springbok is his son-in-law's cousin. I was speaking to someone just last week about it. Who was it? Dawid I think it was."

Tannie Hettie nodded and brought the phone back up to her ear.

"Precious had one bit of good news, Marius," she said after she'd rung off. "Sarie's been in the shop and you know she never comes in herself. Always sends Agnes to get the groceries. She came in for flour and eggs and that special cocoa powder you ordered for her last week…"

"Are you going to go through Sarie's grocery list, woman, or are you going to tell me what happened?"

Tannie Hettie flashed her husband a stern glance. "You want to phone her yourself?" she snapped.

Oom Marius shook his head, "Not now, Hettie. My nerves are shot. Just tell me, what happened?"

"After she'd paid, she walked right out the front door with the plastic bags in her hands. Koos and Herman and Bertie blocked her way. She ignored them and turned round to Frikkie, asking him what his ma would say if she were to see him standing there, not bothering to help an old lady with her shopping.

"Frikkie got that confused look on his face that he always gets when someone mentions his ma. Without even looking at the others, he held out his hand for Sarie's bags and walked away quietly with her. The people gathered outside cleared a pathway for them to get through. And this is the best part: Frikkie hasn't been back."

She looked expectantly at Oom Marius, hoping this bit of good news would melt away some of the creases on his forehead.

"Maybe not today but he'll be back tomorrow. You know Frikkie can't think for himself. They'll talk to him tonight and he'll follow them back to the shop tomorrow morning like the sheep that he is. They need their sheep, Hettie. Don't forget that. Without sheep there'd only be Karel and Oom Hans on that stoep. Maybe Bertie. No more."

Oom Marius shook his head. Tannie Hettie saw him glance at the clock on the dashboard: an hour and ten minutes before her appointment with the oncologist.

"Do you know how to switch that thing off?" her husband asked. "There's nothing we can do about Klippiesfontein anymore and I don't want it to start ringing when we get you to the hospital."

Chapter Ten

Precious was snooping around the General Store. Well, not snooping exactly, more like exploring. Of course she'd been in there many many times before, but as a customer, not as an employee. You could find practically anything inside the shop and what you couldn't get there, you wouldn't find in all of Klippiesfontein. The last couple of years, Baas Marius had even taken to stocking beauty products for black people, so now she didn't have to go all the way to Springbok when she ran out of hair-straightener.

"What are you doing, sister?" Petrus called from behind the counter.

"Just looking at the things you sell in here," she answered idly.

As an employee she had more leeway, even a half-time employee who came in from eight 'till one Mondays to Fridays and all day Saturday.

"You got any pencils?" she asked.

"Pencils?"

"Yes, I need to take some home for my brothers."

"Over there by the stationary. No, no, more to the left. Close to the fridge."

Precious looked over the products in the gently humming fridge. So many kinds of yoghurt. Not exactly an item that featured frequently on any black person's shopping list, preferring instead to drink *amasi*, traditional sour milk. But now that they had a fridge at home, the second-hand one Precious had bought off her boss two months ago, she decided to take home some of the fruit yoghurts as a treat for her five younger brothers.

"So many flavours," she marvelled out loud, half to herself, half to Petrus. "Have you tried them all?"

Petrus wasn't very interested in discussing the range of products they stocked in the store, "You want to see something really special?"

Coming out from behind the counter, he crossed the floor and went to stand next to her. "Here. Over here," he gestured to a cardboard cut-out for Surf washing powder.

"What, brother? I don't see anything."

"Here, behind this advertisement."

What was he up to, she wondered. Precious strolled over to the cut-out.

Petrus waited expectantly, his arms crossed, "Look there, behind that thing."

Stepping behind the cut-out, Precious saw some kind of water tank thingy shining blue. There was a strong fishy smell. What was it for? And what were those... She went closer. Precious jerked to a dead standstill. "*Hauw*!" she shrieked. "*Hauw*. What on earth!?"

Looking over her shoulder, she saw Petrus standing three steps behind her, his hand covering his mouth, laughing quietly behind it. "Ugly devils, aren't they?" he said.

Precious stepped closer to the tank, "What are they? Crayfish or lobsters?"

"Lobsters," Petrus answered with authority, secretly grateful he knew the answer. "The baas he calls them lobsters."

"And do people buy them hidden away here in the corner?"

"No one buys them, sister. They are too ugly."

"People don't eat things because they're beautiful or ugly. They eat things because someone else has eaten it first and tells them it tastes good. We don't eat sheep's intestines, brother, because they look good."

"Then no one in Klippiesfontein is telling anyone that these things taste good because no one is buying them." Petrus was smiling, chuffed with his acute observation.

Stepping even closer, Precious bent down to eyelevel with the tank, her face close to the glass. She tapped on it with her long, pink fingernails. Behind her, she heard Petrus suck in his breath.

"Are you scared of them, brother?" she asked, turning round and smiling.

"I am not afraid," he stated matter-of-factly but she could see the whites of his eyes huge and round in his face.

Turning back to the tank, Precious fiddled with the lid. She heard a click and the thing came off in her hand. She stared down at the blue water and the dark backs of the creatures. "Do you dare to come closer?"

"How do you think I feed them every day if I don't come close?" he asked, without taking a step forward.

"Yes, how *do* you feed them, brother?" Precious grinned at him. "Do you stand here like I'm doing now and drop their food into the water?"

Petrus shook his head.

"Then how?"

He made his way to a small table in the back against the wall. On it was a chopping board, a long knife and a pile of slimy, white things. He picked one of them up. It was the shape of a large ring. Leaning up next to the table was a broomstick. Taking hold of it, Petrus threaded the white ring onto the end. He threaded on two more. Then, very carefully, he took hold of the broomstick at the other end and elevated it so it was hovering just above the tank. He brought the broomstick down hard on the edge of the glass, banging it a few times so that the white rings became dislodged and fell into the water.

The lobsters, by now, had flown into a fit of activity. Petrified by the banging on the tank they were crawling all over one another. At the same time, they had also come to realise that this banging brought food. The white rings sunk slowly down to the floor of the tank where the lobsters started attacking them with their mouths, their claws being taped up.

"That," said Petrus, quite clearly chuffed with himself, "is how I feed them." He leaned the broomstick back up against the wall.

Precious couldn't stop herself from laughing. She saw Petrus look at her uncertainly, a smile just twitching on his lips, not all the way convinced that he wasn't being ridiculed.

"I will help you from now on," she offered. "Or else these creatures will die from heart attacks."

Petrus nodded, more convinced now that her intentions were benign, "Yes, that would be good."

"But why? Can you tell me why you don't like them, brother?"

His smile was gone and his eyes were big again. "It's the *tokoloshe*. I think maybe he's hiding inside those creatures."

"You still believe in the *tokoloshe?*" her voice was gentle. She understood this fear even though she'd long since stopped believing in the evil little dwarf herself. He would wait under unsuspecting beds, to crawl out at night and rape innocent maidens or terrorise and bring bad luck to men. The *tokoloshe* could change his form and take on the shape of an animal.

"My mother says it's true," Petrus insisted.

"Your mother is still from the old school. So is my mother. These are old wives' tales. You mustn't believe them, brother. They are not true."

"If you say so," he acquiesced but nothing about the way he stood there, watching her, told Precious he believed her.

Putting the lid back on the lobster tank, she came out from behind the cut-out. Petrus followed her. "What do you usually have for lunch round here?" she asked.

Chapter Eleven

Frikkie was a twenty-two-year-old Afrikaans male. Previously that would have meant being the most powerful and the most revered, just a couple of steps below God, but now it had devalued him to being a member of the least loved of all species. It wasn't easy for Frikkie to get used to this fact in the new South Africa, and that's why he was back in front of Oom Marius' shop on Main Street.

If he was going to be honest then he'd have to admit he was more than a little embarrassed to be there after being marched off so mortifyingly by Tannie Sarie. But honesty wasn't the name of this game, so he sauntered casually up to his pals with exaggerated steps and upturned elbows. A man's walk – or, at least, that's what he hoped.

"Hey, what you wearing that baseball cap for? Don't tell me you're going all American on us, Frik?" Bertie called when he spotted his friend.

Frikkie cursed under his breath. He'd been hoping no one would say anything about the cap. Kind of like a disguise for if one of his ma's cronies came down Main Street. From a distance, of course. Close-up, he knew they'd all recognise him.

"*Ag*, this old thing," Frikkie answered, taking it off his light brown mop of hair and flinging it into the corner of the stoep. "My gel was finished and, since we're boycotting the shop, I can't buy a new pot," he laughed nervously. Frikkie ran his thumb and forefinger over his thin brown moustache.

"We're not boycotting anything, you idiot," Karel barked.

Frikkie hadn't been aware that Karel was listening. If he had, he would've been more careful with his words. As he dropped his eyes, he spotted Karel's revolver gleaming on his hip.

He'd held that thing once before. Just like he'd held his dad's gun when he was a lightie. He hadn't liked it then and he didn't like it now. Guns made him nervous. But Karel had insisted that he feel the thing. Cold and heavy and ready for death. Frikkie hated the idea that something was created with death as its sole purpose. But he never said anything. Just like he wouldn't be saying anything today.

Karel continued, "To boycott something means you refuse to go there, to use their services. Boycotting is for pussies. For women. We're barricading the shop. *Pro*active, you see. Not *re*active. We're showing everyone that Klippiesfontein isn't going to end up like the rest of this banana republic. So watch what you say or I'll make you eat your words."

"*Ag,* sorry man, Karel," Frikkie stammered, going red. "You know me. I'm no good with these big words. They all seem more or less the same to me."

"Well wake up then and pay attention. We can't afford to keep ourselves dumb like the blacks. Educated. Sharp. Ready for action – like soldiers. And why is that, Frikkie?" Karel barked like a real army *komandant.*

"Because we're at war, Karel. Like you said the other night. Defending our way of life."

"Good. Good. I'm glad you were listening, Frikkie, my boy. Now, come stand here next to me so we can take on the day."

Frikkie took his place in between Karel and Bertie. At least Oom Hans wasn't there, he thought, because he would've given him a serious grilling for walking out on them the day before to carry Tannie Sarie's shopping bags. To be honest, he was becoming a little bit tired of these serious grillings.

Petrus saw the men outside rearrange themselves in a straighter line, like a whip that had just been cracked. Quickly he stepped back from the window before one of their white faces caught sight of his black one. He knew that would just antagonise them and if there was one thing Petrus was adamant about, it was not to provoke this particular group of men. Simply peering at them like this, through the bottom corner of the dusty window, caused him to breathe shallowly and made his palms sweaty.

The worst one was their leader, that Baas Karel. He stood out there in his khaki shorts, his khaki shirt tucked in at the waist, a pair of leather *veldskoene* on his feet and socks pulled up to just below his knees. His stomach bulged at his shirt from all those meals cooked for him by his poor black maid, his mouth was fixed in a permanent grimace, scouring the world for so-called injustices to the white man. He'd probably never smiled in all his life, Petrus thought, probably not even when he was a fat little white baby being tickled by his old black *ousie*, his child minder.

Petrus didn't like him one bit. In fact, if it wasn't against what the preacher preached under the wild fig tree on Sundays, Petrus would've said that he hated him. He didn't only cross the street when he saw Baas Karel coming towards him, he clean ducked in behind the first building or bush just to avoid the horror of running into that man. Petrus watched Baas Karel as he barked crossly at the other men and then took his place in the centre of the line.

Next to him stood *Kleinbaas* Bertie, the small boss, Oom Hans's son. He didn't seem too bad just yet, but Petrus had spent his whole life watching young white men like him grow into old ones and he knew he'd get worse. Somehow being young made them look softer, hid their fathers' traits that they carried deep inside. But once they got older, had sons of their own, they turned mean just like the *groot* baas, the big boss, their fathers. No, this one he didn't trust, this *Kleinbaas* Bertie.

In fact, the men standing outside Baas Marius' shop this morning were just about the worst group of men in all of Klippiesfontein. Without a doubt. Now Baas Herman and Baas Koos and all the rest of them, they weren't as evil as their leader but, one thing Petrus was sure of, they all wished they were. Every single one of them aspired to have a heart as cold as Baas Karel's when he saw a black man. And all the black men in Klippiesfontein, their hearts went cold when they saw one of these men.

Petrus turned to look at the man at the end of the line, the one who'd just joined. As he focussed on his face, he shook his head as if to shake something out. He looked away and back again to make sure he was seeing correctly. He was. The sweat running down Petrus' back, causing his shirt to stick to him, had turned cold as the ice inside the ice-cream freezer. It happened each time he saw him. *Kleinbaas* Frikkie. Even after all these years, Petrus couldn't stop himself having this reaction no matter how hard he tried.

"Hey, you got a cigarette for me?" Frikkie asked his friend.

"No, I smoked my last one last night," Bertie said, producing a green comb from his sock and running it through his hair a couple of times.

Frikkie stared out across the empty road. Two chickens had escaped again from Mister Scott's run. They were pecking at loose pebbles on the road's surface. Soon everyone would be out and about, thought Frikkie. And they'd all see him. Standing there, to attention, next to these men with their extreme views. Lenny would see him. So would Shawn, and so might the dominie. And that was without even mentioning what would happen if Tannie Sarie came to the shop again today...

Yesterday she'd dragged him away like a naughty schoolboy being tugged off by the ear to the principal's office – but even back then, in his schooldays, it hadn't been the headmaster's wrath he'd been most scared of. It had been his ma's. And it was still the same today. If you rolled up Karel's hatred and Oom Hans' pig-headedness into one person, they'd still be no match for Frikkie's ma. And the problem was that Tannie Sarie and his ma were good friends.

Well, most of the women in town of a particular age, it seemed, were well acquainted with one another. Women liked to run around in packs. But then, he supposed, so did men. Or else, what was he doing here?

Tannie Hettie and his ma were cousins – he'd had the same grandparents as her sons, before his *oupa* and *ouma* died, of course. And since Tannie Sarie was Tannie Hettie's best friend, she often ended up having tea and cake at his house with his ma. That's how he knew her well enough that she felt she was entitled to rebuke him like she did yesterday. Plus there was the fact that he'd been in the same class with her daughter, Henriette, and he'd been to the weddings of all of three her children.

In fact, Frikkie had enjoyed a privileged seat at the table of the most renowned baker in the region for years. She'd made him that three-tiered cake for his twenty-first birthday bash last year – one tier with milk chocolate, one with white chocolate and the last with dark. Standing out there like that, baking in the hot street, watching the mirage shimmering just a couple of metres away while his stomach grumbled, he'd give anything for just one bite of that cake...

"Why are you standing there watching them, brother? You're only making yourself nervous," Precious called from where she was perched on the counter, legs swinging, paging through a magazine full of famous white people.

"Have you seen who is out there?" Petrus asked in a cold, stilted voice.

"Same men as yesterday. I don't have to peep out the window like a scared child to know that," she continued.

"*He* is out there with them."

"*Who* is out there with them, Petrus?" she asked, flicking over another page.

"His son is standing there."

"Who's son, brother? And why are you talking in circles today?"

"The one who came to our house when I was a boy. The policeman."

Precious' hand froze in mid-air and she turned her full attention to Petrus, "When they took away your father?"

"Yes, look. It's *his* son standing there. *Kleinbaas* Frikkie."

Precious slid off the counter and onto the floor. She put down her magazine and walked over to Petrus. Laying a hand on his shoulder, she drew him back from the window, "Come with me to the back, brother. I will make us both a nice cup of tea."

Like a ghost, Petrus followed her.

"Karel, you got a smoke for me?"

"No," Karel barked.

"What we going to do about cigarettes, man? We can't stand here all day without a smoke."

"Stop whingeing Frikkie, before I lose my patience."

"Sorry Karel."

His parents had had six children. Frikkie was the youngest of the lot. He'd enjoyed (if enjoy was the right word) a strict Calvinist upbringing where rods weren't spared and children weren't spoiled. Sundays were spent on hard church benches in the morning and Bible study in the afternoon. Fearing God, fearing his parents, fearing his older brothers; that was the stuff Frikkie's childhood was made of. The only people he hadn't bothered fearing, in fact, were the maid who'd worked for the family for almost forty years and her husband, the old grey-haired garden boy. Black people hadn't been made to fear, he'd learnt from an early age, they'd been made to serve and that's why Frikkie was secretly fond of them. Fearing so many people sometimes got on his nerves.

His dad had been a police inspector in Springbok and the surrounding area for thirty-five years before he dropped down dead from a heart attack, but his dad had been just as scared of his wife as his children were. Frikkie often imagined that his ma had caught his dad doing something she'd forbade him and that's why his heart had given out. But it wasn't the kind of question he could put to her. If he was going to be honest then he'd have to admit there weren't too many questions he could put to her except for the standard, "*Hoe gaan dit met Ma?*"

How are you, Ma?

So, if Tannie Sarie went through with her threat to phone his ma with the news that he was hanging around with the likes of Karel and Oom Hans, blocking Oom Marius' shop so that no one could buy from that poor black bastard Petrus, he'd be in big trouble. Without a doubt his ma would make his older brother drive her straight back to Klippiesfontein to deal with her youngest son – whether she'd just become a grandmother for the sixth time or not. And Frikkie did not want to be the reason his ma drove straight back to Klippiesfontein. Ever.

"Has anyone got some coke? I'm dying of thirst in this bloody heat," Frikkie said.

There was no answer. The men stared resolutely down the road.

"Fanta? Anyone got a Fanta?" he pushed.

Again, no answer.

"Are we going to stand here all day without anything to drink or smoke?"

Bertie leaned over and whispered urgently, "Shut up man, Frik."

"But it's just so damn hot…"

"Don't you have any brains? Karel's going to come over and *klap* you if you keep on whinging like a woman."

Frikkie wasn't happy. How come they were expected to act like soldiers but they weren't fed like them? He felt his mind start to wander off again in the unyielding heat.

Now Frikkie's ma was no kaffir-lover like Mister Scott or Mrs Joubert or even Charlie. He'd heard her say how she knew as well as the next person that blacks were scientifically proven to be inferior to whites. But just like animals, she would add in her Sunday voice, they had to be kept separate and treated with a certain amount of kindness. After all, weren't they God's creatures too, she would ask. And Frikkie would nod in profuse agreement.

But she did not agree with what she called *radicals* and he had no doubt she would judge Oom Hans and Karel's campaign as just that. And though he'd never say it to her face, maybe not even mention it at her graveside when she had one day left this earth and gone to be with the Lord, (like he sometimes spoke with his poor dad), there were some things she would simply never understand.

Like what it had been like to be at school with Bertie, Oom Hans' son, his whole school career. They'd been caned by the headmaster together countless times, smoked behind the school hall during assembly, put that frog in Lana's schoolbag and made her scream so loud she peed in her pants, and they'd laughed about it until they both got detention. Those kinds of friends just didn't hang around waiting for you on every street corner. Especially not now they'd grown up and he couldn't even find a girlfriend, let alone a job.

Frikkie had always wanted to be a policeman when he was a lightie, just like his dad. The blue uniform, the badge that twinkled like that in the sunlight – nothing else had interested him. He'd tried several times to get into the police force but he'd been turned down every time. Didn't fit the profile, they told him, failed the entrance exam, but he didn't believe them. Didn't believe them one bit! It had to do with the colour of his skin and it not being dark enough, of that much he was sure, though of course, there was no way of proving it. They'd be sorry, he would pacify himself after each failed attempt. He'd have made the perfect policeman and they didn't even know it. It was their loss. Yes, their loss.

Maybe it was nothing more than logical for him to be standing in this line, he thought. Judging someone by the colour of their skin was just plain inhumane. That's what he called it, inhumane.

"Where are the others?" Frikkie quickly asked Bertie when Karel went over to talk to one of the other men.

"We had a meeting last night after the shop closed," his friend replied.

"Why didn't anyone call me, man?"

"My dad sent me to get you but then I saw that Tannie Sarie was visiting Tannie Rita across the road and they were drinking tea outside on the stoep. You know, keeping an eye on you so you didn't come running back to us or anything. So I just walked right on past…"

"What did they say at this meeting?"

"That we're going to take shifts. You know, the men who have to be at work or on the farm, they can go about their business but at five o'clock, when they get home, they must come relieve us for a few hours. Oh, yes, on Saturdays too. That way there will always be someone outside the shop."

"And you don't have to help your father on the farm?"

"No, he said this was more important. Having someone from the family here showing everyone that we won't be tolerating this liberal bullshit."

"And do you..." Frikkie started.

'Do I what?' Bertie asked.

"No, it's nothing."

"No. Say."

"Do you believe everything your father says, Bertie?"

"*Ag*, you know how it is? Better to just shut up and do what he says. Besides, I do reckon he's right most of the time. You know, you're not going to tell me we're the same as those *moents* from the township?"

"No, no, I agree with you. We're definitely not the same. It's just that sometimes..."

"Sometimes what?"

"*Ag*, nothing, Bertie. Say, is someone going to bring us some breakfast or what? I'm starving."

"You're not starting to doubt the cause, are you?"

"Don't even say that. You know I'm not. I'm one hundred percent behind this. But if I'm going to be honest, I don't like this idea of violence that Karel keeps talking about. I mean, even if Petrus is a dirty old kaffir, he's also just a man. We bought our sweets from him when we were lighties, man. I wouldn't like to see him getting hurt."

"You know Karel. He likes to shoot off his mouth. Pretends he's in some movie. But this is Klippiesfontein, man. Nothing interesting ever happens here. Not even a kaffir getting a *paksla* when he deserves one. So don't worry about it."

"No, no, I'm not worried. You know me, Bertie. I'm just shooting crap to pass the time."

"Of course. Of course."

"Don't say anything about our talk to the others, OK?"

"Hey look, there's Karel's wife coming down the street. He

91

said she was going to bring us some fresh coffee and *vetkoek*," Bertie said.

"It's about time too. Now that my mother's not home, I don't have anything to eat except bloody cornflakes."

Petrus sipped the hot *rooibos* tea.

"Be careful, brother. You are going to burn yourself," Precious warned.

Petrus hadn't noticed how hot the tea was. Now that she mentioned it, he realised he'd burnt the tip of his tongue. He looked down at his mug as if he'd never seen anything quite so out of place before. In fact, it didn't even feel real being in the shop with her. All he could think about was *Kleinbaas* Frikkie standing outside, about breaking the promise to his mother, breaking the promise to himself. He'd spoken to a white man and look where it had gotten him. As hard as he'd tried to escape his father's fate, it seemed like now it was catching up to him.

Chapter Twelve

"Where is Petrus today?" Precious wondered out loud.

Coming from the storeroom where she'd been expecting to find Petrus just waking, she tip-toed into the shop. But he wasn't there either.

Inside, everything was dark. She waited for her eyes to adjust to the weak light and looked round but she couldn't see him anywhere. Probably outside taking care of his ablutions, she thought.

Precious decided to get the bar of soap her mother had asked her to bring home. She walked to the back of the shop and was startled to see Petrus standing motionless in front of the lobster tank. She gave a little yelp. Petrus turned to look at her.

"*Hauw!*" he said.

"What are you doing there, brother?" she demanded.

"Thinking," he answered in a dull voice.

She knew something was wrong. Petrus' voice was usually so full of excitement when he greeted her first thing in the morning.

Her hand flew up to her mouth, "About what? Is Missies Hettie alright?"

"She's alright."

"So, what's wrong?"

"Baas Marius phoned me last night."

"He phones you every night, Petrus," she snapped. She wasn't in the mood to drag every detail out of him like this.

"He went to eat in a restaurant in Cape Town."

"Yes? Carry on."

"Baas Marius said the restaurant had one of these things," he pointed to the gently humming tank. One of the creatures slowly lifted its front claw, like it was waving at them. They both shuddered.

"And?" she pushed on.

"And you have to change the water every two weeks, Precious, and you know who Baas Marius wants to change the water? Me.

Yes, me. I have worked for the baas now for many years and I've always done what he's asked me to do. He took me off the streets when I was a little boy. I was able to earn money so I could look after my mother. He's a good man. He's been kind to me. So when he asked me to cut up those, what do you call them, squids that the delivery guy brings every week, I told myself it would be alright. That if I close my eyes and think it is ox liver then it will not be so bad. So I do it. Every week I chop up those slimy creatures and throw them in here and feed them to these horrible things and I say nothing to Baas Marius."

Petrus stopped. Precious looked on with big eyes. She saw him think for a while and take a deep breath before he carried on, "But now he wants me to change the water, Precious. This is going too far. I think I would rather go back to the streets than touch those things. I'm telling you, they have evil in their eyes. *Hauw*, he asks me this thing like it's the same as sweeping the stoep."

Precious stared at Petrus. She had never heard so many words come out of his mouth at one time. Seeing the surfaces of his eyes shiny with tears, she reached out and touched his arm, "We will ask Mrs Joubert what we must do, brother. And then we will do it together. It will not be as bad as you think. Yes, their eyes are beady but I do not think they are evil, Petrus. Look again. It is only because they are so dark. But just because something is dark does not mean it is necessarily evil. You know that."

"Baas Marius he says I must do it today. I do not think I can do it today, sister. I do not think I have the strength for those men outside in the street and this thing here – both on the same day. It is asking too much. I think I would rather go back to the streets than to..."

Gently, Precious put her arm around his shoulders and steered him away from the lobster tank. "Come brother, let us not think about this thing now. Let us put on the kettle for a nice cup of tea, yes?"

An hour later, Precious and Petrus had breakfasted on thick brown sandwiches with watermelon jam. They'd swept the floor and dusted the shelves. Still apprehensive of their responsibility, they turned on the cash register together. Taking up their positions behind the counter, they watched fresh dust particles dancing in a shaft of light that poured through the window.

They were startled by the sound of knocking on the back door. They stared questioningly at each other.

"I hope those men haven't come to the back door," Petrus said, the whites of his eyes wide in his dark face.

Even though Precious was nervous too, she wasn't going to let it show, "It's not the men, brother. Do you think they would knock politely like that?"

She knew he was depending on her to seem brave. Even if inside he was the strong one, the one who slept alone in this building every night, he still needed someone else to wear a fearless face. So, with a little spring in her step she didn't really feel, she walked to the back door.

"Baas Alan?" she said, surprised, when she saw Tannie Hettie's hairdresser standing on the step below her.

"Just call me Alan, Precious. You know I don't like this baas and missies nonsense. Look, let me in quickly before those apes outside see me and start making trouble. You know me, I never miss a chance to be in the limelight, but I think I'm going to sit this one out."

Precious stood back and let him in.

With his shuffling gait and swishing hips, Alan flounced into the shop and went straight over to the toiletries shelf. A waft of sickly sweet aftershave remained in his wake.

"Oh, my good man, good morning," he said when he saw Petrus staring in bewilderment at him. "Everyone tells me you're talking these days? I couldn't believe my ears so I decided to come in and take a look. No, I'm only teasing. I'm here because I asked Oom Marius to get me some salon conditioner with his delivery last week. Do you know if it's come in yet?"

Petrus nodded and went back into the storeroom. He fetched a plastic bag with a few bottles where his baas had written *Alan* on. He went back inside and stood behind the counter, waiting for Baas Alan to finish flinging creams and powders into the shopping basket on his arm.

"Oh, there you are. Listen, have you heard anything from Oom Marius and Tannie Hettie? Do they phone to hear how things are going? How is Hettie? Is the treatment making her sick? Tell me Petrus, how is she doing?"

Precious saw Petrus looking dazed. Alan was simply rattling off too many questions at once and Petrus didn't know where to start with his answers. She was about to open her mouth to help him out when she heard his voice, deep and slow, "The missies is sick, Baas Alan."

"Yes I know she's sick Petrus, otherwise we wouldn't be in this pickle with those baboons out front in the first place. But how is she responding to the treatment?"

"This treatment it makes Missies Hettie's cancer look small. It makes her very sick and very weak. Baas Marius he says she only sleeps and cries. The baas, he is worried."

"That's just what I was afraid of."

Alan walked over to the counter and started packing out his purchases. Precious rushed to his side to put them into a plastic bag as Petrus carefully typed each item's price into the cash register.

"I spoke to Tannie Sarie last night and she says she's tried to call Hettie on her cellphone but that the thing is always switched off. She even tried to phone Stefaan to find out about his mother but there was no answer. I feel absolutely awful, hearing this news. Tell Oom Marius we're thinking about them. No, tell him that we're praying for them. Not everyone in Klippiesfontein is..."

"I will tell the baas this when he phones tonight," Petrus said with a touch of finality in his voice. "That will be two hundred and thirty-six rand and forty-two cents, Baas Alan. Must I write it in the book?"

"No, no. I reckon Oom Marius needs all the cash he can get to keep this place running. I'll pay my bill and anything else that's outstanding. Do you want to look in the book, Petrus and tell me what I owe?"

After paying, he headed to the back door, "Is it true that Mrs Joubert cut through their tape and walked out the front door?"

Precious nodded.

"I wish I had the guts to do that, my dear. But these blokes give me a hard enough time as it is."

"Yes *Baa*- just Alan?" Precious smiled.

Even though she agreed in theory that calling white folk baas and missies came from an era long gone, in practice this first-name-basis thing still took some getting used to.

"If I can give you a little advice: move those bins away from the back stairs. They stink the place to high heaven. I suspect this will become your main entrance over the next couple of weeks. Maybe a little potted geranium or two. It never hurts to spruce a place up a bit. I just potted out mine yesterday. Gorgeous pink colour. I think they're even prettier than last year. Do you want me to send you over a pot or two?"

Overwhelmed by the sheer volume of words that ran from this man's mouth, Precious and Petrus nodded simultaneously. Friendly as he was, they were relieved to see him disappear.

"What are gera- geramiu- ger-?" Petrus asked.

"Flowers, brother. Like the ones my mother has in the front garden."

"Do you think flowers will make the back stairs look better?" he continued sceptically.

Precious nodded.

"I'm not so sure Baas Marius would like this idea."

"It can't do any harm, Petrus. And besides, we're in charge now."

She looked around the shop to find something to do. She wished there'd been a TV standing in the corner somewhere so she could at least watch her soapy. These were going to be long days holed up in the shop with nothing to do besides talking to a man renowned for his few words.

Finally Petrus spoke, "When do you think Mrs Joubert will come in?"

"I don't know, Petrus."

He was quiet.

"Are you still worried about the lobsters?"

He nodded.

"We'll wait. She'll come. You'll see."

Again he nodded. Full of trust. Precious hoped she could be worthy of that trust. And above all, she hoped she was right. Because if Mrs Joubert didn't come in, she had no contingency plan for cleaning out that tank.

Chapter Thirteen

Panic was about to set in.

By six o'clock that evening, Mrs Joubert still hadn't come into the shop. Other people, yes, but not the one person they'd been paining to see. Didn't she need something at home? Fresh milk, maybe? Surely her bread was getting low, Precious thought.

Even though they tried their best to ignore it, the problem of the lobster tank just grew bigger and bigger. It loomed over them like Henk Coetzee's big Alsation with its tongue hanging out. But, by some kind of unspoken agreement, Precious and Petrus refused to mention it. They were relieved by each sporadic customer who came in through the back door and temporarily chased the problem away.

Patty had popped her head in the back door to fetch cigarettes for her and her husband. She'd enquired after Tannie Hettie's health and expressed dismay when Precious told her that she was reacting badly to the treatment. She asked how Oom Marius was doing and wondered when he'd be coming home but Precious hadn't been able to give her an answer.

The dominie's wife, Dalene, had also been in. "Aren't those just the loveliest geraniums you've got out there on the back steps, Petrus?" she'd exclaimed. "Is that Hettie's handiwork? You know, I never took her to be much of a gardener but the dark pink in the middle against those light pink petals, I must say, is just charming. It would look so good in the baskets in front of the church. Do you think she'd mind if I sent the garden boy over for a few cuttings later on?"

"You are right," Petrus began slowly. "Missies Hettie she doesn't plant those flowers. Baas Alan he gave them to us. If you want to send your gardener then you can ask him to go to Baas Alan's house for these cuttings."

"I think I'll do that. Now be a good man, Petrus, and fetch me this stuff on my list quickly? I've had the most terrible pain in my feet lately. The doctor says it's water retention. Besides, you must be going out of your mind with no customers here all day."

"We have customers," Precious replied curtly. "They come round the back just like you do."

"Oh," was all she said.

Precious suspected the dominie's wife wasn't very amused to be referred to as *you* instead of with the customary Aunty or Missies. Dalene was her elder, and a white elder at that. It was very bad form indeed but Precious didn't care.

Taking the list, Petrus scuttled round the shop collecting the wares. Precious stayed behind the counter and stared seethingly at Dalene. There were two reasons for this: firstly, Dalene was the only person to come into the shop that day who hadn't enquired after Tannie Hettie's health – and that for a dominie's wife! Secondly, her garden *boy,* as she had referred to him, was, in actual fact, not a boy at all. He was a man in his fifties, married to the cousin of Precious' mother which made him a kind of uncle to her. Surely the fact that he was at least a decade older than Dalene herself should've earned him the right not to be referred to as a boy? But, of course, Precious couldn't voice her objection to this age-old term. She had to shut-up and swallow because Dalene was a powerful woman in Klippiesfontein and she was supposedly on their side. She was grateful to see Dalene's back when she turned round and left the shop.

The whole day long they waited for Mrs Joubert. It was a Saturday and Precious didn't have to go to her other job at the petrol station so she had nothing to distract her. She'd run out of ways to keep her friend's mind off the lobster tank. She'd shown him some very basic bookkeeping skills. Turning the dial on the radio to her favourite station, she spent a good thirty minutes trying to teach him to dance. Eventually she'd given up, exasperated – Petrus was possibly the only black man she knew with absolutely no sense of rhythm at all.

"*Hauw,*" he'd told her, "I'm thirty. I can't dance like you young ones anymore."

"Thirty is hardly old, brother," she told him.

He looked pleased when she said this, "No, maybe it is not

so old next to your twenty-three years."

At lunch time she'd gone into the back and cooked them a simple stew of chicken feet with tomatoes and onion gravy and *pap*. Afterwards they'd scrubbed the back stairs with bleach, rearranged the dry goods shelf and wiped down the sweet jars until the colourful contents inside glistened like jewels.

Precious glanced at the front door, willing Mrs Joubert to step through it in that proud, authoritarian way of hers, so they could put forward their questions about lobster tank maintenance and wipe off some of the dread on Petrus' face. If she hadn't been so squeamish herself, she would've tried to tackle it alone just so he'd stop stealing glances at the four creatures staring at them from their watery prison. But there was no way Precious was going to touch one of those things. No matter what Oom Marius said.

They weren't surprised to hear another knock at the back door. They were becoming more frequent.

Charlie came in, "I've got a list of things my mom sent me to get." He took a basket and started walking around the shop.

He wasn't bad-looking for a white man, Precious thought. He had what the magazines referred to as a square jaw line which made him look strong and in control, but then, to soften that, his eyes were light blue and his hair somewhere between light brown and blonde – there was probably a hair colour just like that for sale in a bottle on the toiletries shelf. Almost golden, but not quite. She liked that in a man, contrasting features. It made him seem more interesting, not so one-dimensional.

As she stood there watching him, Precious heard his cellphone go off and watched as he took it out his pocket. That was no ordinary cellphone, she noticed. If she were to take a guess she'd say it was one of those Blackberry things. Precious had an idea.

"Excuse me, Charlie," she asked when he'd put it back in his pocket. "Do you get the internet on there?"

"No, I don't."

Her face dropped in disappointment.

"There's no wireless out here. Why? Is there something you

want to know?"

Pleased that the offer had come so spontaneously, she nodded.

"I can always check it out for you on the internet at home?" he continued.

"That would be great... "

Petrus watched Precious and Baas Charlie huddled together by the Illovo Golden Syrup. He wondered what their conversation was about. At last they separated and Charlie came over to pay for his purchases. Precious hurried to join Petrus behind the counter, her eyebrows raised as if she wanted to tell him something but he had no idea what.

As Charlie reached out to take his plastic bag, Precious suddenly nudged Petrus, "What about a little token of gratitude for our loyal customer?"

Petrus looked at her quizzically.

Leaning in towards him, she whispered in his ear, "Give him something."

"What? For free?"

"Yessss," she hissed.

Obviously she must have gone mad. "The baas he doesn't want us to give things for free, Precious. This is a shop. We're here to make a profit."

"He's going to help us, Petrus," she spoke urgently. "Just listen to me and give the man something."

Petrus and Precious turned their eyes back to Charlie and flashed him two uncomfortable smiles.

Petrus had no idea what had got into this usually level-headed woman but he knew he had no choice but to obey her. Looking around, he spotted a box of lighters on the counter. On the lighters were women with big boobs and small bikinis. When the flame of this lighter was on, the bikinis would go away and the women would sit there wearing only their smiles. Baas Lenny he liked these lighters so much he bought one with each of the different ladies on. Even Petrus had one at home next to his bed that he used to light his candle if there was a black-out.

Grabbing one from the box, he pushed it across the counter towards Charlie.

Charlie stared at the little plastic offering lying before him. He looked up at Petrus who didn't know what to do except smile. Clearing his throat, Charlie waited. Suddenly Petrus jumped. He'd felt a dull stab in his arm. Precious had punched him. He stared at her, confused. What had he done wrong?

"Charlie doesn't smoke, Petrus," she tried to make her voice sound light but it wasn't working. It only sounded more panicky. Like that time when Petrus went to Springbok wearing his new pants and shirt but underneath his shoes with holes stuck out and everyone could still see he was poor. If he'd just worn his regular clothes, no one would have noticed anything and they wouldn't have laughed at him on the taxi. That's how Precious' voice sounded when she pretended to be speaking normally to Baas Charlie.

Petrus didn't understand anything about Precious today, "You said to give him something for free?"

He looked at her. She was smiling at him but he could see there was something hiding behind that smile. Petrus was sure he didn't want to find out what that something was. Reaching out, she took a Bar One chocolate from the box next to her and slid it across the counter to Charlie, "Like I said, for our loyal customers."

Charlie looked uncomfortable, "Ah... thanks, but it's not necessary."

"I know," Precious said, flashing him quite a different smile from the one she'd just given Petrus, "but we like to do it. I hope you like chocolate."

Charlie looked puzzled, "I do. Thanks." He nodded at the shop assistants and left.

"What did you do that for, sister?" Petrus demanded. "You starting to flirt with a white man?"

"Oh stop being so ignorant, Petrus," she snapped. "I told you he was going to help us, didn't I?"

Petrus nodded. Yes, she had told him, but what did that have to do with the lighter and the chocolate?

"He's going to look on his computer and see how to clean the lobster tank."

"*Hauw!* The computer can clean the tank?" Petrus was flabbergasted.

"No, brother. It's going to tell Charlie how to clean the tank and he's going to tell us."

"Oh," he said, deflated. "How is telling us, helping us?"

"Then at least we'll know what to do."

"I know what to *do*, sister. I wash the windows of the shop all the time. Take the lobsters out of the tank and put them in the bucket. Wash the glass with Windowleen and put in clean water. Put the lobsters back inside. It is not with the knowing that I need help, sister, it is with the *touching* of the lobsters."

"But Petrus, you can't wash the tank with Windowleen."

"Why not?"

"The lobsters will die."

"Why?"

"Because they may not have soap in their water."

"I will rinse out the soap, sister. I am not stupid."

"Petrus, those lobsters don't live in tap water, you know. They live in the sea."

"I know this, sister. The rivers and the damns aren't filled with tap water either. They're filled with rain water."

"But the sea is filled with salt water."

"Salt water? What for? Who can drink salt water?"

"The fish in the sea. The lobsters. The squids."

"But we have salt in the shop, sister."

"Yes, I know. But Charlie has to look on the internet about how much salt we must put in the water so we don't kill the lobsters."

"One teaspoon."

"Why one teaspoon?"

"My mother always says one teaspoon is more than enough."

"Honestly brother, sometimes I don't know what to do with you."

A while later, Charlie was back. Petrus let him in sceptically. "You know how much salt?" he asked.

"What do you mean, how much salt?"

"To give to the lobsters so the water changes from tap water to sea water?"

"Oh, that. It's much more complicated than that. Look, I've printed it out. Do you want me to read it to you?"

Precious came up behind Charlie, "Let's go sit somewhere. Then we can give you our full attention. Do you want something to drink?" She laid her pink-nail-polished hand briefly on his arm.

Petrus flashed her an angry glance but either she did not see it or she pretended not to. Petrus was not happy with her. He would tell Baas Marius to take the money for the drinks and for the Bar One chocolate from her pay, he decided resolutely. The baas had not left them behind in the shop so they could start handing things out for free.

Charlie was sitting on top of the counter, his legs swinging casually while he read out the instructions, "For exterior tank cleaning use a vinegar-water solution of three tablespoons vinegar to half a litre of water. Always use a clean rag. Never use chemical cleaners, soaps or spray detergents on any part of the system. Interior tank cleaning – remove algae growth with a manufacturer recommended acrylic cleaning pad or non-abrasive foam aquarium pad on-a-handle." Charlie looked up, his eyes fixed on Precious. Flashing her a smile, he carried on, "Hey, this sounds neat. Do you guys want me to help you with this?"

Precious and Petrus nodded urgently.

Maybe Precious had been right to give Baas Charlie the chocolate, after all, he thought.

Chapter Fourteen

Charlie trotted down the back steps of Oom Marius' General Store. Now he was going to have to walk all the way round to Church Street to get his car. Couldn't they see they weren't achieving anything other than irritating everyone in town? Did they honestly believe, with their little flags and so-called military precision, that they could go back in time to when the white man was God? Just look at them in their shorts, their thick socks pulled up to their knees. Jesus, Bertie even had a comb sticking out of his. Ridiculous.

"Hey Charlie," someone called from the line of barricaders. Probably Frikkie.

Nodding his head ever so slightly, he hoped the girl in the shop, Precious, wasn't standing at the window. He wouldn't want her to see him acknowledging these idiots. She seemed like a nice girl. Maybe nice wasn't the right word. Special. Yes, that was a better way to describe her. It wasn't too much, was it? Special?

"Hey Charlie," Frikkie called again, his voice more insistent. "What's up, man?"

Shoving his hands into his pockets and staring down at the pavement, Charlie pretended not to hear. He reached his car, unlocked the door and dropped down into the driver's seat. He turned the key to start the car. The engine gave one or two feeble mechanical purrs and then stopped completely. Damned car! The technician who'd used it before him had driven it to pieces. It urgently needed to be replaced but Charlie's supervisor at work wouldn't hear of it. Damned Telcom!

There was no getting around it: he should've spent more time studying at university in Cape Town and less time checking out the big city, acting like some country boy *moegoe*. He'd known, going in, that he wasn't the brightest, that he'd have to work harder than the rest if he was going to achieve something... and still... He'd chosen to hang out in the student bars instead of behind his books and where had that gotten him? Failed each and every one of his exams, that's where.

"I'm warning you, Charlie," his mother said before he left, "I only have enough money to give you this one chance. If you mess it up then you're going to have to come home and find a job."

It was true, she had told him. Setting off to university he'd known all of that. Charlie had matriculated from Springbok High School amongst the top thirty percent of his class. OK, thirty percent wasn't exactly the top five or even the top ten percent, but it was something. And it was this something that Charlie was after. Something more. Something more than a life in Klippiesfontein. And he'd hoped that Cape Town University would be the answer to this quest for *something more*. His mother, ten years divorced, receiving no alimony from his father, working for twenty years as a receptionist, did not have the money to afford his mistakes. And yet he hadn't managed to do it. To find the self-discipline. To make her proud. To do something more. So now he was stuck in this stinking car in this stinking job his mother had had to ask her stinking supervisor at Telcom for.

"Can't turn back the time, Charlie," he scoffed bitterly to himself, banging his fist on the steering wheel, his blonde fringe flopping over his eyes.

Turning the key one more time, the car suddenly chortled to life. He grinned to himself, put the car into gear and started off down the road. Maybe it wasn't *that* bad, he thought. That Precious, she wasn't half bad-looking.

"Fool!" he scolded himself out loud. "Idiot!" Precious was black. He was white. They both lived in Klippiesfontein. There was nothing more to say about it.

Charlie pulled up in the driveway of their small, neat house where he'd lived all his life. With his dad for the first fifteen years, without him for the next ten. One thing was sure, when Charlie got married, when he had kids, he wouldn't walk out on them no matter what. And definitely not for a blonde bimbo like Shelley with her leopard-print leggings and fake eyelashes. He still didn't understand how his father could prefer her over his mother. Wouldn't understand it in a hundred years.

Climbing out of the car, Charlie entered the house by the side door. "Ma, I'm back," he called. Walking to the fridge, he pulled open the door, grabbed the carton of fresh milk and glugged the cool liquid straight from the spout.

"Where were you?" her voice rang from the lounge.

He could hear the TV on. Probably watching her soapy. He called back, "Over at Oom Marius' shop. I was helping his assistants to clean the lobster tank. To tell you the truth, I think they're a bit scared of the things."

"Yes, I heard about the tank," she called back lazily. "Antoinette was telling me they've had nothing but trouble with the thing from the minute it arrived. And now he's got those two looking after it with all their wretched superstitions. Oom Marius should be jolly grateful that they haven't run off yet."

Charlie put the empty carton of milk back in the fridge, grabbed a slice of salami and popped it into his mouth before making his way to the lounge. "Have you ever eaten lobster, Ma?" He dropped down into the sofa next to her.

"I have," she said. "A long time ago. Before you were born. When your father and I were..." she stopped.

"What was it like?" Charlie asked.

"It was lovely. One of the best meals I've eaten in my life."

Charlie smiled to himself. He had an idea... It was her birthday in two day's time...

"Your plate's in the microwave, if you're hungry," she said, patting him gently on the thigh.

It was the end of another shitty workday at Telcom. He'd been back to that idiot's house for a third time, only to be yelled at that the internet wasn't working properly when the guy was simply too thick to send an email. But somehow the day had been more bearable than others. He'd carried around with him the thought of two events that would make his day end well.

The first one was the fact that he'd see Precious when he stopped off at Oom Marius' store. Fair enough, he shouldn't be feeling this way, he realised that. This was still Klippiesfontein.

She was still black. He was still white. That ought to be enough to put the idea right out of his head. But he couldn't do it. Simply couldn't stop himself grinning each time he thought of her. Her shiny brown cheeks, those long eyelashes, her pert, round bum that bounced so pleasingly when she walked, her voice that sounded as if it was just a hair's width away from breaking into laughter...

"Not very smart, Charlie," he told himself sternly, but his lips defied his thoughts and broke into a grin all the same.

The second event that cheered him up was the prospect of surprising his mother for her birthday. This year he'd really come up with an original idea, even if he had to say so himself. He had the recipe printed out and folded up in his pocket and now all that was left for him to do was to make his purchases...

Forty minutes later, Charlie walked into the kitchen at home, the cuffs of his shirt suspiciously wet, carrying a white polystyrene box in his arms. "Happy birthday, Ma," he called out proudly.

His mother came in from the lounge, her red hair falling tiredly around her face, grey sticking out at the roots where she hadn't dyed it yet. The white blouse that she wore to Telcom was hanging out of her pencil skirt, the zip on the side let down so she could curl up on the sofa more comfortably. Her shoes had been kicked off her dainty stockinged feet.

"What have you got there?" she asked, coming to take a closer look.

Charlie leaned towards her and kissed her on the cheek before putting the box carefully down on the kitchen table. "For you," he beamed.

Gingerly taking a step forward, she stretched out her hand to touch the white lid. Quickly she pulled back again. "What's in there?" There was almost a giggle in her voice.

He congratulated himself again on how smart he was to get her this gift. Then he stepped forward and pulled the lid off the box. Two lobsters sat inside, side by side, without moving, waiting to be ogled over by Charlie's mother.

Her hand flew up to her mouth to cover a shy smile. "You didn't," she gushed.

"I did and I've even got a bottle of sparkling wine in the car. We're going to celebrate in style tonight."

"What about the macaroni and cheese I made?"

"Put it in the fridge. We'll have it tomorrow," said Charlie, turning round and heading for the door again.

"Why are your sleeves so wet?" his mother called.

Facing her again, he spoke, "I had to catch the lobsters myself. Petrus was too scared to touch them. I tried grabbing them with a set of tongs but they're slippery little bastards. Eventually I had to go in after them with my hands."

"You know how we have to kill these things, don't you?" his mother asked.

Charlie nodded, "That's the bit I'm not looking forward to."

Charlie and his mother stood in front of a boiling pot of water on the stove, sweat and steam running down their red faces. Behind them the kitchen table had been painstakingly set with crystal champagne flutes that had been a wedding present many years before. A candle stood flickering in the middle and two stiffly starched serviettes had been folded into little swans.

"Try again," Charlie's mother urged.

"But we've tried twenty times already," he sighed.

"One more time. Come on. This time it's going to work."

Taking a deep breath, Charlie plunged his hand into the sink filled with cold water where the two lobsters waited apathetically. He grabbed one by its dark brown back and moved quickly to stand in front of the pot of boiling water. The lobster, suddenly drenched in steam, started wriggling in his outstretched hand.

"I can't," he all but screeched while his mother hopped from one foot to the other next to him.

"Just let go," she shrieked back. "Let go!"

"Look how it's looking at me, Ma. Like it knows it's going to die," his voice was high-pitched and panicky.

"Just let go!" she kept on screaming.

"I'm trying."

"Open up your fingers."

"Don't shout like that, Ma. You're making me nervous."

"Let go, I said."

"I can't," he said with a sense of finality in his voice and stepped back from the stove. "I'm sorry. I just can't, Ma." Charlie brought his arm down to his side, the lobster still dangling from his hand.

His mother took a step back too and stood next to her son. The smiles had been wiped from form their faces and both pairs of blue eyes were cast down at the floor.

"You want to give it a try, Ma?" Charlie asked feebly because, of course, he knew the answer.

"I can't even kill a spider. How do you think I'm going to boil that creature to death?"

They stood there. Side by side. The forgotten lobster suspended between the two of them.

All of a sudden, Charlie's mother gave a loud, high-pitched scream. "Get that thing away from me!" she yelled.

He spun round to face her, making a wide arc with his hand, swinging the surprised lobster through the air, "What, Ma? What's wrong?"

Her mouth was formed in a tight little O, accentuated by the lines around her lips from years of smoking, "Get it away from me!"

"Ma, what happened?" he insisted sternly.

"It stroked me. It touched my thigh."

"It what?" Charlie asked in disbelief.

"I swear, it stroked my thigh," she said.

Charlie stood there staring at her. He tried to take her seriously, he really did because he could see she was genuinely frightened but... he couldn't... A smile cracked his serious expression, broke out unreservedly on his face. "It stroked your thigh, Ma?" he said more slowly.

"Yes, it stroked my damned thigh," she smiled back. He could see her shoulders relax as she heard her own words. "I must be getting desperate if even the lobsters are making passes at me."

"I'm glad you said it," Charlie laughed, "so I don't have to. We really need to get you a date, Ma."

His mother was laughing too, "You mean to tell me the lobster's not my date?"

Charlie thrust the creature close to her face, "Give it a kiss, Ma. Come on, give it a kiss."

"I mean it Charlie," she spoke sternly, though she was still smiling, "get it away from me before I scream."

Sticking his hand into the cold water in the sink, Charlie caught hold of the second lobster, "Why, Ma, do you prefer this one?" He brought his hands together and held them outstretched, side by side, twisting his wrists as though they were doing a dance. In answer to the sudden movement, the lobsters swayed their claws. The laughter of the mother and her son bounced off the stark white kitchen walls. A moment of distilled happiness. After a few seconds it died down again. Grins remained plastered on their faces.

"What are we going to do with those damned things now?" his mother asked at last.

"You can dress one of them up and take it to the movies," Charlie smiled.

"No, I'm serious. What are we going to do?"

"We could shove them in the deepfreeze?"

"Freeze them to death instead of boiling them to death?" she asked, her hand going up to her hip. "I won't be able to get a wink's sleep, lying in my bed thinking of them shivering from the cold before they finally... No, Charlie, we can't do that."

Charlie's eyes moved back and forth rapidly as he thought about the possibilities. "What's the time?" he said at last.

His mother turned her head to look at the kitchen clock, "Ten to eight. Why?" The last remnant of her smile had scuttled off her face.

"If I hurry I can still take them back to the store." Swinging into action, he dropped both lobsters into the box, located the abandoned lid lying in the corner and popped it back on again.

"Must you go tonight?"

"If I wait 'til tomorrow they'll be dead."

"Do you think they'll take them back?"

"As long as I don't tell them they tried to get fresh with my mother," he said, trying to lure back her smile.

"Watch out or you'll be sleeping outside tonight."

He was halfway out the door when his mother called after him, "Shall I heat up the macaroni and cheese for us?"

"Sounds good," he said and the screen door slammed shut after him.

The smile still on her face, his mother stared after her disappearing son. Three seconds later it flew open again and Charlie's face popped back inside, "I'm going to take you out to a restaurant, Ma, where they serve fresh lobster. OK?"

"Sounds lovely, my boy," she spoke gently, "At least in a restaurant they won't be as squeamish as the pair of us."

And with that, Charlie's face disappeared again.

Charlie knocked urgently at the back door of the shop, the polystyrene box balanced on one arm. Just as he was about to twist the handle to go inside, the door swung open. Above him, at the top of the geranium-bedecked stairs, stood Precious.

His breath petered softly out of his lungs and he forgot to take in more. From her earlobes dangled pink plastic earrings, a shocking pink skirt flared from her soft, round hips, white high-heeled sandals on her feet and a white blouse with a round neckline which revealed nothing but only just hinted at the swell of flesh beneath. It was truly astounding, he told himself, how well the pink and white set off against her chocolate skin. He wasn't sure if he'd ever seen such a beautiful black woman in real life before.

"Charlie," she exclaimed, flashing him a smile that matched perfectly with her white blouse. He drew in a gulp of air.

"I was just leaving," she said.

"You can't!" he protested in a panic.

"I can't leave?" Precious slowed down. "Why? What's wrong

and why have you got that…"

"We couldn't do it," Charlie explained, looking sheepishly down at the box. "We couldn't kill them so I've… I was hoping… hoping that you could, you know, take them back before they die on us?"

Precious smiled, "I'll never understand you white people. You want all your meat wrapped up neatly in squares of plastic so you can pretend it doesn't come from a live animal. I bet you've never even killed a chicken before?"

"Of course I haven't killed a chicken," Charlie said indignantly. "Why would I kill a chicken?"

"You see, that's what I mean. What's the word you use for people like that?"

Charlie shrugged. "Non-animal killers?"

"Wimps," she stated flatly.

Charlie looked away.

"I'm just joking. I wouldn't be able to kill one of those creatures either. Mrs Joubert said you have to boil them to death. Is that true?"

He nodded. Precious turned round and headed back into the shop. "Come then," she called over her shoulder, "let's get them back in the water."

"You sure Petrus won't mind?" he asked, following her up the stairs. In her wake she left behind a trail of her perfume. Something with flowers. No, no roses. She smelled like roses. Charlie sniffed deeply.

"I'll speak to him," she answered self-confidently.

A few minutes later the three of them; Charlie, Precious in the middle and then Petrus, stood watching the two remaining lobsters welcome back their departed comrades. There was a lot of claw waving going on.

"You are lucky I did not phone the baas tonight," Petrus stated. "I was going to tell him we sold two lobsters. I knew this news would make him happy. Now I will tell him nothing and he will not have to be sad that the lobsters are back."

"Thanks again, man, Petrus," Charlie said. "I don't know

what the hell we would've done if you didn't take them back."

"It is alright, Baas Charlie. You help us also to clean the tank. We can help you too when you cannot kill the ugly lobsters."

Precious was the one to break away from their contemplative row, "Come on, it's past eight. Let's close up and go home."

The two men followed her. Charlie and Precious waited on the back steps for Petrus to lock up. Once it was done he nodded, satisfied, and they started manoeuvring down the narrow stairs so they didn't knock over any of the plants.

"Bye," Charlie mumbled feebly when they got to the bottom.

"See you, maybe tomorrow?" Precious sang in that melodic voice of hers.

Precious and Petrus headed off together. Charlie stared forlornly after them. "Precious," he suddenly called out. He couldn't bear to let that voice get away. What was he going to say? Think, Charlie, think. Quickly. "I… I… I can give you a ride. I've got time."

"To Rifilwe?" she asked.

"I'll drop you off just outside the township, if that's OK?"

"You sure?"

He nodded urgently.

"That would save us the taxi fare, thanks. Where are you parked?"

Charlie jerked his head in the direction of the street. "Out there, on the side. I'm sure those idiots out front have gone home by now."

Precious changed direction and followed Charlie. Petrus stood still and glared after them.

"Come on, brother," Precious called out. "Don't you want to ride in Charlie's car?"

Petrus said nothing. The look on his face didn't change. He put one foot in front of the other and slowly followed them to the car.

Chapter Fifteen

Oom Marius' beige bakkie drew up in front of the store and stopped right in front of the men. He turned his head to look at the shop and saw Precious and Petrus watching from the window. Then he looked at the barricaders and scoffed: they thought they looked like soldiers but no army in the world would want that bunch. They were sprawled out on the steps, passing cigarettes backwards and forwards and calling out to one another. Karel and Oom Hans were nowhere to be seen, that was probably why. Oom Marius knew from his nightly phone calls to Petrus that the townsfolk had started using the back entrance to the store. With so little action out on the street, the men of the barricading movement had become bored.

So when the proprietor of the store they were barricading pulled up suddenly in a cloud of red dust, they scrambled to an embarrassed attention.

"*Is julle bliksems nog altyd hier?*" he called as he climbed out of his bakkie.

Are you bastards still here?

Trained since boyhood to greet their elders, Frikkie and Bertie blushed and immediately answered him with a "*Môre,* Oom."

Good morning, Uncle.

Oom Marius turned his head away from the youngsters in disgust and they suddenly seemed to remember he was the enemy. Their expressions turned stoic and they stared at the horizon, army style. He walked up the steps and through the front door. Probably the only one to take this route in the last ten days besides Mrs Joubert.

He saw Precious and Petrus scramble upright from where they'd been leaning on the windowsill. The radio was on and a black voice was talking animatedly.

"Petrus!" Oom Marius shouted.

He stopped before the pair of them and looked them up and down quizzically as if surprised to find them in the shop. They stared back guiltily.

"How's business?" he barked.

"Business it is slow, Baas. People come in through the back to buy but many they go to Springbok for shopping now."

"Who comes to the shop?" Oom Marius asked.

"Mrs Joubert, Missies Sarie, Missies Patty, Baas Charlie..." At this last name Petrus glanced spitefully at Precious.

She looked away and Oom Marius wondered what exactly was going on round here.

Muttering under his breath, he stomped off to the counter. Opening and closing the till, he coughed bitterly at the few bank notes he saw there. He slammed the tick book open and ran his finger down the column of everyone who owed him money. Suddenly he looked back up again at Petrus and Precious. They were standing side by side a few metres away from the counter, watching him with big eyes.

"How are the lobsters doing?" he wanted to know.

Not bothering to wait for their answer, Oom Marius crossed the floor to where the freshly cleaned tank was standing. They'd done a good job on it, he noticed. It seemed to hum now with a little more pride. Oom Marius bent down to be at eye level with the lobsters. He tapped his finger on the glass. "I still don't know what we're going to do with you lot," he spoke to them. They stared back, emotionless.

Behind Oom Marius, Precious cleared her throat before speaking, "How is Missies Hettie doing?"

He looked down at his feet and cursed loudly but didn't give her an answer. He reached up and ran his finger along the top of a shelf to check for dust, more out of force of habit than anything else. Looking across the room at her, he spoke, "Karien is spending the weekend with her in the hotel. That's why I'm here."

He could have added more. He could have told her that if he'd had to stay in that hotel one more day they'd have had to bloody lock him up in a madhouse. He could have told her that the only thing worse than the hotel was sitting at his wife's side in the hospital, watching them pump shit into her veins that made her sick and not being able to do a thing to help her. He couldn't stand that hospital smell that hit the minute you walked through the door. He wanted to hit every nurse who spoke to him in that sickenly sweet voice they all seemed to be trained to use. He wanted to take out the doctors with his shotgun and he wanted his wife not to need him so much. Yes, that's what he wanted most of all. For his wife not to need him so much. But he could hardly admit these things to himself, let alone talk to Hettie about it, so mentioning it to Precious seemed quite ridiculous.

He'd opened up a black ledger and was studying Precious' neat recording of credits and debits. "*Bliksem!*" he shouted.

Petrus jumped but stayed rooted to his spot close to the lobster tank. Maybe Baas Marius was in a cursing mood, he concluded. Maybe Missies Hettie wasn't doing very well. Sometimes an attentive daughter-in-law like Karien and a fancy hotel weren't enough to stop the bad news.

"How long have you been sleeping inside the shop now, Petrus?" Oom Marius asked.

"Fifteen days," Petrus explained. "Just last week Sunday I went home to see my mother and take her some food."

"Today's Friday. I'm going back Sunday night. Go home, both of you, and take the weekend off. Make sure you're back here on Monday morning. Oh, and Petrus, take your mother a box of chocolates. And you, Precious? You still live with your mother?"

She nodded.

"Take her a box too."

Staring bewilderedly at him, they didn't move. One minute he looked like he was going to kill them and the next he was handing out boxes of chocolates?

"Come on, get out of here before I change my mind!" he snapped.

They started to move. Petrus went in back and combed his hair in front of the small mirror. Precious walked over to the chair where her handbag was lying and touched it half-heartedly.

Both kept stealing glances at Oom Marius. He looked ragged and old, like he was the one with the cancer. Petrus and Precious couldn't begin to imagine what Missies Hettie must look like.

"I don't mind, Baas. I'll stay here till the shop closes tonight. You go lie down," Petrus ventured.

Oom Marius' face started going red and Petrus realised he shouldn't have said anything. But it was too late.

"Are you getting white with me?" he exploded.

"No, Baas."

"If I wanted to bloody well lie down I would've stayed in Cape Town and spent the whole weekend doing just that. Don't tell me what to do in my own goddamned shop, do you hear me? Now get out of here!"

Petrus and Precious scurried to the storeroom out of his way. As they tried to slip out the back, they heard his voice again, "Don't forget the chocolates."

"You go," Petrus whispered and pushed her back inside the shop.

She glared angrily at him before hurrying over to the shelf and grabbing the first two boxes she saw – Cadbury's Milk Tray. She rushed back to Petrus and they exited through the back door. Precious was imagining her mother's face when she presented her with this gift from her boss.

Oom Marius stood proud and upright behind the counter in his store. He stared out across the shelves piled high with kitchen sieves, corkscrews, and cake moulds. He listened to the familiar purr of the fridge, the little hiccough it made every few seconds, before it restarted its hum with a wheeze. It felt good to be back. Good not to be in that blasted hotel room with its fancy TV and room service and three kinds of eggs for breakfast in the morning. He ran his hand over a gleaming glass jar filled with red boiled sweets. He touched the neat pile of plastic bags he used for the sweets; he'd seen many a child grow up in Klippiesfontein, and every one of them was equally painstaking in the important matter of choosing their sweets. He smiled as he thought of their grubby fingers pointing at the different bottles.

His hand reached out involuntarily and touched the bottle with the gold-and-purple wrapped chocolate éclair toffees. Hettie's favourite. Grabbing a handful, he shoved them into his pocket. He'd give them to her on Sunday night when he got back to the hotel, he decided.

He felt a pain in his gut. A dull stab. And how often did you take her chocolate éclairs when she was right behind that door, Marius? Not once. Not one bloody time. It was in the little gestures that Hettie seemed to see love and Oom Marius realised he'd never been one for little gestures.

Hell, how about two years ago when his brother had turned up unexpectedly for a visit? He'd closed the shop early and they'd both gone to the bar at the Royal Hotel for a drink. They'd stayed there until well past twelve when the manager kicked them out and they stumbled home.

The next morning the three of them were sitting down for breakfast when Hettie spoke, "Where were you last night, Marius?"

"Damn it woman, can't a man even go out for a drink anymore without having to answer to his wife?" He'd been furious that she had the gall to talk to him like that in front of his brother.

Looking down at her plate, she continued, "I was waiting for you to come home and have supper with me. I even baked us a nice milk tart."

"Can't you think about anything else but food?"

She bit her lip and said nothing more. Even his brother had looked at him, his eyebrows drawn up questioningly, "If you've got any of that milk tart left, Hettie, I'd like a slice."

But she hadn't jumped up from the table as she usually would have to cut him a piece. She remained in her chair, pushing her spoon around in her bowl of Jungle Oats.

It was only later that day that Oom Marius remembered that it had been her birthday.

And the worst part was not that he'd forgotten her birthday, not even that he'd snapped at her like that at the table the following day. No, the worst part was that he'd never done anything to make it up to her. Not even a feeble *I'm sorry* had passed his lips.

He came out from behind the counter and strolled in between the shelves. Coming to a stop in front of the tinned vegetables, he straightened a displaced tin of sweetcorn. He looked out of the front window at the backs of the men, in a neat military-style line. He noticed that Karel had joined them and Oom Hans' bakkie was approaching down Main Street. Showmen, he scoffed. That's all they were.

Back behind the counter, he decided to take stock of the cigarettes. Looking up at the shelf above his head, he started; Camel Filters, yes. Peter Stuyvesant, yes. Benson and Hedges, or, as Patty would call them, Bennies and Hennies...

"Patty," he said out loud. Oom Marius took a deep breath and shook his head slowly. Not because he was in any way pining for the gentle, blonde woman but because the thought struck him that his Hettie might have guessed his feelings for this other woman. No, it couldn't be, he told himself. Surely Hettie hadn't been around when Patty came in to fetch her cigarettes. She was always in the kitchen busy preparing supper, wasn't she? Wasn't she? Oom Marius came out from behind the counter, away from the cigarettes, from the Benson and Hedges and paced the floor.

Behind the soap-powder cut-out, he discovered Petrus and Precious' socialising corner. He stared at the two plastic garden chairs, the radio, the coffee mugs and empty crisp packets lying on an upturned crate. Lazy, bloody bastards. He should have known not to trust a...

No, that wasn't true. He stared at the lobster tank. He knew how scared they were of the things yet still they'd cleaned the tank. It was positively glistening.

Crossing the floor again, he reached up and took a bottle of *brandewyn* from the shelf before returning to the lobster corner.

Dropping down onto a chair in front of the tank, Oom Marius was suddenly overwhelmed with exhaustion. He stared at the crustaceans. The yellow sticky tape had come off one of the creature's claws and it was opening and closing it, looking straight into Oom Marius' eyes. Unscrewing the lid off the bottle, he took a long, deep drink. He wiped his mouth with the back of his hand and placed the bottle down next to his feet. He dropped his head in his hands. For a while he was quiet and finally he began to sob. He didn't stop for a long time. In between the sobs a single word bubbled from his lips, "Hettie... oh, Hettie..."

There was a knock at the back door. Oom Marius wiped his eyes and nose on his sleeve. "Come in," he croaked.

The door opened. Patty stood there.

"Patty?"

"Oom Marius?"

Saying nothing more, she went over and sat down on the chair next to him. For a long time they didn't speak.

Looking up at the lobster tank, she said at last, "You still got these things, Oom Marius?" She laughed gently.

"Just call me..."

"Marius, I know. I'll try, OK?"

"She's very sick, Patty. I don't know what to do."

"She'll be alright, Marius," Patty spoke confidently because she knew that confidence was what he needed to hear. She was good at knowing what men wanted to hear. In fact, it was probably one of her best skills, having learnt it so young.

His voice was flat, "I want things to go back to the way they were. I want her to come out of that door and moan at me because I'm late coming to table."

"Wouldn't that be nice? But when things like this happen, nothing goes back to the way it was before."

She reached out her hand and closed it over his. The two of them sat like that for a long time. They took no notice of anything, not even the sun going down. When Charlie popped his head in the back door to ask where Precious was, only then did Oom Marius pull himself reluctantly up to switch on the lights.

Chapter Sixteen

The wedding photograph that Patty held in her hand had long ago been forgotten on a window sill, and had subsequently been swiftly and harshly punished by the merciless African sun. Even though it was only a little over ten years old, it looked much older. The smiling couple were tinged yellow, the once white wedding dress now beige. The background – the trees and shrubs and stretched out lawn – looked like it'd been dipped in cold tea, that sepia effect that Patty used on her handmade Christmas and birthday cards that she sent to the people she'd left behind in Cape Town. In fact, if the curled edges of the photo were to be ironed flat, it might even seem as if the effect had been done on purpose.

But, of course, it hadn't.

Patty would've loved for this photograph to be as pristine and crisp, so full of vibrating colours and grabbing smiles, as was the one of her first marriage all those years ago, when she was just nineteen. With a deep sigh she reached for her box of Bennies and Hennies and the lighter next to her. Tapping out a cigarette, she lit it and drew long and hard on the little white stick. Sometimes it felt like this was her only solace in this hard, sad world. She exhaled a plume of white smoke from her red lipsticked lips.

She was sitting on the steps of the back porch of the small house she shared with Shawn. Ten years they'd lived there. Ten years they'd been working on their so-called new life. Ten years they'd tried to outrun the sadness that had enveloped them in Cape Town, the sadness that seemed to have enveloped Patty since the day she was born on that cold and wet July morning forty-two years ago. And run as she might, hide wherever she tried, it always seemed to catch up to her.

Even here. In this remotest of *platteland* towns, the sadness still managed to catch up with her.

Laying the photograph down on the step next to her, Patty

took another drag of her cigarette. Her left hand stretched out to take hold of the glass of semi-sweet white wine. The ice blocks clinked against the side of the glass as she raised it to her lips. The sun had long since left the vast African plain and in its place was the cool blackness of the night and the frenzied chirping of the crickets, trying to be sexy for one another.

Patty had grown up in a two-bedroomed flat on the wrong side of the city, blocked by other apartment buildings so that no view was possible of either the mountain or the sea. What was the point of living in Cape Town, she'd often asked herself, if you couldn't even see Table Mountain or False Bay?

She'd been an only child. The result of a tumultuous two-month love affair and a subsequent shotgun marriage. When Patty's mother received her husband's fist in her face for the first time just a week after the wedding, she realised she'd made a mistake. But it was too late. A promise had been made before God and there was a little one on the way so there was no going back. But after her daughter was born, a scrawny, long-limbed baby with a sad expression in her eyes right from the minute she opened them (did she realise, even then, that the black colouring over her mother's lip wasn't supposed to be there?), Patty's mother decided there would be no more babies.

And so Patty grew up as an only child and perhaps it had even been a good decision not to bring any more children into a loveless, violent marriage or, perhaps it hadn't. Patty wasn't sure. She did know, however, that having a younger brother or sister to share those terrifying nights with her, huddled up in the corner behind her wardrobe as she listened to the dull thud of her father's fist in the other room, would have been less lonely.

Not astonishingly, the little blonde girl never did particularly well at school and her prospects in life would not have seemed very promising had it not been for a surprise that occurred in puberty. Blonde hair, blue eyes, curvaceous hips and a set of pert bosoms very much improved the sad young girl's circumstances. It resulted in a whole string of boys running after her; for a while anyway, that made Patty forget the sadness of her daddy.

But somehow she seemed to have inherited her taste for men from her worn-out mouse-grey mother, and there was many a boyfriend who thought it fitting to plant a fist in Patty's face whenever an altercation occurred. But where Patty did differ from her mother in this regard was that it only ever happened once with each of them. At the first sign of aggression, she was out of there. She didn't care what the man would be like who eventually loved her, what mistakes he'd have made, as long as he kept his fists to himself.

And so it happened that Patty met Gary. She was eighteen and had just finished high school. He was twenty and worked as a mechanic at a bike shop. He was by no means the most perfect specimen of manhood to stroll the streets of Cape Town, but he knew where to keep his fists. For Patty that was good enough and she accepted his proposal of marriage a year later.

Affairs with other women, debt collectors on their doorstep, a series of jobs he kept getting fired from and quite a lot of beer drinking were the details of Patty and Gary's marriage. Oh, and a string of miscarriages. And it was these miscarriages, these babies who refused to get born, that haunted Patty the most. She was convinced that if she could bring a child into their home all of Gary's little quirks would disappear, and he'd become a responsible, doting father and husband overnight. So in a way Patty blamed herself, or at least her defunct body, for the disappointment of their marriage. (Then there was the fact that she would've loved a little baby all of her own to cherish, a little baby who could drown out her loneliness.)

By the time Patty was twenty-nine she'd lived through enough sadness to fill the life of someone three times her age. Every drop of naïveté or hope had evaporated from her soul and she simply didn't believe she could do anything to save her marriage anymore. She had the names of twelve dead babies painstakingly written on twelve heart-shaped cards to prove it: Billy, Christine, Angela, Pearl, Davy, Joanie, Gary Junior, Michael, Michelle, Stevie, Colin and May. She went to court to apply for divorce and was granted it three weeks later because Gary didn't contest it. Just before her thirtieth birthday, Patty found herself living alone for the first time in her life.

Somewhere, somehow, at this point, some or other god looked down at Patty and decided she'd had enough for the meantime. Along came Shawn. Actually, he'd been there all along since he was Gary's younger brother and was two years younger than Patty, but he did a very good job of comforting his sad, beautiful ex-sister-in-law. He would visit her in her tiny bachelor flat (unbeknown to Gary, of course) where he would make her laugh and take her for rides on the back of his motorbike. Shawn didn't take long to propose to Patty but she didn't want to rush into marriage this time round. She wasn't quite sure how they could solve the problem of Shawn and Gary being brothers. That was besides the fact that Shawn was not going to be able to offer Patty a place to live with a view of either the mountain or the sea. Slowly it became clear that Cape Town had no more use for her and that she and her young would-be husband could better start a new life somewhere else.

Patty and Shawn sat on cushions on the floor round her tiny coffee table, a half empty bottle of Old Brown Sherry between them, and took turns closing their eyes and poking randomly at the map of South Africa that lay sprawled out in front of them. The rule was that if they'd heard the name of the town before, they couldn't go there.

Now, South Africa is a big country and has many towns and cities. But between Patty and Shawn, even though they weren't the best educated people in all of Cape Town, they still recognised most of the names their fingers landed on: Durban, Welkom, Margate, Uppington, Oudtshoorn. Finally, the bottle of Old Brown Sherry now empty, Patty's finger landed close to Springbok on a tiny dot called Klippiesfontein, and they both agreed they'd never heard of it before.

Shawn went out the next day and bought an engagement ring while Patty packed her twelve heart-shaped cards into a bag. With the two of them sitting snugly on Shawn's motorbike, they set off for the little uknown place.

That had been ten years ago. Ten years ago that the population of a previously unheard of little town of four thousand, one hundred and thirty six increased by two in a single day. Ten years ago that this had become their new home.

Patty stubbed out her cigarette and threw the remains of her semi-sweet white wine into the Agapanthas, picked up the sepia-coloured wedding photograph and went inside.

Chapter Seventeen

Oom Marius was woken up on Saturday morning by the cry of a *Hadeda* right outside the window. Stupid bird, he cursed, before sitting up on the sofa and looking round. He saw the half empty bottle of *brandewyn* on the floor and remembered where he was. Sleeping in a bed without Hettie wasn't something he wanted to get used to.

At the kitchen sink he splashed a few handfuls of water onto his face and went into the shop. He felt his stomach grumbling and realised he hadn't eaten anything since he'd left Cape Town the previous morning. Walking over to a shelf, he grabbed a tin of bully beef and proceeded to eat its contents straight from the can using the pocketknife on his belt. He tossed the empty tin into the dustbin, turned on the cash register, and threw open the front door. The familiar sound of the floorboards creaking under his weight pacified him.

Oom Marius looked out the door. The line of men wasn't there. Instead they'd taken up position on the low wall outside Henk Coetzee's Hunting and Fishing store. Wordlessly, glinting in an early, spiteful sun, they sat watching him.

Oom Marius stomped down his steps and crossed the road to stand in front of them.

Bertie straightened up and spat out the piece of grass he'd been chewing on, "How is Tannie Hettie, Oom?"

Oom Marius ignored him. Instead he let his eyes travel down the entire row of men. Slowly. Patiently. Not resting longer than a few seconds on any one of them. Not even on Karel.

At last he spoke, "What's wrong? Why aren't you bastards in front of my shop this morning?"

Karel pushed himself off the wall and walked over a few steps to where Oom Marius had planted his feet. Karel's shoulders were thrust back and his chin jutted out but when he spoke, his voice was less aggressive than his body language. Oom Marius was still, after all, his elder. "Because as long as you're here Oom, as long as you're in charge, we have no problem with your shop. The way things used to be, you know."

Oom Marius was in no mood to be mollified. Rage and the ghost of *brandewyn* coursed through his veins in equal measures of ferocity. He stepped forward and shoved Karel at the shoulders with both hands, "Nothing is the way things used to be, you bastards. Don't you understand that? Do you really think you can stop things changing? Stop this country changing? Stop people getting sick? Just by being *hardegat*?"

Hard-arsed.

He let out a bitter laugh, "Then you're even thicker than I thought."

"Now there's no need for this hostility, Oom Marius," Karel spoke, taking a step back. His arms hung at his sides and he looked Oom Marius openly in the face.

People were starting to gather round. They came out of Botha's Butchery, the hunting shop, the petrol station. Word spread fast in a town like Klippiesfontein and soon the front doors were opening and folk were taking up positions wherever they had a good view. A group of children gathered in the shade of the stoep. Young Daan produced a bag of marbles from his pocket and tried to interest his playmates in a game but no one was biting. The possibility of a fight was more interesting.

"It's not you we have a problem with, Oom," Karel continued. "You're one of us. It's letting that stinking kaffir of yours take over that we have a problem with. It's sending our wives and children into a shop where the only adult is a black man. Who knows what he could do to them?"

"I'd be the first one to castrate him if he so much as looked at one of your wives in the wrong way. And you know it."

"Look, it's simple. We don't want this. It's not how we do things around here."

"Who made you the bloody mayor? I've lived in this town my whole life and this is how *I* do things so get off your lazy backsides and come stand in front of my shop. If you're going to barricade it with Petrus in there, then you bloody well better barricade it with me in there too because as from Monday I'm promoting him to manager."

Oom Marius turned and walked away. Half way across the road he turned round and looked back at the bewildered men, "Well, are you coming or not?"

The men looked questioningly at Karel. He turned around, with his back to them and flipped his cellphone out of his multi-gadgeted belt. Everyone heard him talking in muted tones to someone at other end, probably Oom Hans, so he could figure out his next move.

Oom Marius shook his head and retraced his steps, long, angry strides, until he was standing at Karel's back. Stretching over his shoulder, he grabbed the phone out of his hand and brought it up to his own ear. Karel swung round to face Oom Marius, his chest pushed out. He took a step closer so that his face was right in Oom Marius'. Wordlessly, the two men stared at each other.

Oom Marius turned his attention back to the phone, "Hans, did he tell you? I've just promoted Petrus to manager. So you better leave your lambs and get your arse over here because if ever there was a reason to protest then today is the day. First black manager in Klippicsfontein. First black manager in Klippiesfontein!"

Oom Marius tossed the phone down on the ground and it lay there, cushioned in the red dust, its screen shining blue and a garbled voice coming from the speaker.

Bertie looked from one man to the next before bending down to pick up the phone, "*Pa, dis Bertie hier.*"

Dad, it's Bertie here.

"First black manager in Klippiesfontein!" Oom Marius shouted again as he crossed the road, his fist raised in the air. "You want war you bastards? You've got it."

Oom Marius disappeared inside the shop and emerged a few seconds later, carrying a chair. He put it down in the open doorway and sat down. A shotgun lay across his lap. He stared at the backs of the men who had scurried across the road at Karel's orders and regrouped in a line in front of the shop.

Fifteen minutes later the scene was still the same. The only movement came from a couple of flies circling the men's faces. In the distance they saw Oom Hans' bakkie driving up.

Oom Hans pulled up outside the shop and climbed out, wearing his veldskoene, knee-length socks and a broad-brimmed hat. Walking up to the steps with long, confident strides, he addressed Oom Marius, "Come now Marius, there's no need for this."

Oom Marius said nothing. He simply raised his shotgun to his shoulder and pointed the barrel at Oom Hans.

"Let's be reasonable here," Oom Hans tried again.

"If you don't get off my property, Hans, I will be forced to use this thing."

"You're going to regret this," Oom Hans spoke through clenched teeth.

"I'm sure I'll regret a lot of things but blowing your head off won't be one of them."

Shaking his head, Oom Hans walked back to his men and took up his position next to Karel.

The heat of day was taking its toll. Flies buzzed lazily and no one bothered swatting them away. Dust blew onto sweat-soaked skins and formed small deposits of red mud. Onlookers fanned themselves with scraps of paper or limp hands. No one approached the shop. The group of children had moved across the road and found shelter in the spindly shade of an Acacia tree. Young Daan had taken off down Main Street when he'd seen the shotgun. The line of barricaders slackened. Feet burned, knees bent, and bodies leaned up against flagpoles. Someone passed a bottle of luke-warm water down the line and everyone took a half-hearted swig from it.

At one point Oom Marius disappeared inside his shop again and everyone thought the impasse had been broken. He emerged a minute later sipping from a bottle of ice-cold coke. Once empty, he tossed the bottle down at the men's feet, the condensation droplets running down the glass into the dust. He went inside again and came out with a box of ice-creams. Taking one for himself, he called over to one of the children to take the box from him and share it out amongst themselves. Gleefully they obliged. After the ice-cream, Oom Marius produced a six-pack of Castle beers. He poured one after the other down his thirsty throat. Staring out over the scene in front of him, his chin started to drop onto his chest. It wasn't long before he was asleep. In the distance a lawnmower roared into life and woke him. It was late afternoon.

Just as the sun was starting to relent, they spotted the figure of the dominie coming down the street towards them.

The men in the barricade straightened up.

"*Goeie dag*, Dominie," they muttered more or less in unison, not quite sure whether to be proud or embarrassed of their presence.

The dominie nodded curtly at the men and started up the steps, "Marius, good to see you back, man."

Jumping up, Oom Marius blushed and tried to kick the empty beer cans under his chair. Then, shotgun held down at his side, he offered his right hand to the dominie. A vigorous handshake followed.

"Now tell me, Marius, how is Hettie doing?"

Oom Marius dropped the dominie's hand like a hot stone and shook his head dejectedly, "Not well, Dominie. Not well at all."

"We will all remember her in our prayers tomorrow in the service," he said.

Oom Marius stiffened, his lips pulled tight. "Thank you, Dominie, but I'd rather you didn't do that."

"What?"

"That lot," he jerked his head in the direction of the barricaders, "they'll be there too."

"Now Marius, we shouldn't go round judging our brothers when there are logs in our own eyes. Didn't the good Lord teach us that?"

"I'm sorry Dominie, but we don't need this congregation to pray for us. I don't want those hypocrites speaking my Hettie's name. One of the reasons she's not getting better is because she spends all day worrying about the shop and..."

"You seem to be a little short in the supply of tolerance, brother..."

Oom Marius' jaw clamped down and he took a step closer to the dominie, "Don't stand here on my stoep and preach to me about tolerance with that lot standing over there..."

"It is to everyone that I speak of tolerance. You too Marius, you need to learn..."

Oom Marius brought his shotgun up to his waist, "I am not in the mood to learn anything today, Dominie. Why don't you try teaching *them* something?"

"This is the beer speaking. Come, let us go inside where we can talk alone," he reached out to lay a hand on his shoulder.

Oom Marius shrugged it off impatiently and turned the shotgun vertically, "It is *me* speaking, not the beer. Marius from Klippiesfontein. Owner of the General Store. Husband of a dying wife. And I do not want those men praying for her. Is that clear, Dominie?"

The dominie stepped forward and reached out to take hold of the gun. Oom Marius jerked back his hand. Suddenly an enormous bang rang out and the dominie tottered back a few steps. The crowd took a collective intake of breath. Not letting the air out of their lungs they stared at the stoep, expecting the dominie to fall down in a heap at Oom Marius' feet. Instead, both men looked up at the corrugated iron roof. A huge hole gaped just above them. A shaft of sunlight poured in and shone down onto the tops of their heads.

The dominie shook his head and backed away. Turning to walk down the steps, he muttered, "How many times have I told them? Alcohol is the fuel of the devil? And do they listen…"

Oom Marius carried on staring at the hole in his roof.

Everyone was quiet. Men wearing guns had their hands on their holsters. Mothers rushed out, located their children amongst the crowd and took them home, the children complaining as they were marched away from the action.

Not long afterwards, Mrs Joubert appeared walking primly down Main Street in her crisp, emerald green pencil skirt, sensible walking shoes and long, grey hair caught up in a loose bun. Short, determined steps.

Not many people in Klippiesfontein knew this about Mrs Joubert, knew that she hadn't always been quite as assertive as she was now. In fact, it was probably safe to say that no one did.

Mrs Joubert hadn't always been Mrs Joubert. A long time ago, approximately sixty-eight years ago, Mrs Joubert had been a chubby little baby called Eileen Crawford, the last child in a row of four girls. Now, her parents were English-speaking South Africans and deemed themselves to be much more open-minded than their fellow white countrymen, the Afrikaners. Although they told their friends and family they didn't mind which sex the baby was as long as it was healthy, the truth was, they did mind a little bit. After three girls, Eileen Crawford's parents were rather desperate for a boy.

But as fate would have it, Eileen turned up instead of the much awaited Eric and she was never really forgiven for this betrayal. On the surface, Eileen got everything her older sisters got: the material necessities of this world, mental stimulation, good schooling, a strict upbringing, love. No one's trying to imply that she missed out, but somehow Eileen Crawford always had the feeling that these things came to her begrudgingly. She felt guilty for being a girl, for being the reason behind that ever-present look of disappointment in her parents' eyes, for using the emotional and financial resources that had been destined for someone else.

Eileen Crawford's sisters, each one a little more unwanted the further down the line of girls they came, saw their youngest sibling as the pinnacle of failure, the perpetrator of an unforgivable crime: that of being the fourth daughter. Now, had she been the boy everyone had never vocally wished for, their own sins of being the first, second, and third daughters, would have been exonerated too.

So Eileen Crawford grew up in a very precarious position and it was this position that got in her way of developing any self-confidence whatsoever. The shy, grey little girl turned into a shy, grey teenager and would have continued on this path to a shy, grey womanhood had something extraordinary not happened to her.

Wendy Foster.

Eileen was almost seventeen when the sassy, stroppy sixteen-year-old walked into her class at the start of that school year. Now Wendy had everything counting against her, much more so than even the shy, grey Eileen Crawford. Her parents were divorced, her mom was poor and more interested in wine and a string of men than in her curly-mopped daughter. But in spite of all of these disadvantages and several others not even mentioned here, Wendy Foster was a self-assured, loud-mouthed, independent teenager who, for some or other inexplicable reason, or perhaps simply because of the grace of God, took a shine to Eileen Crawford. And this, in turn, taught the shy, grey girl a very important lesson: *You needn't be the product of your past. It was possible, albeit very hard, to shape yourself into the person you'd like to be.*

And this is exactly what Eileen Crawford did over the next couple of years. Like a snake, she shed her shy grey skin, and emerged strong and self-confident with a cigarette in her hand and high-heeled shoes. She matriculated at the end of the following year with five A's and a B. Leaving her open-mouthed sisters behind her, she marched on to university. She shocked her parents to such an extent that their disillusion evaporated almost overnight and they started professing how thrilled they'd always been with their quartet of girls, especially the youngest one. (They didn't actually voice this last part out loud – favouritism wasn't a quality found in open-minded English-speaking white South African stock.) At last Eileen Crawford was forgiven. Her sisters were forgiven. But for Eileen it came too late. It came

135

when she didn't need it anymore.

Wendy Foster went on to study law and later became a women's rights activist. The new and improved Eileen Crawford graduated from university, and the rest you could say, besides a happy marriage to a young university lecturer and his unfortunate death a few years later, is history. You could say this, or you could say thank God for Wendy Foster.

Passing the gathered crowd, Mrs Joubert nodded at one or two acquaintances before striding towards the line of men. As if it had been rehearsed, they fell away and made space for her to go up the steps. Once on the stoep, she walked up to Oom Marius, "It's good to see you back home, Marius. It's a pity Hettie couldn't come with you."

Oom Marius dropped his eyes at the mention of his wife, "I'm not sure if she'll be coming home again."

"And if she was here, what do you think she'd say about all of this?" she made a sweeping gesture with her hand, taking in the shop, the line of men and lastly, the hole gaping over their heads. "Would she be proud of the kind, rational man she'd married?"

"Don't talk to me about being rational. Not in this..."

"No, you're right. I suppose this whole thing has gone past rationality. But what good are you going to be to Hettie if you're locked up in jail?"

He scoffed, "As much good as I am to her now, I imagine."

"Right, right," she nodded slowly, "I don't suppose a man wrapped up in self-pity would be much use to her in the current situation."

The red of Oom Marius' sweaty face turned a shade darker, "A man wrapped up in self-pity?"

"Then tell me what you'd call this nonsense?"

"I'm trying to... I'm standing up for... can't you see, this is our livelihood they're threatening?" he sputtered.

"And I'd say you're doing a bloody good job of threatening it too. For God's sake Marius, put away that gun and come inside. Leave these fools out here to themselves."

Their conversation was interrupted by the sound of a car moving slowly past. They turned to look and saw a police van, the driver's elbow out the window, his head turned to face them, taking in the details.

Oom Marius laughed bitterly, "Yes, now you're here, aren't you? When the dominie phones you. But where have you been these last weeks while they've been wrecking my business?"

The police van drew to a stop at the intersection and the driver leaned out, speaking threateningly, "Sir, we've had a call-out about a disturbance of the peace and the unlawful use of a firearm."

"The peace has been restored, Constable. Thank you. You can go back now," Mrs Joubert called out. Quickly she took Oom Marius by the elbow and steered him into his shop.

Once inside, Mrs Joubert said, "Now where do you usually keep that thing, Marius?"

"Behind the counter," he muttered, suddenly feeling a little foolish inside the dark interior of his shop.

"Why don't you go put it back there and I'll put on the kettle for a cup of tea?"

She walked to the back of the shop, "My God Marius, are these damned lobsters still here? When are you going to throw them into a pot and put them out of their misery? You know, I make a lovely Thermador sauce."

Chapter Eighteen

Frikkie stood at the intersection, a raging, black cloud in his head, getting in the way of his thoughts. Take a left and he'd be home where he could heat up the stew his sister had sent him – God knew, he was hungry. Take a right and he'd be at the school where the men would be gathering in the assembly hall. Bertie would be there by now, given the task of setting up the room, putting out the drinks and the snacks baked by various wives and mothers of the Afrikaner Resistance Movement.

Frikkie turned right. He didn't feel like being alone. Not after the day he'd just been through.

Frikkie's pa had always taught him, his ma had taught him, that he was a member of the superior race. He was white and he was male: there was no higher state to strive for. This is what he'd been taught. This is what he believed because, as a matter of fact, it was a hundred percent true: it was as the world should be. But now, coming back from the job interview, the meeting with the manager of civil servants in the police force, the black manager at whose feet he'd had to grovel and received a negative reply all the same, Frikkie was disappointed. To say the very least. The very, very least.

"Hey Frik," Bertie called when his friend walked through the door. "You here to help me? Grab those serviettes over there, would you?"

Frikkie nodded glumly.

"Hey man, what's wrong? You look like someone died," Bertie said.

"I had that interview today," he replied.

"Oh shit, that's right, man. How did it go? Or shouldn't I ask?"

"It was another BEE position," Frikkie spat bitterly. "Black Economic Empowerment," he spoke the words as if they were poison in his mouth. "Why didn't they just tell me that from the start and I wouldn't have bothered showing up?"

"I know what you mean. My old man says the days of the white man being in employment are over. You've got to have your own business in this country or starve. Those are the only choices left to us these days."

"Bastards!" Frikkie continued. "I swear they get a thrill from making us grovel before them like that. Reverse racism, that's what I call it."

"Yeah, and they talk to us about tolerance. But look now, who's judging who by the colour of their skin?" Bertie said.

"Makes me feel like planting a bomb under one of their fancy executive chairs and blowing the whole lot of them sky high."

"Here man, have a beer," Bertie popped open one of the ice-cold cans and offered it to his friend. Frikkie took it from him and guzzled it down in a few deep, angry gulps. He tossed the empty tin into the dustbin and helped himself to another one.

"Come on, give me a hand with these chairs, Frik. The men are going to be here just now."

Petrus greeted everyone sitting in the taxi and wished them a safe journey home before getting out on the outskirts of Klippiesfontein. He waved after it as it took off in the direction of the township, a cloud of red dust billowing in its wake. Since it was dark already, he decided to take a back route to the shop. No good looking for trouble with the mood around town being what it was.

Petrus was going over the details of the Sunday afternoon he'd spent with his friend, Jacob. He was thinking about the soccer match they'd attended until half time, about the four goals that were scored by the visiting team, about Jacob's on-the-verge-of-tears despair and Petrus' quick decision to take his friend away from the soccer match to spare him from any more devastation. Petrus was thinking about the ice-cream van and the way Jacob's eyes glistened when he saw it. He thought about his friend's urgent nodding head in response to Petrus' question, "Do you feel like an ice-cream?" How the two of them had sat down under the thorn tree, savouring their strawberry and vanilla soft serves with a Flake sticking out the side and hundreds and thousands sprinkled on top. He thought about his one-sided conversation with Jacob where he told him all about Precious, every last detail he could remember about her, while his friend sat quietly next to him and licked away at the ice-cream. These were the details Petrus was thinking about as he made his way back to the Klippiesfontein General Store.

With the sun having taken its leave, the air had cooled down and Petrus was enjoying his walk. He thought he could smell a storm blowing in on the wind, but maybe that was just wishful thinking. It'd been so dry lately, the borehole in the township where most of the people got their water was drying up. He listened to the crickets chirping to one another and the odd snatch of dialogue as it drifted out through an open back door. He heard a woman laughing and looked inside the lighted window. A family was sitting around the kitchen table, just finished with supper. He saw the domestic worker at the sink, washing up the family's dishes.

It made Petrus think of his mother. He was just back from a short visit with her to restock the kitchen cupboard. Over the weekend he'd seen that her food was low. Now that he slept at the shop at night, he didn't take supplies home often enough. His mother wasn't one to complain about having little to eat, having gotten used to hunger many years ago after his father disappeared. He made a mental note to send a bag of food home whenever someone from the township dropped by the shop.

As he walked his mind wandered over to Precious again, as it seemed to do at every chance it got these days. The way she touched his arm when she spoke to him in earnest, or when she threw back her head like that and laughed when she was teasing him. It made his step lighter and he was less anxious about walking through the dark streets.

"We're going to have to intensify our actions, men," Karel was standing up in front.

His voice was much too loud for the size of the room. The gathered men squinted at him in discomfort. They were seated in three rows arranged in front of Karel. Frikkie was in the second row next to Bertie. He probably thought he was addressing an entire army, thought Frikkie, sipping his third brandy and coke of the evening. And that was without counting the five beers he'd had before. Frikkie could feel his concentration oozing away. He should've gone home instead of coming to the meeting. He was tired of Karel preaching to them as if he was the dominie in church.

"Is everyone up to date about the latest development at the General Store?" he asked and several voices murmured in assent.

"What development?" Frikkie nudged Bertie.

"Haven't you heard?" Bertie asked incredulously. "Where the hell have you been?"

Frikkie whispered, "I spent the weekend with my sister in Springbok, Bert. You know that. So I could make it to my interview on time this morning. Now tell me, what happened?"

Karel was still droning on in the front.

"Oom Marius made Petrus manager."

"Manager?"

"Yes, can you believe it?"

"Manager!"

"Yes, that's what I said, man."

"That black idiot, who's never seen the inside of a classroom in his life, gets to be a manager while I have to beg like a dog for a simple clerk's position?"

Frikkie hadn't realised he'd spoken out loud. Everyone turned round to face him.

"That's right, Frikkie. That's exactly right," Karel exclaimed, fired up because someone was taking the bait of white indignation.

Frikkie was fired up too. Suddenly he was on the same wavelength as their leader, and, since Frikkie seldom managed to be on the same wavelength as anybody, he was very excited.

"You go to school for twelve years. Well, thirteen in your case, Frik," Karel continued. "And where does that get you? How many jobs have you had?"

"None," Frikkie mumbled.

"That's right. None," Karel exclaimed and held his finger up in the air. "Not one. And why is that? Why does Petrus get to be manager while you are forced to sponge off your mother and her small pension?"

This wasn't going quite the direction Frikkie had thought. He looked down at his shoes. "I don't know, Karel," he muttered.

"Because you're white and he's black, that's why."

Yes, that sounded more like it. It wasn't Frikkie's fault. He lifted his head to face Karel again. "Because I'm white and he's black!" Frikkie shouted.

His fervour seemed to whip up more animation amongst the men and Karel honed in on it, "And what do you suggest we do about this?"

Frikkie jumped up from his chair, stood to a rather wobbly attention with one fist thrust proudly at his side, and the other clutching his drink, "We teach that stinking kaffir a lesson, that's what I say."

"And I say you're exactly right," Karel answered.

"Come on, let's go find him," Frikkie said, draining his glass and banging it down on the chair behind him before pushing past several men's knees to get to the door.

"Bertie," Karel said, "you better go with him."

Bertie stood up and followed his friend to the exit, an excited glint in his eye, an eager nod.

"And stop off at my place on the way and ask the wife to give you two balaclavas."

"Yes Karel."

Frikkie lunged at the drinks table before he went through the door and grabbed two cans of beer, "For the road," he muttered sheepishly.

Petrus was digging in his pockets, looking for the back door key. He hoped he hadn't lost it – he wouldn't like to phone Baas Marius with that bit of news. Pulling out a fistful of coins, he inspected them in the dark. There, glittering amongst them, was the single silver key. He sighed with relief and resolved to get himself a key ring. Petrus looked up and was about to climb the back stairs.

Two men oozed out of the shadows in front of him, their faces covered in black. He could just make out white skin round the eyes and lips. His heart raced, his breath was shallow and panicky, cold sweat dribbled down his back. This is what he'd been fearing from the very start. There was nowhere to run. They blocked the way back to the street and there was no way he'd get up those four steps and unlock the door before they could grab him. Petrus heard a rumble of thunder in the distance.

"*Asseblief* Baas?" he pleaded.

Please?

"Mr Manager now, are you?" one of the men spoke.

Petrus thought he recognised the voice but he was too panicked to put a face to it. He smelt beer on the man's breath. "What?" he asked.

"You think you're white now that you're the manager?" the man said.

Petrus was confused. He saw the other one move round behind him, the short, stocky one with a green comb sticking out of his sock. He felt his arm wrenched behind him and his elbow twisted. Petrus reached up on his toes as his arm was forced up higher behind his back and the pain shot through his shoulder.

Green comb…

"*Kleinbaas* Bertie? Is that you?"

"Hit him, man, hit him," urged the voice at Petrus' back. He felt *Kleinbaas* Bertie grab a fistful of his hair and wrench his face upwards. "He knows my name. Hit him, Frik."

"*Kleinbaas* Frikkie?" Petrus gasped in shock.

"You say anything about this and we go after your mother. You hear me? Huh? You hear me?"

"I hear you, Baas," Petrus' voice was small.

"Mr Manager of Klippiesfontein? Huh? Huh?" *Kleinbaas* Frikkie pushed on.

Petrus saw him raise his fist above his shoulder. It loomed big and dangerous. What was all this talk about manager? Did they even know who he was? It was very dark here behind the shop.

"It's me, Baas. It's Petrus. Why are you doing this?"

"I know who you are," the *Kleinbaas* was saying.

Kleinbaas Frikkie's fist was coming down fast, headed straight for Petrus' face. Everything moved slowly. He dropped to his knees and felt *Kleinbaas* Bertie being pulled down with him. He looked up, one last time, to try to appeal to *Kleinbaas* Frikkie's goodness but he could see by the gleam in his eye that there was none.

Just like his father, he thought. And all because he hadn't kept his promise to his mother.

Petrus felt a fat drop of rain splat down on his forehead followed by the crunch of knuckles on his cheekbone.

Chapter Nineteen

Precious noticed only three men standing outside the shop this morning as she swept the stoep. Maybe it was like Oom Marius had said: they'd get bored eventually, go back to their old lives and things would go back to normal. Precious would be grateful if that happened. These men clinging to the previous century as if their lives depended on it gave her the creeps.

Her mind flitted back to the previous evening when Charlie had taken her out in his little white car with Telcom written on the side to the Wimpy in Springbok. She'd had a vanilla milkshake. Charlie had ordered chocolate. The families at the other tables had stared at them.

Precious wondered where Petrus was; she'd knocked until her knuckles were sore and he still hadn't emerged. The only explanation she could think of was that he was sleeping off a *babbelas* in the storeroom and that he'd be up in a little while. She wouldn't have pinned him as a drinker though, but she was already thinking of a few jokes she could tease him with.

Precious looked up as the school bus wheezed into life at the intersection and took off down the road. Come to think of it, Precious hadn't seen Patty get on the bus this morning either. *Hauw*, could she be round back, knocking at the door to buy her cigarettes? Precious propped the broom up in the corner of the stoep and descended the steps. Trying not to look at the men, she turned the corner and walked round to the back.

Kneeling on the floor, her hands cradling something dark, Precious spotted Patty.

"Precious, thank God. Get inside and phone the ambulance!" Patty shouted at her as soon as she saw her.

Precious didn't move. She stared at Patty's face. A smudge of dirt across her chin. A smear of something red on her cheek. Horror in her eyes. Precious couldn't figure out what was going on.

"Precious!" Patty screamed again.

"I can't get in. Petrus is still asleep," she spoke in a dull voice.

"Petrus is here," Patty called, her voice edging towards hysterical. She looked down at the dark thing in her hands and started to sob.

Precious rushed over to where Patty knelt. She drew a sharp breath. In Patty's hands lay what looked like it might once have been a head: a mass of split skin, brown on the outside, pink on the inside; welts; the exposed white of an eye; dry, crusted blood. Her eyes travelled over the rest of the body. The arms were pushed up underneath it, one leg lay at an unnatural angle to the torso, fabric was ripped and stained red.

"Petrus?" Precious spoke, her voice shocked. There was a pressure in her ears making her feel dizzy. The sky, the back door, the wall of the building next door, all seemed to be spinning round.

From somewhere far off she heard sobbing and then someone called out her name. She shook her head and looked in the direction of the sound. She became aware of Patty again and she was saying something, "Take my cellphone out of my bag and call one-one-two. Hurry up."

Precious saw a handbag lying two metres away. Dropping onto her knees, she started digging through its contents. Locating the cellphone, she flipped it open and proceeded to dial the number Patty had yelled to her.

Precious heard a crisp female voice on the other side, "Hello, what is your emergency? Where are you phoning from?"

Buzzing in his ears. That was the first thing he became aware of. Buzzing. An incessant buzzing. A bright light behind his eyelids. Flashes of red. Then the pain flooded in and clouded over everything else. He couldn't figure out where it was. The pain. It seemed to be everywhere. Especially, especially... Petrus gave up and allowed himself to be swallowed up by the blackness again.

Patty felt cold despite the heat of the sun beating down on her bare arms and legs. She stared after the ambulance, feeling no emotion. Cold. As she watched it getting smaller, it seemed to swallow up all the horror of that morning. It had swallowed Precious and driven away. It could have her too, she thought. The ambulance could take all the misery of that morning and drive off and never come back.

She was dying for a cigarette. She looked round for her bag. It wasn't there. She saw a couple of housewives and some maids staring pityingly at her. Frikkie and Bertie were there too. She shook her head. God, she needed a cigarette right now. Where the hell was her handbag!

Patty remembered it was still lying in the dirt behind the shop. In a trance she started walking. Frikkie rushed up to her, "Are you alright, Patty?"

She pushed past him and carried on to take the corner.

In the alley she saw the handbag. Looking down, she noticed her pantyhose were torn at the knees and the flesh-coloured nylon hung down her shins in shreds. That's what she'd been doing here, she remembered. She'd been on her way to buy a packet of cigarettes because she'd run out. Damn it!

Next to her bag, Patty spotted a silver key lying in the dirt. It wasn't one of hers. Maybe it belonged to Precious or to... to... Petrus – a sob escaped her throat. Maybe it was the key to the shop.

Patty bent down to pick it up. Cigarettes, she thought triumphantly. The first good thought that had entered her mind since... since... since... another sob... since she'd found Petrus. Walking up the back steps, she slid the key into the lock. It fitted. She turned and heard the mechanism give way. Crunching down on the handle, Patty entered the shop. It was dark inside and her eyes needed several moments to adjust. She smelt paraffin and soap powder. Crossing the floor, she walked in behind the counter. Locating the Benson and Hedges, she took a pack from the shelf and tore off its plastic wrapping. With grubby, blood-stained fingers she pulled out a cigarette and brought it to her mouth. Her hand was shaking. Lighter? Lighter? Then she spotted a tray of lighters with buxomly women in swimming costumes. She reached out and grabbed one, lit her cigarette and exhaled with the deepest contentment as she felt the smoke travel back up her throat again. She stared at the lighter in her hand. The woman's swimming costume had disappeared.

Patty heard someone knocking at the front door. Taking another drag from her cigarette, she crossed the floor, turned the key in the lock and opened it. In front of her stood two policemen.

"Were you the first person on the scene this morning, ma'am?" the blonde one enquired.

She nodded, "Come inside."

His skull was going to burst. Any second now. He could feel it. And it wasn't as if it was just coming from his head. Each time he breathed in a pain shot across his chest. And his arm. What was going on with his arm? Why was it hurting so much? Disinfectant. Like at the clinic. The smell filled his nostrils. But he could hear nothing. Not a sound. The silence was eerie. Where was he? A bright light shone right through his closed eyelids. He turned his head away from the source and felt again like it would explode. Slowly, with the greatest of effort, he opened his eyes.

Precious! Her face was right in front of him, her eyes were boring into his. He tried to speak but only a croak came from his throat.

"Be still, brother," he heard her sweet voice. "You must rest."

He did as she told him. He shut his eyes and this time there seemed to be less pain. Precious was sitting next to him. Precious was taking care of him. Precious loved him. He allowed the darkness and happiness to overwhelm him.

Precious didn't bother with the back steps the next morning. Defiantly, she walked up the front and put the key into the lock. She pushed down the handle and went inside. There'd been only one barricader outside the shop but Precious didn't care. She would've taken on the whole lot of them if they'd been there. They didn't frighten her anymore.

Herman, that was his name, she remembered. She watched as he took his phone from his pocket and started talking into it. Calling for back-up, she scoffed. The coward couldn't even take on a single girl.

Precious turned on the cash register before going to check on the lobsters. "Yes, don't look at me like that," she spoke to the creatures. "I know your house is dirty. I'll phone Charlie later and see if he's got time to come over and help me, OK?"

She went to the fridge to check the sell-by dates of the milk and removed six cartons before turning on the kettle for her morning cup of tea. By the time she walked past the window again, the whole group of them was gathered outside. Eight, she counted. A little distance away she spotted the police van. Yes, you bastards, she thought, it's a little late now.

Precious was startled to hear a prim clicking of footsteps on the steps. Looking up, she saw Mrs Joubert walk through the door.

"Good morning, Precious. How are you this morning?"

"Good morning," she muttered, not quite ready for the first customer. She'd better get used to it, she thought quickly. There'd be a fair share of people coming in this morning, wanting to hear the full account of what happened. But she hadn't thought Mrs Joubert would be one of them.

"What can I do for you?" Precious asked in her politest voice.

Again she was startled. Patty stood right behind Mrs Joubert. Precious hadn't noticed her come in.

"No, it's what we can do for you, my girl." Mrs Joubert spoke in her matter-of-fact voice. "Patty and I are here to help you run the shop until Petrus or Hettie gets better. One of the two. We know you have another job you have to get to and we won't give them the pleasure of seeing this shop closed for a single minute during business hours."

"We're here to help," Patty smiled triumphantly. "What can we do?"

Precious looked from one woman to the next and then back again. She couldn't believe this was happening. It was the last thing in the world she'd expected: allies. But she sure could use them, she decided quickly.

Precious beamed, "Well someone can take the list lying behind the counter and phone in this week's order and maybe one of you can help me clean the lobster tank?"

Chapter Twenty

Petrus was sitting up in bed. He tried bringing a spoonful of soup to his mouth but he was clumsy with his left hand and messed it down the front of the new set of pyjamas his mother had brought him when she came to visit. Frustrated, he dropped the spoon in his bowl and turned his head away. He stared out across the ward.

Twenty beds. Twenty broken men. Knife fights, several victims from the same taxi accident, a gunshot wound, someone who'd fallen off a ladder. And him, Petrus, a thirty-year-old man who'd been beaten by the son of his father's killer. Plaster casts, bandages and stitches decorated the men. Some in pyjamas, some in their loosest everyday clothes, two in nothing but their underwear. He'd been in the hospital for almost five days so he'd gotten used to the putrid smell of disinfectant mixed with unwashed sweaty bodies.

There weren't enough nurses on the ward to help the patients bathe so, unless a family member came in and did it, they remained unwashed. The men on the ward told him that the nurses all went away in aeroplanes to work in hospitals in England. And the doctors too. They made more money there. That was why there weren't enough of them left to wash the men. Some of the men came from far away. Their families couldn't come to visit so they hadn't been washed in weeks.

There was a TV mounted in a corner but it didn't work. Its screen flickered black and white. Several men were staring at it; it was better than staring at nothing. Faint strains of music drifted into the ward from the nurses' station nearby.

Petrus heard a prim, rhythmic clicking of heels on the cold hospital floor. It was different to the sound of the nurses' rubber-soled shoes. He listened for a few seconds longer before recognising them: Precious! Several men drew themselves up in their beds. They'd recognised the footsteps too. No one else had such a pretty woman come in to visit them every day and it made them look at Petrus with envy. The men in underwear threw their stained sheets over their lower bodies. Petrus watched as some ran fingers through their tight-knit curls or rubbed sleep from their eyes. He didn't have to smarten himself up. He'd been ready for her for hours.

"Good evening, *Mma*," a chorus of attentive male voices greeted her as she strode into the ward.

"Good evening," she sang back, making her way directly over to Petrus' bed, the last one in the ward by the grimy window.

"Oh brother, what's happened?" Precious exclaimed. "Why are you bleeding?"

"It's only tomato soup. I am clumsy with my right hand in a sling."

"Here, let me help you," she offered and came over to Petrus' side.

"I am not a child, sister," he protested.

Precious threw back her head and let out a peal of laughter that scattered through the room and made the men wish they'd messed tomato soup down their fronts too.

"It is not only children who need help, brother," she stated matter-of-factly, and lifted a spoonful of soup to her own lips first to feel if it was cool enough. She brought her hand over to Petrus' mouth and he slurped up the soup.

"The swelling seems to be down a little more today," she commented.

Petrus replied, "Yes, sister. I am getting better every day. The doctor says I can go home tomorrow."

"I went to see Charlie last night after work. I met his mother. I asked him if he'd fetch you and take you home."

Petrus was not happy. Why was Precious going to Baas Charlie's house? Why was she visiting white people now, like she was one of them, when this is what they'd done to him? Even if it was Baas Charlie, even if he wasn't one of the bad ones, why did she go to his house?

"I will take the taxi, sister."

"You're going to take a taxi with a crutch under your arm, a bandage on your head and stitches all over your face? Don't be stupid, brother. You will frighten the other passengers. Why not make it easy on yourself and accept a lift from Charlie? He is happy to do this for you."

"I do not want to make Baas Charlie happy. I want to make myself happy."

"Then do it for me, brother? I don't want to think of you struggling all alone in the taxi."

"I will not be alone. There will be other people. You know there are always other people in the taxi."

"That's not what I mean and you know it. I don't want you struggling home without a friendly face at your side. I tried to get off work but it's the end of the month and the VAT returns have to be in tomorrow…"

"The faces in the taxi will be friendly enough."

"Please? For me? Else I won't be able to sleep a wink tonight."

Petrus didn't want to give in. He really, really didn't, and he tried his very best to stop his head from nodding but it did it all the same. Petrus sighed. What more could he say after his head had just betrayed him?

Precious smiled. She looked down at her lap and started fiddling with the clasp of her little white handbag. She seemed not to know what to say.

"How are things going at the shop, sister?"

"Good. I work in the mornings and after lunch Mrs Joubert and Patty, they take turns to run the shop. They are getting quite good at it too and business seems to be picking up a little."

Petrus smiled, "I see it takes three women to do one man's job?"

"Hey, don't start getting smart with me," she teased back.

"It will be good to get back to work," Petrus said, growing more pensive.

Precious' expression turned serious, "No, brother, you cannot come back to work. You need to rest."

"What am I going to do at home? I am not used to sitting around like an old woman."

"Baas Marius says you must stay at home as long as you need to."

"Was he here, Precious? Did he come all the way from Cape Town to see me or was I only dreaming it?"

"No, brother. He was here but you were not fully conscious. He wanted to close the shop for good. He wanted to take his gun and shoot all the men outside. But Mrs Joubert, she knew he would want to do this thing so she took his shotgun to her house before he arrived in Klippiesfontein. She told him that he mustn't give in to those men. That none of us should."

"He came all the way back for me?"

"Well, in a way you took this beating for him, didn't you?"

Petrus nodded solemnly, "How is Missies Hettie?"

"I think she is not doing well but Baas Marius, he doesn't say anything anymore. But I can read it on his face. I think he has stopped hoping."

"Then we must pray to God, sister, that He gives Baas Marius back his hope because without hope we are nothing. We are just like animals."

"Yes, brother, we must pray."

Petrus was sitting in the front seat of Baas Charlie's car. The one with Telcom written on the door. Petrus had always admired Baas Charlie's car and thought how he would like a ride in it. But that was before Baas Charlie started visiting Precious in the shop every day with his fancy cellphone and his internet and his white skin and all his money. Before Precious had gone to Baas Charlie's house and met his mother. Now Petrus didn't want to ride in his car anymore. Now he wanted to ride in the taxi with all the other men from the township.

And today Baas Charlie had decided to be very talkative with Petrus, probably because Precious was at her other job and he couldn't be talkative with her. But Petrus had made his decision and he was going to stick to it. Nobody was going to change his mind. Not Baas Charlie, not Mrs Joubert, not Baas Marius, not even Precious.

"So, have the police been in to see you?" he asked.

Petrus nodded.

"Were you able to tell them who did this to you?"

Petrus shook his head.

"Do you know who beat you up, Petrus?"

He shook his head.

"Aren't you going to say anything to me?"

Again Petrus shook his head.

"So how will I know where to drop you off?"

Petrus shrugged.

"Is it even safe for me to drive into the township? You know, I've never been there before."

Petrus was tired of nodding and shaking his head at Baas Charlie the whole time. He turned his face away and stared out the window.

Charlie took a left turn into the road that lead to the township, Rifilwe. He'd driven past it many times before on his way to Prieska to see clients. From the road all you could see was a row of Bluegum trees and behind them a few flashes of colour: red from a tiled roof, blue from a sheet of plastic serving as someone's wall to their shack, yellow from a bucket of water on top of a little girl's head. He knew they were poor. He knew they lived in squalor. But he'd never seen it close up.

Petrus' good arm suddenly shot up from his lap and pointed left.

"Do I turn here?"

Petrus nodded.

He focused intensely on the road. He had to. There were potholes everywhere. Hell, some of them would count as full-blown craters, never mind potholes. There were chickens to dodge, children running alongside the car, hands cupped at his window. "Sweets, sweets," they cried. Charlie rolled down his window and was met with the smell of wood-fires, a comforting smell. It was late afternoon and many people, he assumed, were starting supper.

He drove past several make-shift shops, square frames built from wattle branches, a piece of metal sheeting for a counter, and a corrugated iron roof on which the sun beat down mercilessly, even at this late hour. One was selling live chickens, all squashed inside a home-made wire cage, destined for the cooking pots of those lucky enough to permit themselves some meat.

At the next stand, Charlie saw a lady attending a couple of teenage boys. *Airtime* said the handwritten sign scribbled on the side of an old box. She was helping one of the boys to top up his cellphone. Cute enough, Charlie thought, but not half as pretty as Precious. The next stall sold sweaty dilapidated vegetables: tomatoes, cabbages, onions, spinach. He passed an improvised carwash – a car stood beneath another wattle and corrugated iron stall, its doors open while two men furiously rubbed at the windows with bright yellow cloths. Close by, on a sawn-off tree trunk, stood a ghetto blaster pumping out loud music.

He felt a tap on his shoulder. He looked at Petrus who was pointing to the right.

"Here?" he asked and his passenger nodded.

Turning right, he drove past the primary school – a long, single-storey building with burglar-barred windows. He noticed the last couple of classrooms at the end of the building were burnt out. "Was there a fire at the school?" he asked.

Petrus shrugged.

He carried on down the road past an array of tiny houses, all of them identical except for the decorations outside. One had paintings of roses on the front door. The next one had a turquoise-coloured door and window frames. There was one with two rose bushes on either side of the door. No lawn, mind you. Just dry baked red clay and then suddenly two flowering yellow rose shrubs. And a dog chained to a pole, no cover or a drop of water in sight for the poor creature. Here and there stood a spindly tree casting an excuse of shade on the red earth. A toddler played outside, not wearing a stitch of clothing, except for the traditional string of beads round his fat little waist.

At last Petrus held up his hand.

"Over here?" Charlie asked.

Petrus nodded.

He stopped the car. Petrus opened the door and climbed out before leaning over the passenger seat to grab his crutch and the plastic bag with his dirty clothes.

"Can you get inside OK?" Charlie squinted out into the sun through the open passenger door.

Petrus nodded. Then he bent down low and looked Charlie in the eyes. He lifted his left hand and touched his brow.

"You're not going back to saying nothing because of what those men did to you, are you?" Charlie asked.

Petrus shrugged and slammed the door. Charlie watched as he struggled into his yard, the crutch under his left arm, his right hand gripping his plastic bag. The front door opened and a scraggly woman appeared. He watched as she rushed up to Petrus and threw her arms around him.

Charlie started the car and drove off.

Chapter Twenty-one

The three women were making their way back inside after their umpteenth break out on the back steps. Precious made them each a mug of steaming tea to sip in their socialising corner next to the humming lobster tank tucked away behind the cardboard cut-out.

Precious glanced at the magazine rack as she went past. All were out of date. They'd stopped ordering new magazines except for Lenny's weekly girlie mag. "Who feels up for a quiz, ladies?" she asked, taking last month's *Cosmo* from the rack.

Mrs Joubert and Patty's interest was immediately piqued. It wasn't a difficult thing to do anymore. An ant crossing the floor could do it, so critical was the tedium in the shop.

"What kind of quiz?" asked Mrs Joubert, just settling down with her thick book on her lap.

"*Are you really in love or are you forcing it? Try our quiz to find out,*" Precious read out loud from the cover.

Patty looked away. "That would hardly be fair on Mrs J, would it?"

"No, I'm game," declared Mrs Joubert. "If I read another page of this insipid book, I'm going to start climbing the walls. I must remember to bring the other one in with me on Monday." She closed her book and looked expectantly at Precious.

"You joining us, Patty?" Precious asked.

"Aw, I don't know," she said, tossing her blonde hair over her shoulder. "These quizzes are so stupid. They never tell you anything worth knowing. Maybe I'll just go outside for a ciggy." She started to rise from her chair.

"Come on. Just for fun," Precious urged.

The aging blonde dropped back down and shrugged. Bringing her left hand close to her face, she examined her cuticles.

"Alright, where's a pencil so I can write down the answers?"

Precious said, chuffed with her temporary role as moderator. "You ready?"

Her audience of two nodded.

Precious had been grateful when they'd stood up from the back stairs in the merciless sun where they watched Patty smoke cigarette after cigarette. The dark interior of the shop was much cooler. The ceiling fan whirred rhythmically, keeping a whisper of movement in the otherwise stagnant air.

The afternoons were the worst. Each one seemed to stretch out for at least a week. In the mornings they had the floor to sweep, shelves to dust, change to count, figures to write down in ledgers, sell-by dates to check and new orders to be noted down. Grateful for the flurry of activity, each woman performed her tasks with the utmost care, postponing the inevitable monotony that lay ahead of them for as long as possible.

Indeed, three women were hardly needed to serve in a shop that saw about a dozen customers a day. But it wasn't the serving of the customers that kept them there, kept them coming back every day, day in, day out, choking on the chalk of boredom. Precious realised this all too well. It wasn't for the money they were earning on behalf of Baas Marius – the takings they made were so meagre it would probably have been more profitable to keep the shop closed. No, they kept the shop open as a sign of protest – their way of sending a message to that line of men out front with their khaki clothes and sunburnt faces. They kept it open so they could receive the odd customer who, in turn, was sending a message too. They kept it open as a proclamation of solidarity.

Sometimes, not that often mind you, Precious thought that all this tedium was a pretty high price to pay for this so-called solidarity. Yes, she'd admit it, there were times, in the middle of an unending afternoon, that she doubted their cause. When she thought how much better it would be if she was out walking with her girlfriends through the streets of Rifilwe, or sitting next to Charlie in his little white car with the radio on, or even cooking a meal for her brothers instead of sitting there like that inside the blasted shop. But as soon as she felt like this, as soon as these treacherous thoughts entered her head, she'd force herself to remember Petrus' broken body lying outside in the dust that day, to think about Missies Hettie fighting for her life in a barren hospital in Cape Town, about Baas Marius so helpless at her side, and as soon as she thought these thoughts, the doubt and desire to give up scuttled shamefacedly out of her head.

It wasn't for lack of trying or imagination that they couldn't beat the boredom. No, every day at least one of them would come into the shop with a new idea about how to whittle away the never-ending hours. Mrs Joubert had brought in an old game of Monopoly. Patty had given the other two facials, though she'd admitted she had no idea how to make up a black woman. Precious played music on the radio and tried to teach Patty to dance *kwaito* style. Mrs Joubert just laughed gently and shook her head when they invited her to join in, saying she was too old.

"This is what it says in the intro," Precious started, reading from the page, "*Sure you like your man, but is your bond bona fide love? Take this quiz to find out.*"

She was interrupted by a loud sigh. Without looking she knew it had come from Patty. She pushed on, "*First question: Which is worse? Being alone or dating a guy you totally don't click with?*" She looked up.

"The second one," said Mrs Joubert.

Precious scribbled down her answer on the page. "Patty?"

"Being alone, actually," she gave a feeble smile. "I've never really been much good at that."

"OK, question two: *When people say 'How's that Prince Charming of yours?' or 'God, I wish I could meet a guy as great as yours,' you A. Switch to a different topic or B. Blush and silently agree with them?*"

"Again, the second one," Mrs Joubert replied.

Patty looked sad, "I'm not sure if anyone has ever said anything like that to me about Shawn. It's not like he's a bad person, or anything. It's just that no one knows him the way I do…" she trailed off.

"You have to pick one. A or B?" Precious said.

"The first one then. I suppose I'd change the subject."

Precious wrote down the answer.

"And you?" Patty asked. "Come on, we're not going to take this quiz alone."

"I don't have a boyfriend," Precious replied.

"Maybe not officially, but there must be someone you like. Why else did you want to do this quiz?"

Quickly Precious looked back down at the page on her lap. "Question three," she stated.

"No, no, no," Patty said. "You're not getting away with it that easily. Which of those answers do you choose? A or B?"

"B then," she said, grateful that neither women could recognise her blush under her dark skin.

"And who is he?" Patty sang.

Precious kept her eyes down. "No one. I can't say anything yet. I'm not even sure if he likes me."

Mrs Joubert spoke up, "What's the next question?"

"*Would you feel the same way about your guy if he suddenly lost his job or his hair?*"

"Of course I would," said Mrs Joubert, taking hold of her mug of tea standing on the upturned crate and taking a sip. "My man practically had no hair to start off with and that never made any difference to me."

Patty laughed, "And mine doesn't have a job, and, I must say, it's a very sore point with us. I think I'd definitely feel different about Shawn if he had a job."

Precious jotted down the answers.

"And you, missy? Don't try to get out of this one?"

"Well," Precious started slowly, "my guy has both hair and a job but I don't think it would make any difference to me if he lost either."

"And what about both?" Mrs Joubert smiled.

"Yes," Patty joined in, "what if he became a bald, good-for-nothing? How would you feel about him then?"

"The same as I do now… I think."

"Sounds like true love to me," Patty teased. "Come on, out with it. Who is the lucky guy?"

"I told you, it's nothing really. Just a bit of a school girl crush. Let's move on," Precious looked back down again. "*Do you ever edit yourself when you talk to your friends about your man? A. There's no reason to make him sound any better than he already is or B. Yes, sometimes you omit unattractive things he's said or don't reveal when you're upset with him.*" Precious looked straight at Mrs Joubert, "I know which one you're going to choose."

"What can I say?" Mrs Joubert shrugged. "I had a good husband. I never had to leave out things he said or did."

"Is that really true?" Patty turned sharply to her. "All marriages have their ups and downs. Aren't you just saying all of this because you've been a widow for so long and you can only remember the good stuff?"

Mrs Joubert took another sip of her tea, "I suppose there's that too. You're right, Patty. If Mark was here with me now I'm sure there would be irritating details I'd have to deal with. But I only have my memory, that's the only place I can answer from. I'm sorry if you feel I'm being a bit ostentatious."

"I don't think you're being a bit anything, Mrs J. I guess I'm just a little jealous because I'm not sure if I'd feel the same way about Shawn if he suddenly decided to drop down dead."

Neither Precious nor Mrs Joubert knew how to respond. They'd heard the comments about Shawn just like everyone else had and, although neither of the women, young nor old, partook in gossip, they also knew that very often there was a seed of truth buried in it.

Precious read the next question silently to herself: *If your man was to dump you tomorrow, what would your biggest regret be? A. You just wasted a chunk of time in your life when you could've been dating someone else and building a future. B. You'll never be able to smell him, to be held by him, to hear his laugh again.*

She knew which answer she'd put down. She knew which

answer Mrs Joubert would give about her Mark, and, sadly for Patty, she knew what she'd be forced to say about Shawn. A Saturday afternoon like this wasn't the time to go rubbing someone's face in things they couldn't change, Precious decided. Closing the magazine with an air of finality, she looked up, "These questions are all the same. Why don't we go outside for some fresh air?"

Mrs Joubert's eyes met Precious' and she nodded, almost unobtrusively. Fresh wasn't the way she would describe the sluggish wave of warm air that awaited them on the back stairs. Fresh wasn't exactly the word that could describe anything in the open air in Klippiesfontein. But it would do for now – as long as it made it easier for Patty to walk away from that quiz about true love.

The three women stood up and started moving towards the back door. All was quiet except for the whirring of the ceiling fan. On the way out, Precious dropped the magazine into the bin behind the counter.

Chapter Twenty-two

Saturday afternoon, and the trickle of business through the back door was slow. Very slow. A couple of kids had come in for ice-creams. Lenny had been in for a six-pack of beer. Standing in front, he nervously fingered various objects lying on the counter, looking down at the floor. Finally Mrs Joubert clicked on to what he wanted, "Aah, yes. The delivery guy brought a magazine for you. Is that what you're waiting for?"

Lenny nodded but didn't dare look into her eyes. She went in back and came out with a plastic-sealed magazine with a bare-chested woman on the cover. She pushed it, face-down, over the counter.

"Thanks," Lenny mumbled, thick-tongued, and slid his money across to her. "You can keep the change." He hurried out.

The three women sat staring at the cards in their hands. Mrs Joubert was teaching them to play Gin Rummy but the game had come to a stand-still, their interest sapped away by the heat. The only sound in the shop was the whirring of the fan blades and a fat, lazy fly bumping repeatedly against one of the windows. The one consolation was that at least they were indoors, out of the sun, and could take ice blocks from the deepfreeze to run over their brows and the backs of their necks while the men outside sipped lukewarm drinks and had only one another's lousy company without even a whisper of shade.

"Send the black girl home and we'll call it a day," Oom Hans had tried negotiating with Mrs Joubert earlier when she'd walked up the front steps. "Then everything can go back to normal."

"Never!" Mrs Joubert retorted and walked right past him.

"You know, one day, woman..." he called after her.

She spun round to face him, "One day what, Hans? You're going to send one of your baboons after me too?"

He didn't answer.

She walked into the shop, her heels clicking primly on the stoep.

Suddenly the three women heard a loud clanking sound on the back steps. Simultaneously, they looked up and across the room to the back door. It was flung open and there, in the doorway, sunlight streaming in from behind him, stood Petrus, propped up on his crutch.

Patty gave a little shriek in fright.

"*Mfowethu, ufuna ntoni?*" Precious asked in their isiXhosa language.

Brother, what do you want?

Petrus nodded at the little company and struggled into the shop, his crutch *doof-doof-doofing* on the wooden floorboards. The women were standing upright, staring at him, jaws unashamedly open. Clumsily he made his way over to the counter. Propping himself up on his crutch, he took the order book from the shelf below, opened it and ran his finger down the list. He pushed a button on the cash register and it popped open with a ping. He started counting its contents.

"Petrus," Mrs Joubert spoke gingerly, "Oom Marius doesn't expect you back at work yet. You know that, don't you?"

Looking up at her, Petrus nodded. Then he turned his attention back to the cash register and started counting the twenty-rand notes all over again.

"Do – do you – do you want something to drink?" Patty tried.

Petrus shook his head.

Mrs Joubert turned to Precious and spoke in a subdued tone, "I think he's gone back to being mute. Why don't you go and talk to him?"

Precious and Petrus were seated behind the soap-powder cut-out next to the gently humming lobster tank. Three of the lobsters were clambering over the fourth one in the corner.

"First tell me, brother, why you have come back to work?"

"Baas Marius, he left me in charge."

"Yes, he did. But you're not well and we've got everything under control here. Baas Marius expects you to stay at home and get better."

Petrus shrugged, "How must I say this, sister?"

"Just say it like it is."

The edges of Petrus' mouth were twitching upwards and Precious could see he was trying to control his face, "Are you smiling, brother?"

Petrus looked down and shook his head but this didn't stop his lips from breaking out into a full-blown smile, "I have worked for Baas Marius now for twenty-two years and the only thing I'm sure of in my life is that I'll be working for him for at least another twenty-two. But I never thought, not even in my wildest dreams, that I would be working for him as a manager. Manager, sister. Can you believe that? And managers, they don't lie around at home."

"No one's saying you should lie around at home, but wouldn't it be better if you took some time off so your body could heal?"

"My body will heal here at the shop just as quickly as it will heal at home."

"Do you think you won't get paid as long as you're not at work?"

"I know I will get paid. It is not for the money that I am here."

"Very well, you stay then. I will put a chair in front of the counter for you and you can manage us from there. OK?"

He was still smiling. A little more shyly. He nodded.

"I have just one more question for you, brother. Why have you stopped speaking to white people? Charlie tells me you never said a word to him all the way back from the hospital and just now you wouldn't speak to Mrs Joubert or Patty. How do you think this will help you?"

"You wouldn't understand."

"Try me. I understand a lot of things."

"Baas Marius he left me in charge because I spoke to him, yes?"

Precious nodded.

"Those men outside, they came here because I was in charge.

166

Then they beat me, sister, because I was in charge. All of this because I opened my mouth. I was never in trouble before I spoke and now look how many problems have come into my life."

"Oh brother, you cannot think like this. It will get you nowhere."

"Nowhere is better than where I am now," with a sweeping gesture of his good arm, Petrus highlighted his broken body. "I have made up my mind and I don't want you to try to talk me out of it."

"But how can you be manager and not talk? How will this work?"

"I don't have an answer for you, sister. I just know that this is how it must be."

For the rest of the day Petrus sat on his chair in front of the counter, watching the goings-on in the shop. Even if they were only women, he thought, three of them were a bit too many for the few tasks there were. He could have told one, or even two of them to go home, now that he was manager. But since he wasn't talking, he couldn't exactly make his wishes known, except, of course, to Precious. And he wasn't about to tell *her* to go home.

Precious went out onto the stoep and washed the front windows. Missies Patty stood behind the counter and served the odd customer who drifted in and Mrs Joubert, she sat by the lobster tank and knitted something. He would have liked to tell her that what she was doing wasn't work, now that he was manager but, again since he wasn't talking, he couldn't. And even if he was talking, he didn't really think that Mrs Joubert would listen to him so somewhere he was also secretly relieved that he didn't have to scold her. If he was going to be completely honest with himself, he'd have to admit that, even though he was the manager now, he was still a little frightened of her. In fact, just about everyone in Klippiesfontein was a little afraid of Mrs Joubert, Petrus imagined. Probably even Baas Marius.

As the sun edged down towards the horizon and the heat of the day extracted its claws, the occupants of the shop heaved a joint sigh of relief. Closing time was getting closer and Petrus' bottom was becoming more and more sore every minute. In fact, it was starting to go numb. There was only so long that a man could sit still and do nothing before his bottom started complaining, and Petrus had reached that point.

He watched the three women get everything ready to close the shop until Monday morning. Patty counted the money in the cash register and wrote the number down in Baas Marius' black book. Mrs Joubert, she wrote down words in the order book and Precious changed the black plastic bag in the dustbin. Then she went in back to chop up some food for the lobsters. She left the bag full of rubbish on the floor.

He couldn't bear to stay seated a second longer. Leaning down, he grabbed hold of his crutch. He propped it under his arm and hobbled over to the bulging plastic bag, a sour stench rising from it. A lone, green fly buzzed lazily around it. Picking it up, Petrus struggled to the back door.

He managed to make it down the back stairs without falling. Lifting the lid of the black container, he dumped the bag inside. He was just about to make his way back when he heard footsteps crunching in the dirt. A man's footsteps. Slow and deliberate. Petrus froze. He didn't dare look back. The footsteps came closer and stopped just behind him.

"Petrus?"

It was *Kleinbaas* Frikkie. Petrus would know that voice anywhere. His crutch fell out of his hand and into the dirt.

"Don't be scared, man. I'm not going to do anything to you in broad daylight."

Petrus anticipated the feel of *Kleinbaas* Frikkie's touch and he was frightened. None came. Pinching his eyes shut, he hobbled in the direction of the back stairs, his shoulders hunched, his face turned towards the wall.

The footsteps followed him. "I wanted to thank you, man, for not saying anything to the cops. You know, Bertie and I, we would've been in deep shit if you didn't keep your mouth shut like we warned. I 'preciate that, man. I really do."

Petrus reached the steps. He tried to manoeuvre himself up the first one but a searing pain shot through his ankle each time he put weight on it.

"But you have to admit, man, it was also a little bit your own fault," *Kleinbaas* Frikkie continued.

Petrus stood still and listened. There was nothing else he could do.

"I mean, I was drunk and I was angry and I took it out on you. That's my fault, I know. But you... you... what were you thinking, man? Becoming manager like that? Why couldn't you just know your place like a good *kaffir?*"

Kleinbaas Frikkie waited. He probably wanted a response. Petrus stood frozen and wondered how on earth he was going to get up those stairs. Next thing he saw *Kleinbaas* Frikkie's hand reach round from behind him.

"Here. This is for you," said *Kleinbaas* Frikkie.

Petrus saw many one-hundred-rand bills clutched in his hand. Slowly he turned round to *Kleinbaas* Frikkie. He looked up into his face.

"Here, man, take it. For your medical bills. Or for your mother. Or some of that *kaffir* beer you lot are so fond of. Whatever, man. I don't care," *Kleinbaas* Frikkie explained, looking suddenly like that young schoolboy again who used to buy sweets from Petrus.

Kleinbaas Frikkie thrust the money forward again. Taking hold of Petrus' hand, he stuffed the wad of notes into his fingers. He stepped back, a satisfied look on his face.

Petrus stared straight back at him. He opened his hand and let the money fall. It dropped with a muted thud on the bottom step and down into the dirt. *Kleinbaas* Frikkie looked down and his eyes grew wide.

Suddenly, from somewhere to his left, Petrus heard a gasp. He turned his head in the direction and saw Precious standing there. She'd come round the side of the building and was close to the dustbins.

"It was you," she said to *Kleinbaas* Frikkie, her voice cold, like a machine.

"Mm... mmm... me what?" *Kleinbaas* Frikkie said.

Petrus read the fear in his eyes. He recognised that look.

Precious walked resolutely forwards and bent down to pick up Petrus' fallen crutch from the dirt. "It was you!" she shouted.

She lifted the crutch above her shoulders and charged forwards, an animal growl coming from her throat.

Kleinbaas Frikkie looked around for an escape route. He turned on his heel and ran away. Faster than Precious, he rounded the corner and was back out on the safety of the street.

Precious came to a stop and looked at Petrus. Walking up to him, she lowered the crutch and handed it back to him. He said nothing. He simply nodded at her.

"You're not going to tell the police it was him, are you, brother?"

He shrugged, "What if they come after me again?"

"Fear cannot be a driving force. That way they will always win."

"What will my mother do without me?"

She looked at the money lying in the red dust at their feet. Puckering her lips, she spat viciously on the wad of notes, "Of course, brother. Your mother needs you. I understand that."

Precious hooked her arm into Petrus' and helped him up the stairs.

Chapter Twenty-three

Precious had been to Springbok many times before but none of her previous visits had felt like this. She was on a mission and nothing was going to get in the way of her accomplishing it. Not even her almost debilitating fear, the fear that still lingered in the hearts of many black South Africans, the fear of the police.

She was sitting in the taxi, seven people squashed onto a four-seater bench, her face pushed right up against the window. She chewed on a fingernail, taking in the sights and sounds of this town. It was much bigger than Klippiesfontein and there seemed to be people everywhere. What's more, they appeared to be more relaxed too. Possibly, because of the sheer number of them, they were simply less worried about what other people would say and think. It seemed impossible to Precious that everyone in this town could know everybody else. It wasn't like Klippiesfontein in that way.

The taxi edged through the black section of town. Shops weren't segregated anymore but unofficially there was still the black section. Someone had set up a hairdressing salon on the pavement. Buckets of soapy water, two customers seated side by side on crates; the man getting his hair trimmed with a razor blade while the lady next to him was having skull plaits done.

Precious touched her own hair self-consciously. It had been a long time since she'd been to the hairdresser, what with her job at the Shell petrol station and helping out at the General Store. She wondered what Charlie would like. She had no idea what white men found attractive.

The taxi stopped at the red robot and her thoughts were jerked back to the matter at hand. The side door slid open and at least half of the vehicle's occupants started pouring out onto the street. The lights changed to green and the taxi remained still, waiting for passengers to climb over knees or pass parcels out the door into waiting hands. Behind them, two other taxis immediately started hooting. The driver thrust half his body out the window, twisted round and shouted at the drivers behind him, "*Kufuneka ube nalo umonde.*"

Be patient – and then he said a word that made Precious blush.

The hooting grew louder, the shouting and gesticulating more heated. Then suddenly, as the last passenger climbed out, the door slid shut. Dropping deftly back into his seat, the driver slammed the gear lever into first and took off with such force that the remaining passengers' necks were whipped backwards. He drove straight through the robot which had turned red again in the meantime.

It pulled off the road in front of the clinic and a woman with two small children climbed out. Stopping again in front of the municipality, another handful of passengers disembarked. Eventually only Precious was left, staring out her window.

"Where to, *Mma*?" the driver asked, leaning over the back seat. "Or do you want me to take you to my special place?" he leered.

"You can pull off at the next corner," Precious replied, "and you better watch how you speak to your lady passengers or one day one of us will kick you in *your* special place."

Grumbling, he turned round and drove Precious a block further. He stopped and she slid across the seat to the door. Opening it, she lowered her feet to the ground. She felt the taxi lurch suddenly forward. She could see the driver grinning idiotically in his rear-view mirror.

"CA 132 546," Precious calmly spoke the letters and numbers.

The taxi driver's eyes widened.

"Yes, I always memorise the number plate before I get in. And don't think I won't go to the police if you don't treat me like you should," she warned.

She saw the grin fall off his face and felt him steady the vehicle. She climbed out and slammed the door shut. He sped off with the screeching of tyres.

Precious touched her hair nervously, straightened her skirt

and lifted her head before setting off round the corner. Somewhere she felt bad for doing this. After all, he was her friend and he'd all but gone down on his knees begging her to forget what she'd seen between him and that *isidenge*, that idiot, behind the shop. But, on the other hand, this conspiring to remain silent was what had got this country into so much trouble in the first place and she'd be damned if she'd participate in it even one tiny bit. Friend or no friend, she was convinced that she was doing the right thing.

A few minutes later she was standing in front of the single-storey, yellow brick building with the blue and gold insignia above the door. *Assist and Serve* it proclaimed boldly in big, black letters. Precious took a deep breath and walked inside. She came to a standstill in front of the counter.

"How can we help you, *Mma*?" the black officer in front of her asked.

"I'm here to report a crime."

Frikkie was just entering the lounge with a glass of *Oros* in his hand for his ma when he saw the van pull up outside. The thin layer of sweat coating his body turned ice-cold in an instant. His toe caught on the carpet and he lurched forward, only just steadying himself, but not before spilling some of the cooldrink on the floor. "*Ag*, no man," his ma reprimanded. "What are you busy with now?"

"Sorry, Ma," he muttered and wiped the outside of the glass on his t-shirt before handing it to her.

Standing next to her, he peered out through the lace curtains and saw two men climb out of the van; one white and one black, both dressed in blue. As they opened and closed the garden gate, Frikkie recognised the white one – Oom Jan, his pa's former colleague.

"Who's there, son?" his ma asked.

"It looks like Oom Jan," he answered.

"Oh, how lovely!" she exclaimed, clapping her podgy hands together in delight. "I'm so glad I baked those cookies this morning. I just had a feeling we'd be needing them."

They heard a knock at the front door.

"Go open up, Frik," his ma said.

"I'd rather not, Ma," he shook his head profusely, feeling his face turn clammy. A single thought rushed through his head: how could he dash out the kitchen door and over the back fence before they came inside?

"What's got into you today? I said open the door for Oom Jan."

Frikkie was unable to disobey his ma. Stiff-legged, he walked to the front door and let the two men into the house.

"Is your mother here, Frikkie?" Oom Jan asked gravely.

Frikkie nodded like a naughty schoolboy who'd been caught looking up the girls' dresses.

"I was hoping she'd be out visiting one of your brothers or sisters."

"No Oom, she's here," he spoke sombrely.

"Because I didn't want to have to do this in front of her," he continued.

Head hanging low, Frikkie gestured towards the living room door, "She's in there, Oom."

Oom Jan walked in that direction.

Frikkie threw a quick glance down the passage, towards the kitchen where the back door and his way to escape lay. The black police officer noticed his darting eyes and immediately laid a hand on Frikkie's elbow, steering him to follow Oom Jan.

His ma was already on her feet. She'd crossed the floor and lifted her arms to throw them round Oom Jan's neck. "How lovely it is to see you," she gushed, all smiles.

Oom Jan took a step back and his ma's arms fell short of their target. "We're not here on a social visit, Marie," he said solemnly.

His ma's face dropped, her features hardened and her eyes glazed over in a severe glare.

"I wish it could've been under more pleasant circumstances that I was standing in your home today," Oom Jan said.

Frikkie watched him. He saw he'd aged a lot; grey temples dotted with beads of sweat, dark rings under his eyes, sagging cheeks. Other than that he looked exactly the same as the man who used to come over to their house on Sunday afternoons all through Frikkie's childhood. The man who played rugby on the back lawn with him and his brothers. His pa's best friend.

"Who is it?" Frikkie heard his ma gasp.

"When I recognised the name I immediately volunteered to come myself, Marie. I didn't want some stranger coming here to do it," he continued, wiping the sweat from his brow with the back of his hairy hand.

"Just tell me, Jan, who's died?" His ma's voice was laced with hysteria.

"No one's dead, Marie," he replied.

"Well thank the good Lord for that!" she exclaimed, her jaw breaking into a smile again. "You scared the hell out of me, Jan. Don't you ever do that to me again. Frikkie, you go to the kitchen and tell the maid to put on the kettle for some tea."

Frikkie needed no further prompting. He moved towards the door but the black policeman was right there, standing between him and the exit, a warning in his eyes: don't make another move.

"I think it's best if Frikkie stayed here with us," Oom Jan said.

"You're scaring me again, Jan. What's going on?"

"I'm sorry to have to do this, Marie. I've known him since he was a couple of hours old, but we've come here today to arrest Frikkie."

A yelp escaped Frikkie's throat. Three pairs of eyes turned briefly to look at him.

"What do you mean? Come to arrest Frikkie?" She looked confused, her eyes desperately searching the faces of the two men standing before her.

"We've come to take him away, Marie, on a charge of assault and battery with intent to do serious bodily harm."

"Frikkie?" she asked perplexed.

Frikkie stared at her. It was unbearable. He'd never felt sorry for her before in his life – she simply wasn't the kind of woman anyone ever felt sorry for. But today he stood there watching her composure break off in great big chunks like the banks of a river after a heavy rain storm and he couldn't help but pity her.

"It's not true, Ma. Don't believe them. That *kaffir* bitch is lying!" Frikkie shouted suddenly.

"Shut up and let me think," his ma ordered but for once he could not obey. His voice protested wildly, trying to drown out Oom Jan, trying to make his ma not look at him that way, "I'm telling you, it's not true. Oom Jan, you've got to believe me? You can't take her word over mine? This can't be..."

"Who is he supposed to have harmed?" Frikkie's ma asked, her voice cold now, calculated. She was no longer speaking to an old family friend. She was addressing her enemy. Frikkie felt himself grow calmer. His ma had taken control. It was going to be alright.

"Petrus. The assistant over at Marius' store," Oom Jan explained, his voice businesslike now, with less emotion.

"Manager," Frikkie mumbled.

"What's that?" Oom Jan asked.

"Petrus is the manager, not the assistant," Frikkie said.

He heard his ma speak again, "There's been some kind of mix-up, Jan. Frikkie hasn't been over to Marius' place in weeks, not with all the trouble going on over there."

"I'm sorry, Marie, there is no mistake. We've got a witness statement and Bertie, you know Hans's son, he broke down like a baby and admitted to the whole thing. I wish this..."

"Out, Jan. Get out of my house," his ma commanded suddenly.

Oom Jan nodded resolutely at his ma. Looking over at the other policeman, he gave him a nod. Frikkie felt his arms wrenched behind and cold steel touching his wrists.

"Leave him alone," his ma stepped forward, grabbing hold of her son, trying to wrestle him back.

The officer ignored his ma and jerked Frikkie round to face the door. Frikkie's jaw hung open: no one ever ignored his ma. "Don't let them take me, Ma! Don't let them take me!"

"I'm only going to say this once, Jan. Let my boy go."

"I'm sorry, Marie."

Frikkie felt himself being shunted forwards. They weren't listening to his ma. How could that be? They were leading him away. Frikkie's shouting started up again, "Ma, it's not true. It's not true. She's lying. They're all lying. Don't let them take me, Ma."

All the way out to the van. Through the gridded window in the back, Frikkie saw Bertie's distraught face staring at him.

He twisted his neck to get one last look at his mother, "Phone Karel, Ma. Tell him what's happened. Tell him to come help us."

He saw his ma standing helplessly in the doorway.

Chapter Twenty-four

Tannie Hettie was lying on the big double bed in the hotel room. Everything was quiet. Almost quiet. She could hear the TV on in the room next to theirs and Oom Marius was moving around in the bathroom. Probably shaving, she decided, judging by the tap-tapping sound on the edge of the basin every couple of seconds.

Oom Marius came into the bedroom and she heard him going over to the window. She was too tired to open her eyes to see what he was doing.

Tannie Hettie heard the sharp zing of the curtain rings against the rail and winced. Bright, heartless sunlight flooded the room and pierced her eyelids. It crawled right into her head, sunk its claws into her, up to that point, sleeping headache, and ripped it right up to the surface of her brain again.

"Good morning, my dear," she heard Oom Marius' voice.

What was on earth was good about this particular morning, she'd ask him if she could find the energy and why did he insist on calling her *my dear*? He hadn't done it in their almost forty years of marriage, so why start now? Did he think it would somehow chase away the cancer? Or that she'd cheer up at the sound of his forced pleasantries? Why couldn't he just act normally around of her? She felt his weight on the mattress at her feet as he sat down on the side of the bed.

"What do you feel like doing today?" he asked.

With great effort she forced herself to answer, "I just want to rest, Marius. For the one day I don't have to go to hospital for treatment, I'd just like to rest." Still she didn't open her eyes.

"You know what the doctors said about too much rest? It's counterproductive." She felt him lay his hand on her ankle.

"I'm tired of listening to the doctors. They haven't been right about a single thing up to now except for the fact that I'm going to die."

"Don't talk like that, Hettie," he snapped. "They haven't said a thing about you dying."

"What do you think they were saying yesterday when they called it progression? *I'm* not the one making progress, Marius, the cancer is."

"Almost eighty percent of cancer sufferers survive nowadays. You know that." She felt him take his hand off her ankle. Even he knew he was lying, that's why he couldn't bear to touch her. Who would've thought he'd become such an optimist in the end? Her grumpy, old Marius. Well, it didn't bloody suit him, that's what she thought. It simply didn't suit him.

"I have no idea where you plucked that figure from, but you can be sure that I'll make up part of the other twenty percent."

Tannie Hettie's eyes remained closed. She heard him sigh heavily before getting up from the bed. "I'm going downstairs for breakfast," he grumbled and for a split second it felt like she had her husband back.

She wanted to call after him to close the curtains but it was too much effort. Pulling the duvet up over her eyes, she blacked out the sun.

Tannie Hettie was dressed and sitting in her wheelchair. Oom Marius had helped her into her clothes. She was wearing the dress with the little pearl buttons she'd worn to Stefaan's wedding and it was hanging on her like a sack. He'd insisted she wear something special today. Her skin felt sore and bruised where he'd handled her with his huge, rough hands. Fumbling with the clasp of her bra like that, it had felt as if his fingers would go right through her skin, through her ribs and into her lungs. Not to mention the humiliation of it, this man, this large, clumsy man fiddling around with her underwear. It wasn't supposed to be this way. Husbands weren't supposed to grapple with sagging, grey breasts at this point in a marriage. It simply wasn't dignified. If only her grandchildren weren't so young, if only they didn't need the constant care of their mothers, she could have asked one of her daughters-in-law to spend a few days with her.

"Where would you like to go shopping, Hettie?" his voice boomed behind her as he came over to take hold of the handles of her wheelchair.

She winced at the noise. "Don't forget to bring my pain killers," she said as loudly as she could bear.

"What!?"

"My pain killers, Marius."

"Right here," he answered and she heard him tap his shirt pocket.

They started moving towards the hotel room door. They hadn't even gone through it yet and the only thing she could think about was returning. Entering that door from the other side, falling down on the bed... "Do we have to do this?"

"I want you to choose a new dress for this weekend. None of your clothes fit you anymore and you can't celebrate our fortieth wedding anniversary in a dress that's too big for you."

"A pair of earrings, Marius," she said. "A pretty necklace. I'd be more than happy with something like that. Then at least someone else can get some use out of it when I'm not around anymore."

Oom Marius walked round to the front of the wheelchair and faced her angrily, "I thought we agreed you're not going to talk like that today?"

No, you agreed, she answered him inside her head. The idea of a confrontation, no matter how small, exhausted her. "Is my wig on straight?"

Oom Marius nodded. Pulling open the door, he wheeled his wife out into the corridor.

"Oh dear Lord," Tannie Hettie started her prayer. She sat slumped in her wheelchair at a table in a coffee shop serving at least a hundred different types of coffee and just as many kinds of muffins. Blueberry – who'd even heard of a blueberry in South Africa? Blue cheese and chocolate. Ridiculous.

Oom Marius had temporarily abandoned her to go to the toilet and there she sat, helpless, shopping bags hung over the handles of the wheelchair like a... well, like a pram. Like when the little ones were babies and she'd gone shopping with her daughters-in-law. On her lap was her white clutch bag. Lying limply on thighs that had once been ample. Anyone who wanted to could just come up and snatch it away.

"Oh dear Lord," she started again. She'd taken to talking to Him regularly these days. Much more often than in the days when she'd been healthy, she realised guiltily. It had to do with the fact that He was the only one who would listen to her, the only one who wasn't in denial. "Please Lord, hear my prayer here today?"

Tannie Hettie imagined the organ in the church in Klippiesfontein wheezing into life, starting up with heavy, dramatic song. She felt better with the musical accompaniment, as if the Lord would take her more seriously with a good, solemn hymn playing in the background. "Lord, I don't want anyone pounding on my chest or shoving tubes down my throat when I stop breathing. Can you arrange for that to happen? Let me go naturally, like you've intended."

This getting closer to the end of life had one advantage, Tannie Hettie felt closer to the Lord than ever before, like He was a protective kind of big brother, more approachable. As if all her suffering made her more worthy. Their conversations came easier.

The music in her head played on. She could see Mrs Van Rensburg, who played the organ in church every Sunday, with her chubby fingers as they pounded the keys with high drama, a faint sweat breaking out on her brow like that Liberace fellow when he used to come on TV all those years ago, before he died. Just like she was going to die. *Da-rum...* the organ sounded.

"Let it come quick, Lord. Don't let me wait too long. I'm a burden to my family and I can't bear it much longer. I can't watch the boys suffering, Lord, or Marius, or the little ones. They don't understand what's going on. Don't let them see their grandmother like this? I don't want this to be their only memory of me when they grow up."

Tannie Hettie closed her eyes and tried to block out the sound of teaspoons clinking in huge coffee mugs mingled with ten conversations going on around her simultaneously. Instead she heard Mrs Van Rensburg hammering on the keys and the lovely deep, baritone sounds that poured out of the organ's copper pipes. "And I realise that this might seem very trivial Lord, but could you arrange for Marius to come out of the toilet now and take me back to the hotel? I'm so tired, Lord. I've done what Marius wanted me to do today. I've done my best to make him happy. We've got the dress, we've got the shoes, we've even got a new pair of pantyhose. Who would have thought, Lord, that I'd ever be a size medium again? I've used up my energy for the day. Please let Marius come and take me back now?"

Da-rum, the organ continued, *da-rum, da-rum, da-rum,* it worked its way to the crescendo. Tannie Hettie kept her eyes closed to concentrate on the music.

All of a sudden Oom Marius was standing next to her, "You want to go back to the hotel, Hettie? You look tired."

"Thank you, Lord," she continued before nodding at her husband. "Thank you for hearing my prayer. Oh, and there's one last thing, Lord, one last thing I need to ask you. If you're feeling merciful today, when my time comes, could you see to it that I'm home in Klippiesfontein? I don't want to die in the hospital. I don't want to die in that blasted hotel room. If it be your will, Lord, of course."

Oom Marius had taken hold of the wheelchair and was wheeling Tannie Hettie towards the door, weaving in between the young coffee drinkers, the satchels hanging on the backs of chairs, a toddler scurrying in between the tables. The organ music had come to an end and Tannie Hettie hadn't really heard the last part, but she was sure it had been done with the deftness and skill that was typical of Mrs Van Rensburg's playing. "Thank you, Lord," she said. "Amen."

Chapter Twenty-five

"Can you believe it? He'll make a laughing stock of us both," Patty spoke, standing at the window, staring out at the dusty street.

Precious heard her let out an angry sigh and, even though it was clear that she was the intended recipient of Patty's comment (Mrs Joubert was in the storeroom and Petrus was nodding off in his chair), she wasn't quite sure how she should react. Precious wasn't used to being the confidante of upset white women. So she said nothing. Instead, she fussed with the bottles of Marmite until they stood straighter than they'd ever done before.

"Ridiculous," Patty spoke again.

"What is?" Precious asked nervously.

"I'm going outside for a cigarette," and with that, she marched to the back of the shop.

Precious stared after her. Was she supposed to follow her to ask what this ridiculous thing was? Was she supposed to leave her alone so she could think about the ridiculousness by herself? What should she do?

At that moment, Mrs Joubert walked in carrying a tray with cups of tea. "What's wrong?" she asked.

Mrs Joubert had read the confusion on her face, Precious realised. With a shrug she directed her raised eyebrows at the back door.

"Patty?" Mrs Joubert asked.

Precious nodded.

"Well, then it's tea time out back today."

Precious stood still, not sure if she was invited.

"Come along, then."

She hurried after her but not before she glanced out the window to see what Patty had been looking at. Shawn was standing in the line of barricaders with the other men.

Patty was sitting on the top step, a cigarette already burning in her hand. Mrs Joubert was standing facing her. Precious took a seat on the bottom step and looked up.

Patty drew long and hard on her cigarette, clearly drawing some kind of strength from it a non-smoker would never understand. "It's Shawn," she started.

Mrs Joubert nodded knowingly.

Precious nodded too, hoping it looked equally knowing.

"He's not a bad man, really he isn't. People tend not to understand him, that's all. But he's gentle and fun and he wouldn't harm a fly. That's why I put up with his sometimes less than spectacular habits."

She flicked the ash from the end of her cigarette. The smoke curled languidly downhill and wafted up Precious' nostrils but she didn't turn away as she would if it had been one of her own friends. Precious wasn't used to being in the inner circle of white women and she didn't want to do anything to offend them.

"He can't hold down a job and sometimes he hangs out with some shady characters but I can live with all of that. He doesn't get drunk. He doesn't hit me like my daddy used to hit my mom." Patty batted her long-lashed eyes at Mrs Joubert, "You know what it's like?" she said. "You were married once too?"

Mrs Joubert nodded but Precious could see it wasn't a very convinced nod. Maybe Mrs Joubert didn't like her marriage being compared to Patty's.

Patty noticed it too. She stubbed her cigarette out on the side of the step and stood up. Running her hands over the back of her pencil skirt, she dusted herself off. "I think I'll just go touch up my make-up," she said and hurried back inside.

Patty walked in the next morning reeking, as usual, of cigarettes. Her eyes were red and bloodshot once again. Precious kept her own eyes fixed on the list she was writing, pretending not to notice.

"God, I need a smoke," Patty said, diving into her handbag to locate her pack of cigarettes.

Precious quickly glanced at Petrus to see what his reaction would be. He wouldn't like Patty taking a smoke-break when she'd only just walked in. Later, when the two of them were having lunch together, she knew he'd complain to her about it. Well, Precious decided, she'd simply tell him that Patty wasn't getting paid for standing in the shop so she could take a smoke-break whenever she wanted. She imagined he wouldn't like hearing that either.

"Do you want to come outside with me?" Patty asked.

Precious looked round to see if Mrs Joubert was standing behind her. She wasn't. Patty was addressing her. "Um, yes."

Back outside on the steps, Precious watched Patty puffing away. She would've given anything to know what to say so it didn't seem like an awkward moment. If she'd been sitting with her township friends out in the sun, she would've gone straight to the point. *What happened?* she would've asked.

Maybe it would work here too?

Precious cleared her throat, "What happened?"

"It's this here," she started, gesturing widely at the shop. "It's not only hard for you and Petrus and Oom Marius. It affects everyone in town in some way or another. Us too. I mean, Shawn and me."

Precious nodded vigorously even though she couldn't see how.

"You see some of those guys out front are Shawn's friends and then I'm inside here all day and that kind of puts him in a difficult position. Herman and Koos were at our house last night. They didn't even greet me. In my own house. Just stood out on the stoep with Shawn, talking quietly.

"Next thing I knew, the men had gone home and Shawn's standing in front of me, talking about traditional values and people needing to realise their place. I sat there staring at him, too thick to click at first what he was on about. Then suddenly he said to me *I want you to stop going to that shop.*"

The back door creaked open. Mrs Joubert stood on the top step.

"Petrus told me you were out here," she said. "Well, he didn't actually say anything," she gave a small laugh while stepping gingerly between the two women to make her way down, "he just pointed at the back door."

Patty dragged heavily on her cigarette.

"Don't let me interrupt," Mrs Joubert said with an expectant expression.

"Did you ever have trouble with your husband, Mrs J?" Patty turned her face trustingly to the older woman.

"Surely you don't believe there's a single marriage where a couple doesn't squabble, my dear?"

"I'm not talking about a squabble."

"No," she nodded sombrely, "I don't suppose you are."

"Well, did you?"

Mrs Joubert shook her head slowly, as if she felt bad sharing the news with Patty. "Not this kind of trouble. Not with Mark. No."

"What was he like?" Patty asked eagerly. Like a little girl asking someone to read her a fairytale.

"Wouldn't you rather tell us what's got you so upset this morning?"

"No. I'm sick of talking about Shawn. Tell us about your Mark."

She cleared her throat and started her tale, "I was one of the lucky ones. You see, I met Mark at a dinner party one night. I'd gone as the date of a friend's brother. I can't even remember his name now. Anyway, it was some university thing. Mark was young and handsome and just starting out as a lecturer at a teacher's training college in the township. For some reason he took a shine to me and we started dating. A year later we were married. He was a wonderful husband," she ended with a satisfied smile.

"And?" Patty asked.

"And what?"

"Surely there's more?"

Mrs Joubert smiled an indulgent smile, "Mmm, let me see… I was very young and naïve back then. Mark gave me books to read. Lots of books. He taught me never to simply accept things. Always ask questions, he'd say. After some years he became a professor at university and we were very happy together but it wasn't to last long. Mark was killed in a train crash on his way to a rally in a township. He left me a wealthy widow but I couldn't bear to stay on in the city where everything reminded me of him. So, I decided to move to the middle of nowhere and that's how I ended up here, in Klippiesfontein."

Mrs Joubert let out a long sigh.

Patty immediately reached for her cigarettes. She exhaled a breath of smoke, "But he wasn't, like, political or anything? I mean, you guys never had to go through anything like this? Like here, outside the shop?"

"Quite the contrary, my dear," Mrs Joubert's eyes flew up to the wall and glazed over as if she was seeing something in the distance. "Mark was quite the political activist. You wouldn't believe how many days, weeks actually, we spent campaigning for the referendum on the abolition of Apartheid. We were out there on the streets every day, talking to just about every person who walked past. Taking the most horrid abuse sometimes, but still, in the end it was all worth it. Wasn't it?"

Precious nodded even though she'd been just a baby when the events Mrs Joubert was talking about took place.

Patty looked at her feet, "And what would you have done if…"

"If what, my dear?"

"Never mind."

"No, come on. Out with it. I can see it's important."

"If you and Mark hadn't agreed. I mean, what if you thought Apartheid was a good thing and Mark didn't. What would you have done?"

"Mmm, that's an interesting one. Let me see. I suppose in the beginning when I was young and impressionable I would've gone along with what he said. But the older me, the one who'd learnt to think for herself, well, she would've stood up for what she believed."

"Even against the man she loved?"

"*Especially* against the man I loved."

Patty didn't respond. She stared down at her red toenails peeking prettily from her high-heeled sandals. Precious stared at them too, not knowing what to say to break the silence.

"We'd better get back inside before Petrus thinks we've gone AWOL on him," Mrs Joubert spoke at last.

Later that afternoon, Precious was tidying a shelf close to the front window when she spotted Shawn strolling up to the men in the sun. He ambled down the line, making jokes with each of them in turn. Precious caught the odd phrase drifting in through the open doorway: *wife-of-yours*, a loud guffaw, *under-control*, some more laughter. Then all of sudden, she couldn't see him anymore.

She heard a pair of footsteps mounting the front steps – a sound they hadn't heard much over the last few weeks except for Mrs Joubert's primly clicking heels each morning.

Shawn was standing in the open doorway.

"Patty," he barked.

Patty looked nervously across at Mrs Joubert before she abandoned her position behind the counter and rushed over to him. She tried to take hold of his hand but he pulled away. They disappeared out the front door and stood huddled together in a corner of the stoep. Precious heard angry tones drifting in from outside. Shawn was gesticulating. Patty was shaking her blonde head.

Finally Shawn stormed off down the steps and Patty came back inside. She went to stand next to Precious and looked out at the street, her arms folded tightly across her chest. Shawn had come to a standstill in front of the line of barricaders and was talking to them.

Realising how nosy she looked, Precious quickly returned to her shelf.

Patty sat staring at the bucket of water that was temporarily housing the four lobsters. Their claws were reaching up, as if they were begging Patty to get them out of there.

Precious was cleaning the inside of the tank with a new cloth and some vinegar, just like Charlie had shown her. She was grateful to Patty for offering to take the creatures out of their tank because, though their health was one of the priorities in the shop these days, both her and Petrus were still too frightened to touch the things. Oom Marius had enough on his hands without them having to break the news that one of his precious pets had died. She knew Petrus felt the same way because he chopped up those squiddy things diligently each day without complaining once.

"So what did you say to Shawn when he asked you to stop working here?" Precious blurted out the question that had been on her mind all day.

Patty looked up and smiled sadly, "I told him I'd have to stop anyway as soon as the school holidays were over. But then he got angry and banged his fist on the coffee table and I almost jumped out of my skin because I'm not used to Shawn banging on anything. The mug fell off and bounced onto the mat. We both sat there just staring at it at first."

"*You're my wife and you'll do what I say*, he shouted and I couldn't help myself, I just burst out laughing in his face because he was being so ridiculous. I know I shouldn't have done that but it just came out. Shawn, of course, stormed out and didn't come back until this morning, reeking of beer. Probably spent the night with Lenny."

"Why is it so important for you to come here every day?"

"I don't know. I guess it's because I'm the one who found Petrus outside in the mud, unconscious and covered in blood. Standing here inside this shop is my small way of saying that that kind of thing is unacceptable. I wouldn't be able to look myself in the mirror if I suddenly stopped showing up here. I'd be saying that what they did to Petrus was somehow OK and I can't do that."

"Do you think that Shawn will leave you?"

"I don't know," she shrugged. "He's threatening to. Talking about divorce. In the ten years we've been married he's never once used that word. I'm hoping it doesn't come to that though. Maybe Tannie Hettie's treatment will work and they'll come back soon and we can all go back to the way things were."

"Do you really think that will happen?"

"What, that Tannie Hettie will get better?"

"No, that things can go back to the way they were before?"

"This is Klippiesfontein. Nothing ever changes around here. This will all blow over. You'll see…"

Precious shrugged and turned her attention back to the lobster tank.

Patty spent her days sighing impatiently and rushing out back to puff on her cigarettes but she didn't go close to that window to look outside anymore. She stopped taking home her daily packet of Camel Filters for her husband which made Precious think he wasn't coming home at night anymore. Her eyes stayed red. Eventually dark rings developed beneath them. Her make-up was hastily applied. Precious thought it was a good thing that Oom Marius didn't see her like this. He'd always been so fond of her prettily made up face.

Shawn kept showing up in the line of barricaders each day but on the fourth day he wasn't there at all. Patty was at the window every five minutes looking out and tut-tutting to herself. Precious wanted to say something to her but, once again, didn't know what. Instead, she made her countless cups of tea and accompanied her out back on each of her many smoke-breaks. She'd sit solemnly on the bottom step, hoping her silence would be seen as unspoken support.

It was lunchtime. They were sitting down on their little collection of chairs and crates by the lobster tank like they did every day. Mrs Joubert opened her lunchbox with neat white-bread sandwiches and offered them around to everyone. Petrus and Precious ate the *pap* with sausages and tomato sauce that Precious had prepared for them. Patty ate nothing. She stared ahead of her, her face pale and expressionless. Mrs Joubert tried making a joke to lighten the mood but it didn't work. Everyone fell silent and concentrated on their food.

Then, from outside, they heard the heavy revving of an engine. They looked up and cast knowing glances at one another: it was Shawn and his beloved motorbike.

The engine roared then dimmed, roared then dimmed again. Precious imagined the plumes of smoke coming out the back each time Shawn twisted the accelerator.

Patty rushed to the window. "Oh my God, he's got his bag strapped to the back," she said quietly. Almost to herself.

Precious put down her plate of food. She crossed the floor and went to stand next to Patty. Mrs Joubert joined them and, after a while, even Petrus clunked his way over to the window on his crutch.

Shawn drove past the shop, up the street and then disappeared from view, though they could still hear his engine. After a few seconds, he was back again. Then he took off in the other direction. Again, he came back. Up and down the street. Engine roaring. Up and down. Children abandoned their games and gathered on the pavement to see what was going to happen.

Up and down.

Patty stayed at the window, her long-nailed hands fingering her lips.

Up and down.

Shawn came to a stop right outside. He steadied himself by placing his feet on the ground. He lifted the visor on his helmet, looked straight at the shop, at the window where his wife stood and let out a blood-stopping cry.

"Patty!" he called.

She didn't move.

"Patty!" he called again.

Again, she didn't move.

Shawn slammed down the visor and, with a deafening roar from his motor, he took off, headed in the direction of the highway. This time he didn't come back.

Chapter Twenty-six

Driving slowly into Klippiesfontein, turning left on Main Street, they passed the familiar sights of their childhood: the church, the dominie's house next door to it, their old primary school, Alan's Hairdressing Salon…

Andre still recalled how everyone laughed when Alan had put up that sign – a hairdressing salon in the middle of Klippiesfontein! What pretention. But now, according to his mom, Alan couldn't keep up with the appointments.

"Is it just me, or does this place seem to get smaller every time we come back here?" Johan said next to him.

"It's not this place that gets smaller," Stefaan piped up from the back, "it's their mentality."

A bitter laugh erupted from the other two.

They were getting closer. Driving past the first handful of shops, Andre spotted his father's store. Instantly, warm memories of lazy summer afternoons playing touch rugby with his friends in the dust in front of the shop flooded over him. Stuffing their mouths so full of Wilson's toffees they couldn't close their lips, spit dribbling down their chins. Daring one another to make a quick dash behind the counter when their dad was busy with a customer, stuffing a hand into one of the glass jars, and coming out with a fistful of boiled sweets. The red ones were the best. Andre could still feel the way they cut his tongue when he ate too many.

That's when he saw them. A haphazard line of khaki-clad men in front of the shop. Two of them were seeking shade beneath the tree on the other side of the street. Sagging red and white cordoning-off-tape, limp flags that wished as hard as everyone else for a bit of a breeze – this was the site of their big resistance. "Huh," Andre scoffed loudly.

He drove slowly up to the front of the shop and turned the car off.

"You ready, boys?"

Several of the men were bending down low, trying to squint through the sun's glare on the windscreen to identify who had the nerve to pull up in front of their barricade. Andre saw a flash of recognition cross their faces.

There was Oom Hans, the one who'd started all this trouble, with Karel standing next to him. Piet, who'd been two years ahead of him at school and Mornê, his brother. Koos had been in class with Johan, and Herman with Stefaan. Men of their own generation. Men, who'd been lighties with them and got into all kinds of boys' mischief alongside them but had now come to turn on their father. Well, they'd chosen the wrong family to mess with. They were going to be sorry.

Andre nodded curtly. Partly to himself, partly to his brothers and almost simultaneously the door handles crunched open. The three men stepped out onto the street.

Young Daan and another boy were playing marbles in the dust close by. They looked up.

"Andre," Mornê spoke first, taking a step towards his former classmate, hesitating, and then dropping his outstretched hand again when he saw no handshake being offered in return. "What… what… what brings you back to Klippiesfontein?"

The two men under the shade stepped out into the glaring sunlight and joined their fellow barricaders on the street. A series of stiff nods were exchanged as the men acknowledged one another.

"How's this weather for you, man?" Piet remarked to no one in particular. "Thirty-nine degrees." He wiped his brow with the back of his hand.

"We're not here for a chit-chat," Stefaan said and took a step closer to the group.

Piet looked at the ground.

Oom Hans stepped towards the brothers and spoke in a grave voice, "How's it going with your mother, boys?"

Andre opened his mouth to give him the answer he deserved but Stefaan got there first, "All the worse for you lot standing out here day after day."

His words were dry and brittle. Small drops of spit flew from his lips and were lit up by the sun streaming from behind.

Men shifted their weight from one foot to the other. One or two turned their faces away, feigning a sudden interest in the crowd of children who were gathering on the other side of the street.

"Dawie, *gaan huis toe*," Piet admonished his young son whom he'd just spotted amongst the kids.

Dawie, go home.

"*Ja Dawie, gaan huis toe want vandag is die dag wat ek jou pa 'n paksla gee,*" Andre said.

Yes Dawie, go home because today's the day I give your dad a hiding.

The child stayed rooted to the spot. His eyes huge with fear.

Behind them they heard the wooden clunk of a crutch. Andre turned his head to look at the stoep. Petrus stood watching them. Next to them stood a pretty black girl. That must be Precious, he decided. And there was Mrs Joubert and Patty.

He turned back to stare at the men. Despite the cruel sun, the metre or so that separated Oom Marius' sons and the barricaders was cold and taut.

"I'm going to say this once," Andre started with the words he'd rehearsed in his head a hundred times, "Pack up your shit and go home so we can all get back to our lives."

"Or what?" Karel challenged, taking a step forward and closing the last of the space between them.

"Or we're going to make you sorry, you bastard!" Stefaan growled unexpectedly. He stepped forward and planted his fist right on Karel's jaw.

Andre tensed up. Glancing around him. Checking to see who was springing into action. Anticipating the first blow. Johan, next to him, did the same.

Next thing he saw was Johan's neck jerking backwards, looking as if his head was going to fly right off his body. His eyes loomed large in his skull. Koos, who was standing next to his brother, drew back his elbow and raised his fist to shoulder level. Andre saw his knuckles were bloody from where they'd split against his brother's face. Before Koos had a chance to land another blow, Andre jumped in between them and brought his forehead down, full-force, on Koos' nose. The crunch of snapping cartilage reverberated through Andre's skull, followed by a deep growl from Koos.

After that, chaos broke loose. The taste of dust mingled with the taste of blood. There was the sound of a tooth breaking off. Skin slammed into skin. Groans. Thumps. Lightning flashes of pain followed instantly by a surge of indignation. Muscles were coiled up and released. Skin burst under knuckles. The softness of a cheek met the stone of a fist. There was a dull thud of leather veldshoes against someone's shin.

A figure stumbled backwards and slammed into the wooden railing of the stoep. Andre was grateful to see it wasn't Johan or Stefaan, but that was the only thing he had time to notice. Before he could identify the man's face he felt something rock-hard slam into his eyebrow. Suddenly he couldn't see out of his right eye. Warm, red fluid gushed over it. The red diluted to a pinkish-orange colour as he turned his head into the sun to identify his attacker. Furiously, he wiped his eye on his sleeve and stormed off in the direction of the fist, roaring like an animal. Human flesh met human flesh as Andre pummelled his fists into it until, at last, the flesh beneath his hands stopped resisting and went limp.

Andre straightened up and gasped for air. Townsfolk stood all around them, mouths agape. Stefaan's elbow was moving swiftly, up and down, up and down, crunching into something on the ground with every downward stroke. Johan, his face covered in blood, was standing over a figure, his leg kicking viciously at it. The figure flinched limply each time it met with the foot.

Andre breathed in deeply. He looked slowly around him. Morné and two other men stood staring at them from the other side of the street. Their eyes huge in dismay. Unharmed, they hadn't taken part in the fight.

He heard the sound of a child crying and he looked over at the group of kids. Young Dawie stood in their midst, sobbing uncontrollably. Snot mixed with dust coated his upper lip. His eyes were transfixed on the figure lying spread out on the road. Andre realised it was Piet, Dawie's father. A little girl with blonde pigtails put her arm around the crying boy's shoulder and Andre felt a rush of gratitude towards her.

No one was coming at them anymore. His brothers noticed it too. They straightened up and surveyed the scene around them. He saw that Oom Hans had been the one who'd crumpled down by the stoep. Andre felt guilty for having laid a hand on a man who was old enough to be their father. But, then again, he told himself, Oom Hans had stopped at nothing when trying to destroy his parents' livelihood. Sixty years old or not, he deserved what he got.

Koos lay at Johan's feet and Karel was curled up close to Stefaan, trying to lift his head and dropping it again into his arms. Defeated. Herman lay groaning on his side, a trickle of spit dribbling from his mouth into the dust, collecting to form a little puddle of mud.

Andre clapped his stinging hands loudly and announced, "And now, that is that. If we ever hear about one of you bastards coming close to this shop, we'll drive straight back here and sort you out all over again!"

Johan dusted himself off. Stefaan walked angrily up to the limp cordoning-off-tape, ripped it down and bundled it into his fists. Johan and Andre each collected a flag. Stamping their feet to get rid of the dust, the brothers trudged up the front steps.

Andre turned round at the top and addressed the gathered crowd, "The beer's on us."

He watched as Alan, his mother's hairdresser, Mister Scott, his old English teacher, and Charlie separated themselves from the crowd and followed them. Once inside, it took a while for Andre's eyes to adjust to the dim light after the blinding sunlight. He saw Petrus standing by the fridge, a grin splitting his face. Proudly he cracked open a beer and passed it to Andre's waiting hand. Andre grinned back at him.

"Give me one of those," Stefaan said, crossing the wooden

floor with a limp.

"You look like Petrus now," Alan joked as he walked through the doorway.

Precious came out from behind the counter where she'd just turned up the volume dial on the radio. Happy beats pulsed through the shop. Bottles of jam and honey vibrated against one another in a victory dance.

"We showed them, didn't we?" Johan gushed. He threw back his head and emptied the contents of his can down his throat.

Andre lifted his own beer to his lips. The sting of the bubbles, the soft foam, rushed into his mouth, over his tongue.

The next thing he felt something vibrating against his groin. His cellphone, he realised, before he heard the first ring. It was a damn miracle the thing hadn't been smashed during the fight, he thought, slipping his hand into the pocket of his jeans to extract it.

"It's Pa," he announced, reading the name off the screen. Andre spoke into the receiver, "Talk about good timing."

"Andre?" he heard his father's voice. Distraught.

"Yes Pa, it's me. What's wrong?"

"It's your mother. She's not doing well. The doctor says you must come. All three of you. Right away."

Andre put his beer down on the closest shelf, "We're coming, Pa. We'll be there as soon as we can."

Chapter Twenty-seven

Oom Marius wasn't opening the shop; it was the second time in forty-two years. The first time had been when Hettie went into labour with Andre at six o'clock in the morning on a Wednesday and he'd driven her to hospital in Springbok. He still remembered it was a Wednesday because the delivery guy was supposed to come that day, and he'd ended up fetching the supplies himself in between visits to his young wife and brand new son. They were just starting out back then and now it was all over.

Oom Marius felt a wave of grief overcome him and he gulped for air to keep at bay the sob that was threatening to escape. But he realised he'd made a sound all the same when his daughter-in-law rushed over to him.

He was sitting on a chair in front of the counter; the one Petrus had reportedly been occupying the last couple of weeks of his absence while he watched the ladies running the shop. For the first time he could remember, the ticking of the seconds of the clock on the wall was audible. He stared at the shelves of produce he'd been seeing for over forty years and noticed that they'd somehow lost their colour. Everything, literally everything, was grey. There wasn't a stitch of colour left in the world.

"*Pappa*," Karien said to him, laying her hand on his shoulder, "*is Pappa oraait?*"

Oom Marius shrugged off her hand impatiently. He knew she was only trying to help but if he'd told these blasted women once, then he'd told them a hundred times he didn't need them fussing over him. All he wanted, if truth be told, was to be left alone and for this day to be over with. Karien dropped her arms at her side and stood uncomfortably next to Oom Marius, not sure where to look.

He tried to forget she was there.

Oom Marius hadn't needed to close the shop for the birth of his other two sons, he reminisced. Hettie had got her timing right by the time they came along. Johan was born on a Saturday night, just hours after he'd closed the store and Stefaan had come on a Sunday. Good boys she'd given him. Right from the start they'd known their place.

Oom Marius looked over at the three of them, huddled together between the Wheatbix and the Rice Crispies. Dressed in black suits, their ties hanging round their necks like nooses, an occasional subdued word passing between them, they took it in turns to glance at the clock counting off the minutes until it was time for them to start their procession to the church.

As Oom Marius looked at his sons, he saw them grow younger before his eyes until there were no longer three grown men in their thirties standing there, shoulders slumped, but youngsters. Motherless brothers.

Andre, scruffy and proud in his rugby jersey the year they beat Prieska High and came home with the trophy. Johan, wearing his black robe and funny square hat in the middle of summer, sweat coursing down his forehead into his eyes, clutching his degree – the first one in both his and Hettie's family to graduate from university. And Stefaan, their youngest, their most sensitive, their most hot-headed, standing before them with a black eye, explaining sheepishly about the umpteenth fight he'd been in, taking it up for some girl or a younger kid who couldn't take it up for themselves.

Oom Marius jerked back his head and gasped for air in an attempt to stop himself weeping. A tormented yelp escaped his lips all the same and every pair of eyes turned to him, filled with pity.

"Stop looking at me, will you? I told you, I'm alright."

Guiltily, all eyes – his sons, his daughters-in-law, his grandchildren's, Petrus' – glanced away, pretending they hadn't been doing any looking in the first place.

Minutes passed. Nobody moved. Least of all the time, and for this Oom Marius was grateful. As hard as it was sitting there, with nothing to do, inside his shop – when the doors should've been open and the children should've been queuing at the counter for ice-creams, and Hettie should've been popping her head round the door telling him his lunch was ready - it was better than walking down the street so he could lower his wife's twinkling green eyes, along with the rest of her, into the ground.

Because it had finally come so far: death had done them part.

Another violent intake of breath but, this time, no one dared to look.

"Pa, it's time to go," Andre finally spoke the words he'd been dreading.

Oom Marius put his hands on his knees and heaved himself heavily up. His shoulders ached. His back ached. His heart ached.

He put one heavy foot in front of the other and started for the front door. His family fell in behind him.

Walking outside, he was dazzled by the sunshine that awaited him and he rubbed his eyes with thumb and forefinger. He was surprised to hear the squall of a *hadeda* as it flew overhead; he'd been expecting, somehow, to find that the world had stopped. Outside on the stoep he looked up to acknowledge the people he knew would be gathered there to take the long walk with him and his sons, down the dusty street, to the church.

The eyes that met his were panicked and once again filled with pity. Lips murmured words that were supposed to bring comfort. He nodded dutifully to give some sign that he had, indeed, been comforted though, of course, everyone knew it was a lie. Everyone playing the roles expected of them because they didn't know how else to act. Oom Marius wanted to scream. He wanted to start running in the opposite direction of the church, aching shoulders, aching back, aching heart and all.

But, of course, he didn't.

He would play his role too along with the rest of Klippiesfontein because it was expected of him and, being a novice at burying his wife, he too didn't know how to act.

His eyes scanned the crowd: Sarie, Mrs Joubert, Mister Scott, Precious, Charlie, Patty. All dressed in black. All eyes downcast.

Suddenly someone broke free from the crowd and rushed towards him. It was Alan, wearing a dark suit and a bright pink tie, tears streaming down his cheeks. Oom Marius couldn't help himself. He burst out laughing when he saw the tie. He laughed and he laughed, tears he had not allowed in grief, now coursed down his face in hilarity. It was true what they said, that tears and laughter were sisters. Best of all, he knew the tie would've made Hettie smile as well.

Alan stopped, confused. He smiled uncertainly at the joke he had no inkling of. When Oom Marius' laughter subsided at last, Alan reached out for his hands, "I just wanted to tell you, she looks beautiful. I went to the morgue last night to do her hair and I can tell you, she was at peace. I thought you'd want to know. Her suffering is..."

"Thank you, Alan," Oom Marius said sternly, fully composed again.

Alan nodded in embarrassment and fell back into the crowd.

Oom Marius heard the heavy thud of his own shoes as he took the first step down to street level. He heard the *clump-clump* of Petrus' crutch right behind him.

At last he arrived at the church, a whole procession behind him. Sweat ran down his temples, his spine and from his armpits. A hot breeze had started up and covered the mourners in an invisible layer of dust. He knew it was there because he tasted it on his tongue, felt it scratching his nostrils. This blasted heat was bad enough without still having to wear a suit. Tugging at his collar, he loosened his tie.

Oom Marius entered the dark insides and relative cool of the church and started his lonely walk to the front pew. For the first time in forty years he was walking down this aisle without his Hettie at his side. His three daughters-in-law and his grandchildren followed. His sons had stayed outside, joined by three of their cousins, to wait for the hearse to draw up in front of the church.

The pews were full of people. Of course, Hettie had been a well-loved woman, but he hadn't been expecting a turn-out like this. People were squashed into all corners, standing in the aisles, fanning themselves with the funeral program. The fluttering of paper was the only sound inside the stifling church.

The last three pews at the back were full of black people. Some whom Oom Marius knew, some whom he had never seen in his life. The men, just like Oom Marius, looked uncomfortable in their suits. The women were dressed in the gaudy prints they seemed to be so fond of. It wasn't often that he'd seen a black face inside the Dutch Reformed Church, and so many of them! It was unprecedented. Oom Marius nodded acknowledgement to his right and to his left before continuing his march to the front. The scent of the flowers as he came closer overwhelmed him.

Amongst the faces of the congregation were people he'd known his whole life; friends, family, youngsters whom he'd seen born and who had since become adults. He also spotted the faces of the men whom he hadn't wanted to see. Oom Hans was there, sitting next to him was Bertie. And there was Frikkie, next to his mom and all her other children. Apparently the two boys had been let out on bail, though he couldn't remember who'd told him that anymore. Karel, Piet, Herman, Koos. One by one he spotted them all but, instead of the anger he thought he'd feel if they dared show up, he felt numb. Just plain numb.

Oom Marius carried on down the aisle, his daughters-in-law clicking behind him on their high heels, his grandchildren scuffling next to their mothers. The youngest one, still a babe on the hip, wailed at the solemnity of the place. But the one sound Oom Marius no longer heard was the *clump-clump* of Petrus' crutch.

He stopped, turned round and scanned the pews. Right there, in the last one, he saw the already cramped line of people shuffle up to make place for his assistant.

"No, Petrus," Oom Marius boomed, "you come sit up front here with us. Hettie would've wanted that."

Petrus looked nervous. He nodded.

Oom Marius heard a whisper start up somewhere to his left. He jerked his head round and glared in the direction it had come from. The whisper scuttled away, humiliated, without betraying its owner. Oom Marius turned round and marched on. At last he reached the front pew and took his seat. His family sat down next to him.

Clump-clump, he heard the sound of the crutch making its way over to join them.

"Is there space, Karien, for Petrus to sit down next to you?" he addressed his daughter-in-law.

"Ja, Pa," she answered.

The sound of the crutch fell silent and, at the end of their pew, right next to the aisle, Petrus' dark, forlorn figure sat down.

Oom Marius nodded slowly, satisfied, and looked out in front of him. Dominie Andries had taken up his position behind the pulpit. The dominie met his eyes and again Oom Marius saw that damned pity directed at him. Looking down the aisle to the back of the church, the dominie nodded curtly. He heard the heavy oak doors creak open. Mrs Van Rensburg wheezed her organ into life and it started moaning a sad song. All heads turned round to see the pallbearers shouldering the coffin. Oom Marius' eyes remained fixed ahead of him. He did not want to see his boys carrying their mother.

When, eventually, the six grown men had completed their solemn march and lowered the coffin in front of the pulpit amongst the wreaths, they took their places in the pew next to Oom Marius. He looked at his stern-faced sons huddled together. No emotion, no tears, just the way he'd taught them.

But Oom Marius wasn't quite managing the control over his own body. Against his will, he gulped once more for air.

Dominie Andries spoke from his pulpit, "Our gathering here this afternoon, dearest family and friends of our beloved sister Hettie, is for the purpose of paying tribute to her life and mourning her death. Life, as we see clearly on an occasion such as this, is always lived in the presence of death, and the brightness of life is highlighted by the shadow of death…"

Chapter Twenty-eight

Petrus was not looking forward to the day stretching before him.

He stood in the dust at the foot of the steps by the back door, biting his bottom lip, waiting to hear the key turn in the lock when Baas Marius opened the shop.

For the first time in ten days.

For the first time since the funeral.

It was going to be a hard day but Petrus had been having a lot of those lately. He could even say he was getting used to them. At least the hardest day was behind him, he thought, remembering how he'd laid in the very dust at his feet, his body broken and bleeding. Yes, at least that day was over.

He heard the key turn in the lock. The door swung open and Baas Marius stood at the top of the stairs, his cheeks hanging down like empty plastic bags. He hadn't noticed before how white people could turn grey. Pink, yes. Red, definitely. But grey?

"Morning," Baas Marius grunted. "Your leg better?"

Petrus nodded and wobbled up the steps. He'd been to the doctor the day before to have his cast cut off. It wasn't easy getting used to putting all his weight on his leg again; it felt as if the inside was soft like a chicken bone that had been boiled in a stew for hours. He'd spent the whole day walking up and down inside his mother's house, getting exercise like the doctor told him, until she'd shouted at him that he was making her *mal*. Crazy. That's when he'd gone outside to sit in the sun to wait for the day to pass so he could get back to work.

The front door of the shop was open and, despite the earliness of the hour, the sun was streaming in, making a bright yellow spot on the wooden floor. Petrus looked out the front window and felt a little happier. They weren't there anymore, those men. At least there was one good thing that had come out of all of this, out of Missies Hettie's... No, he shook his head to get rid of the thought. Nothing good had come out of Missies Hettie's death. He would much rather have her back, taking care of Baas Marius, and have those men outside again.

But still, Petrus thought, at least he could go out front and sweep the stoep like he used to. He went to the storeroom to fetch the broom.

Swish swish it went. Petrus felt the sun beating down on his back and watched the dust particles dancing before his eyes. He couldn't stop himself feeling at least a little bit happy.

Would she walk up the front steps, he wondered, or would she come round the back like she'd been doing for all these weeks? His eyes travelled down the deserted road, a mirage shimmering about halfway down, to see if he could spot her figure making its jaunty way towards them.

"Did you order the fifty kilos of *mealie-meal* last week?" Baas Marius was standing in the doorway, holding his clipboard and pen in front of him.

Petrus nodded.

"Did they deliver it?"

Petrus leaned the broom up against the wall and headed inside. Baas Marius stood back to let him pass and Petrus walked to the storeroom. Hearing the baas behind him, he came to a stop in front of a shelf where twenty-five brown paper bags were lined up, each filled with two kilos of *mealie-meal* from the big hessian sack.

"You've already weighed it off into smaller bags. Is that what you're telling me?"

Petrus didn't want to take credit for a job he hadn't done but he didn't know how to communicate that it was Precious' work. So he nodded.

"Good man," said Baas Marius and laid his hand briefly on Petrus' shoulder. "I see you managed the store well while I was gone."

Baas Marius had never touched Petrus on the shoulder like that before. His lips parted and he grinned.

"Wouldn't it be easier to simply tell me these things rather than showing me every time?"

Petrus shrugged.

"Have it your way," Baas Marius snapped and Petrus felt strangely grateful to be the recipient of his impatience again. Everything would soon go back to normal.

He went back out to the stoep and took hold of the broom again. *Swish, swish.* He scanned the road. Nothing. *Swish, swish.*

Lunch time was strained and uncomfortable. In the old days, before Missies Hettie got sick, she would make sandwiches for the baas for lunch. Sometimes, when the shop was quiet, he would go into the house and eat with his wife. But if there were too many customers, he'd eat his sandwiches standing up behind the counter. Petrus would usually go into the storeroom, open the old ice-cream container he used for a lunch box, and eat his cold *pap* and gravy by himself, perched on a plastic crate.

But there was no one to make Baas Marius' sandwiches anymore and Petrus felt too bad to abandon him to eat his own lunch. His stomach rumbled with hunger and he felt faint in the head but he made no attempt to go to the storeroom. When he stood next to Baas Marius to point out the numbers he'd written down in the big black book, he heard his baas' stomach rumble too.

"What are we going to do now, Petrus?" he said. "Are we going to stand here next to each other with our stomachs sounding like a waterfall?"

Petrus shrugged.

The baas walked over to a shelf and picked up a tin of pilchards in tomato sauce. With the penknife he took from his belt, he opened it. Sharing the contents between two enamel plates he took from under the counter, he pushed one towards Petrus, "Grab one of those half loaves of brown over there."

Once the bread had been torn in two and Petrus had fetched two spoons and two glasses of cold water from the back, the men ate together in silence. The only sound was the clinking of their spoons against the plates. And even though their chattering had driven him mad sometimes, Petrus found himself missing the three women inside the shop. At least there had always been something to think about with them around. Especially with

Precious, he sighed.

"What are you sighing about?" Baas Marius grunted. "You sound like a lovesick schoolboy."

Petrus felt his cheeks go warm and for once he was grateful for his brown skin. If he'd been white, his cheeks would've gone pink just like Baas Marius used to change colour whenever Missies Patty walked into the shop.

And then Precious made her appearance.

"Good afternoon," came her voice from the direction of the front door.

Petrus and the baas turned to look at her.

She was wearing a flared pink skirt with a white top and a thick black belt at her waist. She had pink earrings that dangled happily from her earlobes and some powder shimmered on her eyelids. Petrus caught his breath. He wasn't sure if he'd ever seen her looking so pretty before.

"Afternoon, Precious," Baas Marius said.

Petrus nodded at her.

"You've come for your pay?" Baas Marius asked.

"And to say goodbye," she added.

"Well, come over here. I've got an envelope ready for you. You just have to sign the book for me."

Petrus watched her pretty figure as she made her way over to the counter. After she'd signed her name, she put the envelope away into her little white handbag. He saw Baas Marius raise his hand and rest it on her shoulder just like he'd done with him a few hours earlier.

"You know I'm not one who's good with words."

Precious looked at him earnestly and nodded.

"You mustn't think that I don't know what you did for us. For me, for Petrus, for the shop…"

She nodded again.

"So I just wanted to say thank you," he said.

Petrus thought he heard a crack in his baas' voice.

"Oh, it was nothing," she sang back.

"No, it was definitely not nothing."

"Well, I'm glad I did it," she smiled.

She turned round and looked at Petrus. He felt a lump grow in his throat.

"Do you mind if I speak to Petrus for just a minute, Baas?" she asked.

"That's enough of all this baas business, you hear me? You call me Oom Marius, just like everybody else."

Precious nodded solemnly, "Thank you, Baa... I mean, Oom Marius." She smiled.

Petrus felt a flutter in his heart at the sight of that smile.

"Off you go then," the baas said, turning his attention to the book that lay open on the counter, "take Petrus outside and tell him what you've got to say."

Petrus suddenly realised he was still holding his spoon. It was suspended, mid-air, on its way to his mouth, a piece of pilchard balancing on the end of it. Quickly he dropped it in his plate.

Precious looked at him questioningly, "You want to come outside?"

She walked to the front door and he followed her. On their way out they passed Baas Lenny coming in. Precious reached out and took hold of Petrus' forearm, "I just wanted to say, brother, it was a pleasure working ncxt to you."

Petrus nodded. He opened his mouth to tell her the pleasure had been all his but not a sound came out. Quickly he shut it again, realising how ridiculous he must look, standing there gaping like one of the fish he fed to the lobsters.

Precious threw back her head and let out a peal of laughter. It sounded like jewels tinkling onto the ground. He wanted to catch the sound and stuff it into a box so he could open it up later and listen to it again and again.

"You stopped speaking to black people too, brother?" she asked.

Petrus shook his head violently.

"Then say something."

Again Petrus opened his mouth and again not a sound came out. How stupid he was to have dreamed someone as clever and

208

sophisticated as Precious would ever be interested in someone like him. He couldn't even speak properly. How stupid he was to think his title of manager would impress her. Only the best was good enough for a woman like her. Like men who'd gone to Cape Town to study at the university and who drove white cars with Telcom written on the side. But then again, maybe even men like that weren't good enough for a woman like Precious. Maybe nobody was.

He felt the sting of tears behind his eyes. "I... I... I... I hope you'll be very happy, sister," he finally managed to get out.

Another peal of laughter.

Another stab in his heart.

"You talk as if I'm going away, brother. You will still see me in the township. Maybe you can come visit me at my mother's house on Sunday and we can drink some Koolaid together in the sun?"

"What... what about Baas Charlie?"

"Charlie won't mind if we're friends, brother. He's a modern man."

Petrus smiled sadly, "Maybe I'll come drink Koolaid with you then, sister."

Precious leaned towards him. Lifting her arms, she threw them round his shoulders in a firm hug. He felt his skin tingling. He raised his own arms and placed them carefully around her waist. If only he could die, right there, right then, he'd go to heaven a happy man.

Petrus felt her pull back and extract herself from his arms.

"Goodbye, brother," she said and, with a flash of teeth and a twirl of her skirt, she was down the steps and headed back down the road.

She turned round and gave him a last wave.

He knew his jaw was hanging open as he stared after her but, try as he did, he couldn't get it to close.

"Petrus, get inside here," he heard Baas Marius shouting.

He followed his reluctant feet back inside the shop.

"Come over here," his baas called.

He made his way over to the counter.

"You know what this is?" Baas Marius asked, pushing a bright blue book towards him. On its cover was a big red L and the words *Pass Your Learner's Licence Easily.* Petrus had seen his neighbour's son reading a book just like this one. He shrugged.

"It's for your learner's licence," Baas Marius explained. "It's got all the road signs and things in there. You have to learn what they mean and then write a test about them. If you do well on the test then I can teach you how to drive. And once you can do that, I'll send you to Springbok once a week to collect the supplies. That way we don't have to pay the delivery guy. Whatever money we save we can add to your pay cheque. Do you understand?"

Petrus wasn't sure if he did. If he learnt what all the pictures in the book meant then he could drive Baas Marius' bakkie and get more money for doing it? That's what he thought he'd said but he must've misunderstood something. Baas Marius almost never spoke so many words in one go. He was sure he'd made a mistake somewhere. Petrus shrugged.

"Start learning everything that's written there in that book."

He nodded.

"And let me know when you've finished."

He nodded again.

"And we'll take it from there, OK?"

"Ja, Baas," Petrus answered.

Baas Marius' eyes grew bigger but he didn't say anything about the fact that Petrus had suddenly decided to speak.

Petrus was grateful for this. Somehow it didn't feel wrong anymore that he'd spoken to a white man. He didn't think his mother would be cross with him for doing it. He was going to learn to drive a car, after all. Petrus hoped he'd see Precious in the township that night when he went home. He would tell her about the book and about the licence and then, maybe, just maybe, she wouldn't think Baas Charlie's car was so fantastic.

"*Dankie*, Baas," he spoke again.

Thank you, boss.

Chapter Twenty-nine

She was about to go out on a date. A date. A date. A date... She had an extra spring in her already springy step.

Dare she call it that? Yet? She wasn't sure. She didn't even know if white people actually used the word date or whether that was just the impression she got from watching American TV. People like her, like Precious, they didn't use words like date. No, they just called it getting to know one another.

Walking down the steps of Oom Marius' General Store, she felt a trickle of sweat running down her spine. She hoped the wet patch wouldn't show through her blouse. It felt good listening to the sound of her heels clicking on the wooden steps. Smiling to herself, she looked back and waved at Petrus standing so forlorn on the stoep.

Precious felt the sweat on her back turn cold. She'd just spotted that *isidenge,* that idiot, Karel, pull up outside Botha's Butchery. Her heart racing, she even considered crossing the street so she didn't have to pass him.

But no, she wouldn't do that, she decided. Not for the likes of that man. She had as much right to be on this street as he did. She'd stood up to him and his baboons for all the time Oom Marius was in Cape Town so now, in broad daylight, when the whole ugly business was behind them, she wasn't going to let his presence dictate her movements. She watched him climb out of his bakkie and step onto the pavement. He glanced to his right and caught sight of her. Lifting her chin, she thrust back her shoulders in defiance but realised it hadn't been quick enough for him to notice. He'd already turned his head away from her in disdain.

Precious walked on, looking straight ahead, trying not to think about him. She wasn't going to let him spoil her evening. Nearing the butchery, she read the curly white letters on the blackboard advertising the day's specials: lamb chops. Ox tail. Chicken livers. She saw the dark brown slabs of dried meat, biltong, hanging from hooks on the other side of the shop window. Despite herself, her mouth watered at the thought of its salty taste on her tongue.

He still hadn't gone inside, she noticed. What was keeping him? Surely he wasn't waiting for her…

Just steps away from him, she saw Karel's hand shoot up into the air. Instinctively, she flinched before realising he was waving at someone behind her. He stood still, waiting for the person to reach him. Looking round, Precious saw Charlie coming towards them. Charlie? How had he known she'd be here? They'd agreed to meet at the crossroads where the road lead out of town.

Smiling, Charlie brought his hand up in greeting too. Precious was about to wave back when she realised he wasn't even looking at her. He was smiling at Karel.

The clicking of her heels on the pavement stopped dead.

"Charlie, my man," Karel exclaimed, sidestepping Precious to extend his right hand for a handshake.

"How are you?" Charlie said before turning to nod in Precious' direction.

She felt her jaw drop and raised her eyebrows. Was this how it was going to be in front of the whites of Klippiesfontein? Would he be all attentive only when they got away from this town? Or was even that going to be reserved for the moments they were alone together? Completely alone. Away from white eyes. Her hands flew indignantly up to her pink-skirted hips.

"Man, am I glad to see you," Karel continued.

"Ja, you getting the hang of the internet yet?" Charlie asked.

"No man, that's why I wanted to talk to you. I think the wife's gone and pushed on buttons she shouldn't be pushing. The bloody thing is threatening us with some or other bacteria… I don't know. I think it's sick."

"A virus," Charlie nodded.

"Whatever, man. You got time to come round and take a look?"

"What? Now?"

"Ja, man, I promised this guy I'd, what do you call it…"

"E-mail?" Charlie said.

"Yes, that's it. That I'd e-mail him a quote for fifty lambs."

As Charlie stood there, nodding his head, he turned his attention to her for the first time. "Precious," he exclaimed and his face broke into a wide grin.

Becoming aware of her gaping mouth, she quickly shut it. What was he up to? Was he playing white men's games? Uncertain, she forced herself to return Charlie's smile.

Karel glared angrily at Precious.

She stared right back.

Charlie leaned in to brush his lips lightly across her cheek. "I wasn't expecting to see you here," he said.

She felt her expression soften and smiled back at him, "No, nor you. We said six o' clock, didn't we?" Her eyes flitted quickly over to Karel to see his face. He was looking away from the couple, shifting his weight from one foot to the other.

"Yes, but my mom asked me to fetch a couple of chops," Charlie explained. "Karel, you know Precious, don't you?"

"We've never met but I know who she is," he grunted.

Something about Charlie's eyes made her decide to trust him. Following his lead, she held out her hand and spoke sweetly, "Pleased to meet you."

Karel reached out and touched her hand half-heartedly, mumbling something inaudible.

"Look man," Charlie started, "I was just going to take a drive out to Springbok to go catch a movie."

"But there's a *sokkie* on tonight in the church hall?" Karel answered, a perplexed squint plastered on his leather-brown face.

"Oh, I know. But I wanted to catch that new flick everyone's been talking about."

"And not go dancing?" Karel spoke.

"It's not really Precious' thing," Charlie replied.

Karel's eyes grew large, "You going to the movies with *her*?"

Charlie nodded matter-of-factly.

Precious felt a surge of gratitude towards him that he'd acknowledged her. Almost immediately she was flooded with irritation at herself. What was there to be grateful about? Why the hell *shouldn't* he acknowledge her?

"We could swing by your place on our way, Karel. Your wife home now?" Charlie asked.

What was he doing, Precious thought.

"I... I..." Karel stammered.

"She home or not, man? Because I'm driving up to Prieska tomorrow to see a couple of clients there. I don't know when I'll get another chance to stop off at your place."

Precious stared at the drops of sweat oozing from Karel's brow.

She hooked her arm through Charlie's, "The movie starts in an hour. Are you sure we'll have time to make a stop?"

"You're right. You should get going," Karel said, looking relieved. "Some other time then, when you don't have plans." He hurried away from them, into the butchery.

As soon as he was gone, Precious and Charlie burst out laughing.

"You evil man," she punched him on the arm, "he almost had a heart-attack at the thought of you walking into his house with me at your side."

"Would serve him right," said Charlie.

Still laughing, they crossed the road to where the little white car was parked with Telcom written on the side.

Saturday night, and Precious and Charlie were standing outside fidgeting on Springbok's pavement. Charlie looked nice in his crisp white shirt and freshly ironed jeans, she thought. Hopefully she looked good too in her new pink and white ensemble. She'd come to Springbok especially that morning to buy it so she could look nice for their... date. She fingered the clasp of her little white handbag: open... closed... open... Charlie was rocking slightly from one foot to the other. The smell of the sweaty bodies around them mixed with a concoction of underarm deodorants drifted into her nostrils.

Was he going to take hold of her hand or not?

One part of her hoped he would. She'd thought she would melt into the ground from pure pleasure each time they accidentally brushed up against each other. She couldn't wait for their touching not to be accidental. Another part of her, however, hoped he wouldn't reach for her hand. There'd be plenty of time for that later on. Why rush things?

"Which movie do you want to see?" Charlie asked.

Precious scanned her eyes obligingly over the posters but, being far too nervous, she had no idea how she was expected to come up with an answer. She fingered the white beads at the base of her throat. Trying hard to seem casual, she let her eyes sweep the crowd gathering outside the movie theatre. Did she recognise anyone from Klippiesfontein?

Precious was stunned to notice that Charlie was doing the same. Trying to be just as inconspicuous as her, he was checking for familiar faces. She felt what little courage she had plummet to the pit of her stomach. How she'd hoped he wouldn't do this. How she'd hoped he would be brave enough for the both of them. And how naive of her to have expected anything different.

He'd be counting the other black faces in the crowd – just like she'd done, she thought. Two so far. No, no, there's another one. That made four with hers. Thank God! At least she wasn't the only one.

Despite the fact that blacks had been allowed into movie theatres for more than two decades, it wasn't enough to turn Springbok, at least twenty times bigger than Klippiesfontein, into a buzzing, liberal metropolis like Cape Town. People tried to glance unobtrusively at the other black faces, which meant they were undoubtedly staring at hers too. She craned her neck to see who the others were and realised she was just like the starers – paying special attention to the faces for the simple reason of their being black. Young and hip, she noticed. Neat cornrows, skull plaits, the latest fashion, good looking according to white men's standards... She could see they were nervous too. Their eyes darted around, still feeling like intruders no matter what the laws of the land said.

"How about that one?" Charlie asked pointing at one of the posters.

Precious nodded without registering which film she'd acceded to see.

Was he going to take hold of her hand or not?

Suddenly she spotted a familiar face, "Isn't that Fanus over there?" she whispered urgently, her heart beating.

"I'm sure he won't be the only one here from Klippiesfontein. Despite what Karel thinks, not everyone wants to go to the *sokkie*. Or would you rather have gone there?" he teased.

Precious had seen it once – a *sokkie*. She'd gone with her mother to the church hall to help with the washing up in the kitchen. Each time the doors swung open they'd been able to catch a glimpse of the white women, decked out in their frilly, floral Sunday best, being swung around the church hall, elbows pumping up and down as they tried to keep up to their men, gripping on for dear life. The whites' interpretation of dancing. And to such awful music too. Would Charlie ever expect her to go to one of those things? Would he go with her to a dance in the township? Or was there simply to be no dancing at all?

He gently edged her forwards and they joined the queue.

Feeling something touch her hand, Precious glanced down. She saw Charlie's fingers fidgeting close to hers. Taking a deep breath, she closed her hand over his and thrust back her shoulders. If they were going to do this thing then they were going to do it properly. If it didn't work out in the end then it wasn't going to be because they hadn't tried, she resolved.

Charlie looked at her and flashed her a nervous smile. Together they edged closer to the ticket counter.

Chapter Thirty

His hands were shaking a little as he clutched the piece of paper Charlie had brought him that morning. Would he be able to go through with this, he wondered?

Oom Marius stared at the big pot of salted water boiling on the stove. He'd added white wine, a clove of garlic, half an onion and some green herbs just like it said on the paper. The steam from the pot was settling on his face and he took a step back. Just now he'd stink of garlic, he thought, and that was the last thing he needed tonight.

It was the pot Hettie had always used when she was cooking for the whole family. The one she'd used just a few months ago to cook the potatoes for her famous potato salad for their Christmas lunch; cold-meats-and-salads, like they had every year. Oom Marius remembered how Johan had asked if they could skip Christmas lunch because Karien had wanted to spend Christmas with her own family for a change. Shouting down the phone at his son, Oom Marius had banged his fist on the counter and insisted they come to Klippiesfontein. Afterwards he'd felt guilty that he'd been so unreasonable with Johan.

He didn't feel guilty anymore.

At least Hettie had had all three of her boys around her for her last Christmas on this earth.

And here he was, about to use *her* pot to cook for another woman.

No, Oom Marius was not that kind of man.

He grabbed the pot from the stove using Hettie's oven gloves. Spring green with little pink roses on them. He remembered how proud she'd been of them when she came home from a shopping trip to Springbok with Sarie one afternoon. She hadn't often bought herself things but these particular oven gloves had really caught her fancy. Oom Marius tried to recall what his reaction had been to her pleasure. He was ashamed to think he'd probably said nothing at all. Staring down at his hands covered in Hettie's gloves, he ripped them off and threw them into a drawer. He wasn't sure if his hands deserved to be in the same place as hers used to be.

Taking two dishtowels, he took hold of the pot by the handles and threw the boiling water into the sink. He shoved it to one side.

Oom Marius stomped into the shop. "Petrus," he hollered.

"Ja, baas?" he said, coming out from the storeroom. Face washed and shining with a fresh layer of Vaseline, clean shirt, the smell of soap. Petrus was ready to go home for the weekend.

"Good, you haven't left yet," Oom Marius said.

"No, baas, I'm still here."

"Go over to Missies Sarie and ask her if I can borrow a big pot."

"A big pot, baas?"

"Yes, that's what I said. Are you deaf?"

"Now, baas?"

"Of course now. When else?"

With an almost undetectable shake of the head, Petrus put down his plastic bag and started towards the front door.

"Hurry up. I don't have all day."

Oom Marius thought he heard Petrus *tsk-tsk*-ing but decided it couldn't be. Petrus wasn't one to get too big for his boots. Or was he? Oom Marius would have to watch him more carefully.

He went back through the door, into his home.

Sitting down on a chair at the kitchen table, he waited for Petrus' return. In his mind he went over the list of things he still had to do: put the table cloth on the table – the new one he'd ordered from the delivery guy. He'd decided against using one of Hettie's embroidered ones. Set the table. Don't forget the wine glasses, even though he usually never drank wine. He thought about the bottle of sweet, white wine cooling in the fridge. A touch of sophistication, he congratulated himself for the tenth time. White wine with seafood. He hoped she'd be impressed.

Charlie had reminded him about the wine when he'd brought round the instructions printed on a sheet of crisp, white paper. Instructions Oom Marius had asked him to look up on the internet. He hadn't been able to find a recipe in a single one of Hettie's cookery books.

Oom Marius was nervous. He stood up, crossed the floor to the sink and looked down at the two remaining lobsters submerged in the basin of water, staring up at him with their beady little eyes as if they knew their days were numbered.

He'd given two of the lobsters to Hendrik who was going on a weekend fishing trip with his sons. He'd taken the sticky tape off their claws. The fish in the Orange River were going to get the fright of their lives when they met those two sea creatures at the bottom of the river.

That's when he'd decided to eat the last two. He'd paid enough money for the bloody things and gone through enough trouble. What, with the cost of the tank, all that fresh seafood every week and the two he'd sent off to the river, it would make these remaining ones the most expansive damned lobsters in the world.

"It looks like Klippiesfontein's lobster population is about to be annihilated," he spoke to the creatures squirming in the basin.

Oom Marius heard a timid knocking at the door. He found Petrus waiting on the other side with a pot in his hands. Oom Marius took it from him. "Now go home and get some rest," he said.

"Ja, baas. You too."

"Me too what?"

"Rest, baas. For you also."

"Are you telling me what to do?" Oom Marius snapped.

"No, baas," Petrus said quickly. "I go home now and rest. You, I don't know what you do."

The door closed behind him and Oom Marius immediately felt bad about snapping at the man. Opening the door again, he called out into the empty shop, "Have a good weekend."

He heard shuffling in the back. "Ja, baas," came Petrus' muffled voice, followed by the dim thud of the door as he closed it behind him.

Oom Marius was back at the kitchen table. Putting the pot down, he picked up the paper for what must've been the twentieth time that day.

How to Cook a Lobster it said. He read over it again. Just to be sure:

In order to boil your lobster, you will need a large pot with a lid.

Pour enough water in the pot to cover the lobster completely.

Add 2 tablespoons of sea salt for every 2 litres of water.

Bring the water to a fierce boil…

What the hell was a fierce boil? And how did it differ from a normal boil?

Oom Marius and Patty were sitting on plastic chairs inside the shop, sipping on their glasses of sherry.

Patty had giggled when he offered her a drink. "Oh, Marius," she said, touching his arm with her red-fingernailed hand, "are you offering me an aperitif?"

"*Ag*, no man, Patty," he said. "You know I don't have any of that fancy French stuff here in my shop. Just a bottle of Old Brown Sherry. Do you want some or not?"

She blinked her eyes a couple of times, "An aperitif is what you call a drink before supper."

"I'm not one for complicated words. I just call a thing what it is," he muttered sheepishly.

"Well then, I'd love one, thank you," she'd smiled.

When finally their glasses were empty, Oom Marius knew the time had come to invite Patty inside the house. This was going to be the hardest part: asking another woman to walk into his Hettie's kitchen. Even if that woman was Patty.

She was looking down at her empty glass and seemed almost as nervous as he felt.

Oom Marius stared at his hands and forced his tongue to say the words, "Would you like to come into the house with me?"

She cleared her throat, "Marius, why don't we just eat in here tonight?"

He could've jumped up, thrown his arms around her neck and planted a fat kiss on her lips out of sheer gratitude. "Yes, Patty. That's a very good idea. Very good. You just wait here and I'll bring everything out."

Patty sat neatly on her chair, sipping her topped-up glass of sherry, while Oom Marius made repeated visits to his kitchen, returning each time with a different item in his hands: a small, plastic table, a red tablecloth with blue and green parrots printed on it, a single candle which he put down in the middle and lit with trembling hands. He hoped she hadn't noticed the sweat trickling down his temple, dripping onto the tablecloth. Going back again, he came out with two wine glasses and a bottle of wine. Next he returned with the dinner plates and a dish with baked potatoes and two mealies on the cob.

"You've gone to all this trouble just for me?" she exclaimed, her eyes bright.

Oom Marius beamed back proudly, short of breath and fidgety: it was time for his magnificent climax. He hoped she'd be sufficiently impressed. After all, he'd even managed to surprise himself. He had no idea he could cook this well. Beaming proudly, he went back to the kitchen a final time. On his return, Oom Marius swept across to the table and carefully placed a large dish in the centre, "Lobster Thermidor. Just like they serve in the restaurants in Cape Town."

"Oh, no," Patty squealed, turning her head away and covering her mouth with her hand.

"What is it? What's wrong?"

"I can't possibly eat that, Marius. I just can't," she said in a weak voice.

"But why? I cooked it myself just like it said on the internet."

"It's terribly cruel, Marius. I've told you that before. It's against my principles."

Oom Marius knocked his forehead with the palm of his hand, "You have, Patty. You have. It's my fault. I'm so sorry."

He was blushing like a ten-year-old schoolgirl. What a balls-up. How had he gone and forgotten a detail like that? She'd told him how she felt about the things the first day he brought them into the shop. What an idiot he was! He stared down at the tray and bit his bottom lip. "I'll get them out of here," he mumbled.

Picking up the lobsters, Oom Marius disappeared inside his kitchen. He leaned up against the door, wondering how he was going to go back out there and face her again. He breathed heavily.

Idiot. Stupid, bloody idiot!

There was a gentle knock. "Marius?" he heard her voice.

Turning round to open the door, he realised he still had the tray with lobsters in his hands. Where could he put it? "Wait a minute?" he called.

He looked frantically round the kitchen. Rushing up to the oven, he yanked open the door, shoved the lobsters inside and closed it again. Grabbing a dishtowel, he ran it over his brow to sop up the sweat he felt pouring down. "Come in," he called finally, standing in the middle of the floor, trying his best to look casual.

Timidly she stepped inside. "What are we going to do now?" she asked in a gentle voice.

Patty was standing there inside Hettie's kitchen. He waited for the realisation to knock his breath away. It didn't.

"Steak, Patty? How about steaks? You got principles against that?"

She smiled, "I have no principles against steak, no." The look she gave him was friendly but somehow sad at the same time. Her smile grew faint, "But..." She didn't say anything more.

She'd hesitated. Yes, he'd seen it, she hesitated. Oom Marius was relieved to note her uncertainty; it seemed to mirror something he was just starting to feel but, then again... Why was she unsure? Did she not like...

Oom Marius ignored the thought, "I could go across the road to Dirkie Botha and ask him for two rump steaks?"

She stayed there looking at him with those heartbreaking eyes of hers. She didn't nod, didn't shake her head. She just seemed to stare right into him.

"I can make a mean steak," he tried again.

"Thanks for the sherry, Marius," her voice was soft, just a little louder than a whisper. "Thanks for inviting me this evening and going to all this trouble for me. It's flattering. It really is. But I think we should call it a night. I think it's still too soon."

Oom Marius forced himself to stay composed, "You're right. You're right. You talking about your feelings for Shawn?"

"No, not Shawn. I'm over him. I'm talking about Tannie Hettie. It's too soon, Marius. Even you know that."

He felt as if he would fall over. Oom Marius took a step back to keep his balance and bumped into the kitchen table. The salt and pepper cellars clinked against each other. "Thank you, Patty. Thank you. I mean it."

Her smile was back, laced with pity, laced with kindness, he couldn't decide. She spoke, "Maybe in a couple of months you can cook me that steak? Maybe in a year. We'll see. I'm not going anywhere."

Oom Marius nodded. He felt like Petrus in a way. He was mute. He followed Patty to the front door of the shop and watched as the gentle aging blonde walked down the steps and out onto Church Street.

About the Author

Although Colette Victor has been living in Belgium since 2001, in heart and marrow she's a South African. As a community worker in a disadvantaged ex-mining community in Genk, she works with an array of people from a range of ethnic and social backgrounds.

What To Do With Lobsters In A Place Like Klippiesfontein is her second published novel. *Head over Heart*, a YA novel, was published in 2014. She's currently hard at work on the next one, also for adults.

When she's not working, writing or being a mum, she promotes reading for young children and teaches creative writing to people from disadvantaged backgrounds.

Acknowledgements

I'd like to thank the following people for their support in helping me realise this book: my fellow writers from both the Maastricht and Brussels Writers Groups, Derrick for his faith in me, my family for putting up with me during the really stressful moments, my agent, Jo Hayes, for her invaluable advice on this book, but most of all, to my husband, Taki, for his unwavering support over the years.